# BROKEN

## *Rules*

### The Broken Road Series, Book 3

## MELISSA HUIE

Editorial provided by Emma Mack, Ultra Design Editing
And Dana Hook, Rebel Edit & Design.
Cover Design by Robin Harper, Wicked by Design
Formatting – Cassy Roop, Pink Ink Designs www.pinkinkdesigns.com
Front Cover Photography: Shauna Kruse, Kruse Image and Photography

Models:
Aurora O'Brien www.facebook.com/AuroraOBrien
Zack Salaun – www.facebook.com/Zack-Salaun

Author Photography by Cassy Roop, www.pinkinkdesigns.com

# DEDICATION

To my wonderfully sassy grandmother, Theresa.
Thank you for being amazing, for being so supportive.
I love you and keep on dancing, Granny.

# BROKEN
*Rules*

# PROLOGUE

*Miami, Florida*
*December 2015*

"I NEED SOMETHING HARD and strong to make this day go away."

I raised my eyebrow and stared straight into the bartender's golden hazel eyes, the double meaning crystal clear. His full lips curled into a cocky smirk as he reached for the bottle of Maker's Mark and held it up, his eyes asking if I could handle it. I grinned, as my gaze traveled down the length of his body. The white T-shirt and ripped jeans did nothing to hide the cut of his waist, or his pectoral muscles. I nodded and confirmed that yes—not only could I handle my favorite type of whiskey, but yes—I could handle him as well. I watched as he poured me a double, my eyes tracing the tight cords in his arms. I heaved a sigh and reached for my glass.

"At some point, Paulo, you're going to realize what you're missing," I said with a teasing smile.

"Ah, Kate, I highly doubt that. You don't have the right equipment to fit my needs," Paulo replied, wiggling his eyebrows. Of course, I couldn't keep up with the Cuban Casanova of Miami. I chuckled and sipped my drink. The smooth amber liquid burned as it went down and eased the stress from the day's events.

Not that I anticipated anything else short of drama. Apparently, bitching out my boss, Special Agent in Charge Rapoles, wasn't something that just went away quietly. My rant followed me from FBI Headquarters in Washington, D.C., last week, to the Miami Field Office. I guess the higher-ups didn't take too kindly to agents insisting that one of their own, their golden boy, was corrupt, working for the very enemy they were fighting. In fact, they hated the truth so much, that I was being pulled from the very case I'd helped to build, and was being redirected to the Baltimore office. And from there, a trip to Europe for some white-collar case. Management called it a lateral move, but I called it what it really was— bullshit. They wanted to distance me because I was so close to taking down their favorite agent.

I tossed back the rest of the whiskey and gestured to

Paulo for another. After I received an ass chewing from the Special Agent in Charge here in Miami, I had the humiliating task of clearing out my office, and doing the walk of shame in front of my fellow agents. People I respected saw me walk out, like a criminal. I had made a name for myself as a take-no-bullshit agent. I was proud of my accomplishments, and not for the first time in my life, felt like a complete and utter failure because I didn't go by the 'good ol' boy code.' *Tommy Greene may be their golden boy, but soon, they'll know who they're dealing with.* There was no way in hell I'd let something like that go, but I knew the rules. The more I fought with the Bureau, the more I'd lose. I wasn't raised to lose at anything, so I was going to bide my time and get more concrete evidence before I brought them to their knees.

My orders were to report to Baltimore within a week, but there was no reason to stick around. I returned back to the apartment the Bureau had rented me for the last three years and threw everything into the boxes and bags I had picked up on my way home. Thankfully, my nomad lifestyle definitely came in handy, because all my personal belongings were packed and loaded into my Lexus within an hour. The toiletries, and two extra changes of clothes would fit into my weekend bag. Both my Bureau issued and personal 9mm Glocks were locked safely in their cases, and my messenger bag containing all my notes and files on the Cruz Cartel case were ready to be loaded at first light the next morning.

But after everything was packed up, cleaned up, or thrown out, I couldn't stand the stillness. Below my apartment, Miami bustled with people and noise, excited for the New Year's festivities and fireworks. I needed to feel the city one last time. After living here on and off for the last three years, I truly enjoyed the city. Full of life and vibrant colors, it felt like a vacation from my daily grind of working in the shadows, and dealing with the scum of the city. I had made a friend or two in my short time here, and the desire to say good-bye was overwhelming. So I slipped on a denim miniskirt and white T-shirt, and headed down to Abbey Brewing Company, a local hangout.

"That's a mighty strong drink for someone so small. What's going on in that pretty little head of yours?" His southern drawl made my pussy clench, as it always did when he was near. I turned my head toward the man that just sat down. *Noah Russo.* A casual flirtation in the condo gym two years ago turned into a serial friend with benefits deal. That was as close as it would ever get. I didn't do relationships. And from what I gathered from Noah, neither did he.

I smiled as my eyes took in his blue V-neck T-shirt, stretched to fit his biceps and broad shoulders. His dark jeans hung dangerously low on his hips. His dark blond hair was ruffled from the wind, and his deep brown eyes looked through me, to my very soul, and I shivered. I hadn't seen him since before Thanksgiving, but he was definitely a sight for sore eyes.

"It's been one of those days," I answered vaguely, taking another sip.

He ordered a beer for himself, and pulled my bar stool closer to him. He wrapped his taut arms around my waist and brushed his lips against my ear. "Yeah? What kind of day would that be?"

"The kind of day where I don't care if it's a stiff cock or a stiff drink. I just need something hard to relieve the tension," I replied softly, as I ran my tongue over my bottom lip to catch a runaway drop of amber liquid. His body coiled instantly around mine.

"Aw, Princess, we'll have to remedy that situation," he growled, nuzzling my neck. He straightened to his full six-foot-four height, towering over my five-foot-five stature, and threw forty dollars down to cover my whiskey and his untouched beer, then grabbed my hand. I blew a kiss to Paulo and gave a little wave good-bye as Noah pulled me outside.

The thick and humid air embraced us as we hit the street. My hand clutched his as we made our way up 16th Street, through the holiday crowds. We reached our apartment building and barely made it inside the lobby when he pressed my back against the wall, and crushed his lips to mine. I wrapped my arms around him and molded myself to his body. Noah's large hands cupped my bottom and lifted me up. My legs locked around his waist, my body arching into his. His arousal ground into my already damp panties, and I moaned at the friction.

"Your place or mine?" he grunted against my lips. My head cleared momentarily from an arousal-induced fog.

"Yours."

With my legs still wrapped around him, he carried me over to the elevator and pushed the button for the fourth floor. As soon as the doors closed, he pressed my body against the wall again, this time his rough, calloused hands palmed my breasts.

"It's been way too long, Kate," he growled. He nipped at my neck, then came back to my mouth. My lips opened eagerly for his tongue. His intoxicating scent of leather, soap, and sea air created a sinful combination. Our tongues clashed and I pulled him closer, eager for anything and everything he was doing.

"I know," I breathed, as I ran my nails up his tight back. His lips reached the tops of my breasts, just as the doors opened. He carried me out into the open-air hallway to room 405, and fumbled for the key. Once we were safely behind closed doors, he yanked my shirt over my head.

"God, you're amazing," he muttered, his mouth sucking my nipple through the lace of my bra. He brought me into the bedroom and laid me on the bed. "Do you have any idea how long I've been waiting for this?" he asked, standing at the foot of the bed.

I smirked, then gasped as he yanked my miniskirt and soaked panties from my body.

"Then what are you waiting for?" My fingers glided from my belly to the throbbing ache between my legs, and I plunged into my slick, wet heat.

"Oh no, Princess. That pussy's mine." He grabbed my fingers, and with a slowness destined to drive me crazy, sucked every drop of cream off my digits. Noah fell to his knees and drew my legs around his shoulders. I propped myself on my elbows, and almost had an orgasm just watching him. His lips traced a line of kisses down the inside of my thigh, his teeth gently nipping as he got closer to my core. His lips circled the tight little nub, and I bucked into him with a moan. He reached his heavily inked arm over my hips as he feasted on me. With each lick and suckle of my clit, I was cresting higher and higher. I was so close, and the bastard knew it. Just as I was about to fall over, he pulled back. His face and beard glistened with my juices and gave me that smile—the smile I could never resist.

"You bastard."

"Beg me, Princess. I want to hear you beg me to make you come. I want to make you see the stars." He gently stroked the inside of my core with a featherlight touch, driving me wild. He hooked his finger and pressed on that spot—the spot that only he seemed to be able to find, and I was right back on that edge.

I bit my lip, and looked him dead in the eyes. "Please, Noah…*please.*"

Holding my stare, he leaned forward and tugged on my clit with his teeth. He then inserted two of his fingers, and began thrusting, quickly. I not only saw stars, I saw the freaking galaxy. I ground my pussy into his face, digging my nails into his scalp as I screamed out his name. He lapped up my orgasm, then stood up, taking off his shirt.

"My turn." I sat up and made quick work of his belt buckle and jeans, pushing them down around his ankles. He toed off his shoes, and I pulled him onto the bed. I crushed my lips to his, tasting myself on his tongue, then kissed my way down his body. My tongue traced the phoenix on his hip, then moved down. I ran my fingers under the band of this boxer briefs and gave a good yank. His magnificent cock popped out, and I smiled. I ran my tongue up and down one side, then the other. I circled the tip with my tongue, then relaxed my throat to take all ten inches of him into my mouth. His grip tightened in my hair, and I sucked harder while stroking his sac. The groans coming out of his mouth had me so wet, I clenched my thighs to relieve the ache.

"God damn, Kate. Come here." He pulled his cock out of my mouth and brought me to his chest. Our tongues clashed again, and our flavors mingled together. He rubbed the tip of his cock over my clit, and it had me more aroused than I'd ever been before. I was half tempted—more than half—to sink down and feel him skin to skin.  I needed that ache fulfilled. But my conscious prevailed, and I broke away from his lips.

"Condom," I managed to gasp out. He reached over to the drawer next to him and pulled out a box. I grabbed it from his hand and scooted down. I took my time, gripping and stroking him, while I encased his cock. The second it was on, Noah sat up and pulled me over his body. I sank down, and we both stilled with a groan as my body adjusted to his intrusion.  I raised my hips and rocked onto him, slowly at first, but the pace quickened with more vigorous thrusts. His hands reached out and pinched my already sensitive nipples. That was my undoing. We both climaxed together, my pussy milking his cock as it jerked inside of me. I collapsed next to him, while he discarded the used condom. Panting and sweaty, Noah climbed back into bed, and pulled me into his body, curling his arms around my waist.

I started to get up, when his grip tightened me to his chest. My eyes closed and I sighed.  It was a first. Normally, after a great sex session, we'd have a beer, put on a game, or order dinner. Now, it was as if he wanted me to stay the night. It had never happened before, and it sure wasn't going to happen now.

My eyes opened and my gaze traveled over his face—the sharp angles, his soulful, chocolate brown eyes. Noah was one hell of a sexy man. My fingers traced the sleeve of tattoos on his arms, and he moaned softly in my ear.

"Stay with me tonight," he whispered. I inwardly groaned. *Why now?* That would only make it worse. I could walk away and not think of it as anything more than sex. Sleeping together meant something more.

"You know I can't do that," I breathed. His lips hit the most sensitive part of my neck, right behind my ear. The fire I thought had faded, flickered back to life. I moaned and buried my face in his neck.

"Can't, or won't?" his ragged voice demanded, and he covered my body with his. My legs fell apart as his fingers trailed toward my heat. His lips hungrily took mine, our tongues dancing together, before he broke away, trailing his tongue down my neck and onto my breasts. He sucked and pulled at my nipples, twisting the barbell piercings. The slight twinge of pain sent electric shocks to my core. With his tongue attached to my nipple, he reached over to the nightstand to grab another condom.  He rocked back on his knees and spread my legs, gazing at my wetness while he put the latex over his cock.

"Noah," I gasped. His finger dipped into my slit, finding me more than ready for him.

"Stay with me." The rough command in his voice, combined with the flick of his fingers to my clit, had me screaming, "Yes!"

He pushed into me so quickly, I gasped sharply. He stared into my eyes with each stroke, with each roll of his hips. It was intense, and very intimate. Different than any other time we'd had sex. It almost felt like we were making love.  The tension built, and we crested each wave of pleasure until we exploded together.

This time, I let him pull me into his arms, and sighed when he placed a kiss on my temple. Noah was the guy that any woman would dream of having in her bed. His skills were unmatched by any of my previous lovers, but at the same time, he was one of the best guys I'd ever met. He didn't hold back, whether in bed or in a bar brawl. And good Lord, his laugh. He had the same juvenile sense of humor I did. He was the perfect guy.

*But not for me.* He didn't know who I was. He didn't know anything about my life, my job, or hell, even my real name. Noah only knew me as Kate Parker, a junior assistant for a real estate investment firm, from Toledo, Ohio. That was my story for being here, the reason for me being gone so often. After I left, the Kate Parker he knew would be a memory, just like all the other names I'd used.

Sure, I could have told Noah the truth, that I'd been living a lie for the past three years, that I was constantly putting myself and those I loved in danger. That a man I loved like a brother was presumed dead, but was really tortured in Hell at the hands of a drug cartel. Thankfully, he was home now, in the arms of his wonderful and kick-ass girlfriend. But he lived in fear of that cartel, the same cartel I would give my life to bring down.

The reality was that I couldn't tell Noah the truth. It was bad enough I had my family worried about me. I couldn't do that to someone I cared so deeply about. *Reality will be here soon enough. Let me stay in this dream for just a little bit longer.*

\*\*\*

WHEN I WOKE A FEW hours later, the rays of day peeked through the blinds. I glanced over at Noah, still sound asleep, with his arms wrapped around my waist. *How the hell am I going to get out of here without waking the beast?* I gingerly slipped out from his grasp, and quickly pulled on my white bra and T-shirt. I couldn't find my cotton panties in the mess on the floor, but decided to forget about them. I had just slid on my denim miniskirt when I heard a noise. I froze. Thankfully, Noah had just rolled over. With a sad smile, I tiptoed over to him and kissed him lightly on the head, then picked up my purse and flip flops, and headed out of his bedroom, and out of his apartment.

I slowly shut the door, hearing the knob automatically lock behind me, then hurried down the hallway to my own apartment, 415, and immediately shucked off my clothes as soon as the door locked. Noah's scent, a combination of leather, sea air, and citrus was everywhere—in my nostrils, my clothes, and in my hair. It was a scent that I'd probably never smell again, and it pained me to shower. But, despite my internal struggle to smell like Noah's sex groupie for the rest of my life, I knew I had to get a move on. A seventeen-hour drive was ahead of me, and Lord knew, a shower would be essential for waking up.

After my shower, I put on a pair of hot pink gym shorts and a black tank top, pulled my medium-length brown hair into a messy knot and slipped on my sneakers, and threw my clothes into the duffle bag. After ensuring that everything I needed was packed, I left the apartment keys on the counter for the next occupant and took the two gun cases and the rest of the bags down to the car.

I surveyed the garage as I walked to my spot, close to the elevators. At six in the morning on a Sunday, my only companion was a lizard on the wall. I chirped the car, dropped the bags into the packed trunk and backseat. But I made sure I left enough room in the trunk for the roof. I got inside the luxurious cabin and pressed the ignition button, then lowered the roof. Seeing as how it would be my last drive in Florida and all, I might as well do it up right.

I slid on my cute-as-hell-but-fake-as-sin Gucci sunglasses and pulled onto the street, headed north. It was time to leave this version of 'Kate Parker' and Florida behind, and to go back to being myself. Problem being, I didn't know who she was anymore.

# CHAPTER 1

October 2016

*I'm never drinking again.*

SUNLIGHT STREAMED THROUGH the wooden shutters, right into my eyes. I grimaced at the onslaught of nausea, and drew the blanket back over my head. At twenty-seven years old, I'd had my fair share of hangovers. But today's punishment seemed to take the cake. Ha, make that wedding cake. I chuckled softly at my own joke, only to wince at the slight movement.

A deep groan echoed my pain, and my heart jumped into my throat. Evidently, I wasn't alone, and a quick check under the blanket confirmed I was completely dressed in a tank top and my black boy shorts. I quickly retraced what happened the night before, and sighed with relief. Thankfully, this random hook up wasn't with a complete and total stranger. I shouldn't have been surprised to see Justin McGill at Shane and Megan's wedding. We met once I returned to Maryland this year, when everyone was hanging out at their favorite pub, The Double J. And since then, we'd hooked up occasionally, normally when the stress was too much, and my vibrator wasn't cutting it. The sex was okay— not mind-blowing—but enough to take the edge off.

"Shit, Kate. What the hell did we drink last night?" he grumbled, his voice thick with sleep.

"I blame Cheryl's moonshine cherries. We were popping them like candy," I replied, and rubbed the sleep from my eyes.

"That cousin of Shane's needs to bottle that shit. She'd make a mint." He tossed the thick blue blanket off his legs, revealing his morning wood hidden underneath a pair a boxer briefs. Justin glanced down, then over to me. "Is there any chance you'd want to help me out with this?"

I smirked. "Yeah, because that gets me real wet. Sorry, Justin." I sat up slowly to avoid any lingering dizziness, and managed to roll out of bed. "I'm going to jump in the shower, *alone*," I stressed at his raised eyebrows, "so I'll see you around." I hid my grin at his forlorn look and walked into the attached bathroom. I was no stranger to the walk of shame, but I'd be damned if I was going to do it in front of my whole family.

According to the smells wafting up from the main level of Megan and Shane's farmhouse, the post-wedding brunch was almost ready, so after my shower, I threw on a pair of yoga pants, sports tank, and a hoodie, then headed down the stairs.

The clanging of pots and pans mingled with adult laughter in the kitchen, and the smell of bacon permeated the air. I followed the scent of cinnamon rolls into the kitchen where Megan's mom, Norah, manned the stove while my mom, Cathy, pulled a quiche out of the oven. My stomach, despite its earlier rolling, growled at the sight of the smorgasbord laid out on the antique sideboard. I pinched a piece of sausage and made my way through the dining room. The house was about to burst at the seams with friends and family who spent the night, following the festivities of the day before. Hell, I don't think the bride and groom went to bed until after three in the morning.

"About time your ass got out of bed," quipped my stepbrother, Cole. I took in his dreary brown eyes and pale face, and knew right away he felt the same way I did.

"It's only ten in the morning, jerk." I grabbed a mug and poured myself some coffee from the carafe. "Do you want some more?"

He nodded, then groaned at the movement. "Rough night?" I teased. I handed him his mug, and sat down beside him.

"Kyle's home brew is no joke. How are you so happy? The last I saw, you, Jennifer, and Charlie were downing those moonshine cherries. There's no way in hell you're not feeling it this morning," he grumbled, his head down on the table.

"I'm just a better actor than you are." Better actor my ass. I knew better than to come to the table with a hangover. My mom had no sympathy for hangovers, and would make the nastiest runny eggs and diluted coffee for breakfast, all while playing Frank Sinatra at maximum volume, any time Cole or I would come down to the table from a night of drinking too much. I learned my lesson quickly, and that lesson was to never let Cathy Parker see you hungover.

"She'll see through your act. You aren't that slick," he mumbled, and took a sip of the strong brew. I stuck my tongue out at him. Juvenile, I know, but hell, my brother brought the best out of me. A loud cheer rang out, announcing the presence of Shane and Megan.

"What are they cheering for? Consummating their marriage?" Cole quipped, his eyes somewhat clearer now that he had half a cup of coffee in his system.

I smacked his arm. "Don't be a jackass. Give them

their weekend. They sure as hell earned it."

"Yeah, well, I sure earned those cinnamon rolls Mom just pulled out. Back away, they're mine!" The caffeine must have finally kicked in because he shot out of his chair like a rocket over to Mom and her famous breakfast treats. I rolled my eyes, confident that Mom made more than one batch, and waited my turn. Plus, the fact that she was a stickler for manners, Cole wouldn't get away with cutting in line.

My patience was justified as I watched Mom smack Cole on the hand with the spatula. He'd never learn.

"Watching your brother get in trouble with your mom is not what I expected to be doing on the morning after my wedding," Megan laughed behind me. I twirled around and grabbed the new wife, and my best friend, in a tight hug.

"You're part of the Turner-Parker family now. All get-togethers are like this," I replied, helping her into the chair next to me. Ever since the bullet from Tommy's gun damaged her hip, Megan had had difficulty walking, so she used a cane for support—a cane we decked out with paint and polka dots, specifically for the wedding.

"That's for damn sure," my stepsister Charlie piped in, settling down in the seat next to Megan, with two plates piled high with cinnamon rolls, blueberry scones, bacon, quiche, and fruit. She passed around some forks and small plates, and we all dug in.

"I can't wait for the holidays. That's all Shane has talked about this summer. Apparently, Thanksgiving is a sight to behold," Megan said with a smile.

"Oh, it is. Dad's family is huge, and they all come over to our tiny little house. Shane's parents, Shane, and sometimes his grandparents, would join us, and we'd get packed like sardines in the living room." Charlie's bright green eyes danced brightly at the memories.

Shane and Cole, and by extension, Charlie and I, grew up together in Essex, a blue-collar community outside Baltimore, Maryland. Shane and Cole were joined at the hip from the time they were in diapers, to the day Shane moved away after his parents died in a horrible car accident. After they passed, our Thanksgiving dinners weren't the same. Sure, we had the massive amounts of food and people, but not having Simon and Amelia Turner there didn't feel right. They were our second set of parents. Both sets of parents looked out for us, as if we were all one big family. They nursed our skinned knees, refereed our fights, and made sure we had plenty of s'more fixings and popsicles to keep our weekends full.

When Shane moved away after his parents died, we tried to stay in touch with him, but his world turned upside down. Shane withdrew from everyone he loved, and it was only when he reached the depths of Hell did he finally ask for help. He was in deep with the Cruz Cartel, a dangerous group with international drug and gun running ties, that help came from Megan's Uncle Bob, a federal attorney. Bob assisted him with the deposition and, with some insistence and deal making, Shane became a narc for the FBI. By then, I had already been through Quantico, and had just wrapped up my first case when I was approached to be on Shane's.

"I know he hates the fact that he missed so much with you guys," Megan said wistfully.

I nodded. "I'm sure he does. So do we, but you know what? We're a family again, and now we have you and Katie. You're stuck with us, kid." I rubbed her hand and smiled. The journey Megan and Shane took was a long and tortuous one. To think, that four months ago, we weren't sure we would see the day they would finally say 'I do,' because we didn't know if Megan would be alive to see it. She was collateral damage in a shoot-out with the Cruz Cartel, led by Tommy Greene, ex-FBI agent, my former partner, and crazy enough, Megan's ex-fiancé. Tommy had everyone fooled. Even though I'd figured out the truth at the last minute, the truth was a smack in the face, that Tommy was the ghost son of the head of one of the most dangerous international cartels. That he gave the order to kill two of Shane's close friends, and tried to kill Megan's brother, Kyle. And once Tommy found out that Shane was the narc, he used Megan as bait to lure Shane into thinking he was safe.

After he shot Megan and dropped her into the ocean in Miami, he managed to get away on his father's boat. Despite my best efforts, I wasn't able to get a good shot. I kick myself every day for not taking down that asshole. And more so, because I couldn't get top brass at the FBI to listen to me. Now that Tommy's double-crossing was exposed, the higher-ups finally realized that I wasn't full of shit. That my detective work was sound, and that I was fucking right. So now, my team and I were on the hunt for the elusive bastard. A man that's been one step ahead of us, who knew all our plays and moves, and had more connections than the phone company, which has made hunting him very difficult.

"So, ladies, how are we feeling?" My train of thought was interrupted by Megan's smug smirk. Charlie groaned, and put her head in her hands; her caramel, blonde hair shielding her.

"I'm okay, I guess. Not feeling the greatest, but then again, I don't know who would be after a night like that. I remember changing into sweats with you and Sarah, and coming out to the bonfire by the barn, and dancing with a couple guys from Adrian's shop. Eating those damn cherries and drinking. Definitely, a lot of drinking. Enough to end up in bed with Justin McGill," I quipped, sipping my coffee.

"Justin? He's pretty cute. Where is he, anyway?" Megan peered around the twenty or so people milling around.

"He rolled out. We did our thing last night, and I shut him down this morning." I drained the last bit of my coffee. "He's good looking and all, and we have a good time, but it's just a casual thing. He's not really my type."

"Kate, no one is your type," retorted Charlie, brushing a strand of hair of her face.

*True enough.* "Well, if they have a big cock…"

"Kate Parker, you hussy!" Megan shrieked, and swiped my arm. I laughed and got out of my chair.

"What can I say? I know what I want, and when I want it. And right now, I want more coffee. Anyone want more?" Charlie held out her cup, but Megan stood up slowly, using her cane for minimal support.

"I have to make my rounds. I haven't seen everyone in forever, and I feel that I didn't get a chance to see everyone yesterday." She kissed my cheek. "I'm so glad you're back, Kate."

I grinned. "Me too." Which wasn't a total lie. I loved being back with my family, Shane and Megan included.

But despite bouncing around Florida and New York City over the past five months, the case was at a lull, and I was itching for some action. I rolled my shoulders and cracked my neck. Maybe a little time at the gym would make me feel better.

I ate my weight in cinnamon rolls and quiche, then socialized with family before sliding on my sneakers, and said my good-byes. I lingered over baby Katie, my namesake, my goddaughter, and Shane and Megan's baby girl. At nine months old, the little girl had had so much chaos in her life, and I was thankful that it hadn't affected her little world, the way it had ours. But I was damn sure that I wouldn't let it affect our lives anymore.

Thankfully, the sun was warm enough for me to take the windows out of my Jeep Wrangler. I drove to Tactical Redemption with the wind in my hair and *Breaking Benjamin* in my ears. I missed my Lexus convertible, but the payments were putting a hurt on my wallet. I pulled into the empty parking lot. Normally, the center was busy as hell during the summer months with police and military training, and then again, right after the New Year, with all the resolution-making dummies. MMA had really become mainstream, and everyone and their mother wanted to be the next Chuck Liddell. But nearly everyone dropped out within the first month. As Sketch, Cole's co-owner of Tactical Redemption once told me,

"It's all about separating the dicks from the pussies."

The 10,000 square foot warehouse was divided into three main sections, with one area for mat classes like wrestling, Muay Thai, and Krav Maga. The area on the left was for boxing and strength training, while showers, lockers, and bathrooms were in the back. Weapons and tactical training were done either on-site for the various federal and military teams, or on the five-acre field behind the warehouse.

Heavy metal blared through the speakers, and the smell of bleach permeated the air, telling me that Sketch had already done one of the twice daily mat bleaches. I threw my hoodie into my locker and wandered upstairs to the office, to say hi to Sketch.

If a random stranger walked into his office, they'd run away without saying a word. Especially since Murray, Sketch's huge gray Mastiff, was always the first to greet you. To say Sketch was a formidable looking man was putting it lightly. At six-foot-four and two-fifty, the man was pure muscle. With broad shoulders, narrow waist, and fully covered in tattoos, you would take one look into his almost black eyes and pee your pants. But if someone took the time to get to know him, they'd learn that despite his piercings and tattoos, Sketch was a good man. Quiet and calculating, he didn't need to talk much to get his point across, and he didn't allow many in his inner circle. But whoever broke through, he trusted completely. If anyone knew what that was like, it would be me.

"What's up, Sketch?" I leaned against the doorframe to the bare office. Not much for the pretty things, when Sketch built the center, the office area was an afterthought, preferring to spend his money and creative design on the center itself. He was fine with the bare minimum—a long folding table for his desk, a filing cabinet, and a chair for himself. He didn't even have chairs for visitors, because in his words, "If people wanted to sit in your office, they don't belong in the center to begin with. All talking can be done in the ring."

He looked up, his eyes penetrating mine. "Nothing much, Tink." I sighed at the nickname he bestowed on me last Halloween. *You go as a slutty Tinkerbell to one stupid costume party, and the nickname sticks with you forever.* "How was brunch this morning?" Never one to purposely miss a meal, Sketch had to roll out before the festivities to open up the gym. Of course, once my mom and Norah heard I was going to the center, they made sure to pack a bag for him.

"Awesome, as usual. The moms packed you some leftovers." I handed him the thermal cooler, which he opened with gusto.

"Thank God for mothers," he muttered, pulling out

a container of quiche, and going over to the microwave on top of the filing cabinet. "Are you looking to spar today?" he asked, as the quiche heated up.

"That depends. Are you looking to get your ass kicked?" I asked with a smile.

He snorted. "Yeah, okay, Tink. Sorry to burst your bubble, but I wasn't offering. I have my buddy coming in later to check the place out. I'd take him on, but I have to get this accounting done before the end of the quarter."

I sighed. A new recruit could mean one of two things. Either he'd be completely green and jumping on the MMA bandwagon, or he'd done enough training to think he was the next big thing. Whatever hole he fit in, it wasn't worth my time. "What do you want me to do, Sketch?"

The microwave dinged, and he pulled out the piping hot quiche. "Show him around, answer any questions. Maybe spar a little. You know this place like the back of your hand, so it's not gonna be a big deal. He's a good dude. I used to roll with him back in high school, and he knows his shit."

I shrugged. "Sure, why the hell not." Of course, he was going to owe me big time for it.

"You rock. He'll be here in about an hour, so you have time to hit the bags," he said with a wicked grin.

"Now, get out of here, and let me eat in peace."

I gave him the one-finger salute and headed to my locker to get started. After stretching and going through my warm-up routine, I wrapped my hands with the pink tape from my locker, grabbed my water bottle, and headed to the heavy bags. In the zone, I focused all my energy on the hits, picturing Tommy's body and face at the receiving end of my punches. Fury flowed through me as I remembered the low and terrifying angst in Shane's voice when he called me from Ocean City in May. The rage when I saw the picture he sent to Shane of Megan gagged, bound, and knocked out from the drugs he'd used to kidnap her. The dangerous smile he gave, holding the gun to her head as Cole, I, and the rest of our team barreled down the pier. The cry of agony from Shane when Megan was shot in her side during her struggle with Tommy. The frustration at not being able to take his ass down yet. Every pent-up emotion poured through each of my hits. *Argh!*

I threw my weight behind the last punch, making the heavy bag swing wildly from the impact. Sweat poured down my face and back as I grabbed the bag to hold it steady. My forehead dropped to the bag and I closed my eyes, gulping in air. I was drained, emotionally and physically. The running around, chasing every lead all over the fucking country, was wearing me down. I'd been living out of my suitcase for the last nine months. First in Europe, working a blackmail and security fraud case. Then the Cruz Cartel burst wide open, and all hell broke loose. I went straight from London to Miami, re-establishing my contacts and informants. Flying between Miami, Las Vegas, and New York, tracking down the Cartel had been hell on my body—on my life. I'd been in town for a couple of days, the first good stretch of time since I left back in February. I didn't have a home of my own, so I'd been staying with Cole mostly, but occasionally Megan and Shane, or my parents. I drained my water and went back up the stairs to Sketch's office. He was just hanging up the phone when I walked in.

"Hey, your dude never showed," I said, lingering in his doorway.

"Yeah, it's cool. He just called. Something came up, so we'll figure out something."

I nodded, then my gaze caught on a framed picture on his desk. "Hey, is that your mom and niece? I haven't seen her in forever. I bet she's huge now."

Sketch's eyes brightened at the thought of his precious niece. "Yeah, she's getting so big. She's crawling and getting into so much shit now. Murray loves her, don't ya boy," he said, rubbing the monstrous head of his buddy.

"Good. I'm glad to hear that. How's your sister? Is

she getting the help she needs?" I didn't know much, but from the bits I'd heard from Sketch, his sister had fallen in with the wrong crowd.

Sketch rubbed his massive hands over his face, exhausted. "We haven't seen much of her since Mom applied for emergency custody, until Bree's dad could come back from his mission."

"Argh, that sucks. Did she do her time?"

He scoffed. "Nope. I don't know how she did it, but she's out on probation. The women's prison was full or something, but whatever. Either way, she's back on the streets. She's asked to see her when she's been lucid enough, but half the time she doesn't show up. Ready to go?" I followed him down the stairs, into the front lobby area.

"I'll be right out." Since I had cooled down from my workout, I needed my hoodie. I used the restroom, washed my hands, and grabbed my hoodie and keys. I figured I'd roll out to Megan and Shane's and grab my stuff, then head to Cole's. The newlyweds deserved a night to themselves, without their family listening to every bed creak. Plus, I hadn't given my brother enough hell yet. And who knew when I'd get the chance again.

Unfortunately, the chance to harass my brother had to wait. Just as I was about to throw the Jeep into reverse, my phone chirped an incoming message.

*Got an update. Call me.*

*Shit.* When my partner, Rick Simms, said to call him, I called.

"You beckoned?" I asked when he picked up the phone.

"Yeah. Your informant in Vegas called in. Word on the street is that there's a new Cruz player looking to make a name for himself. A couple hookers were found dead in Old Town Vegas."

"Okay…What's your point? Hooking is the oldest profession out there, and Vegas is the freaking capital for it."

"Because one of the hookers had the card for Yankee's, and Reggie's number in her phone." Ah, good ol' Yankees, the club formally owned by Tomas Cruz, the CEO of Cruz, Inc. A legit and legal entity of the Cartel's many business ventures. The club was just a front, laundering money, and selling drugs and sex to those who could afford the Cartel's high prices. Feds raided the place three months ago, and uncovered a whole treasure trove of goodies, like kilos of cocaine and heroin, and cases of guns. The building was abandoned, and the place went up for auction three weeks ago.

"Wait—hold up. Reggie's been dead for over a year now. Maybe it's old info?" Reggie Cruz was one of the bastards that tried to kill Megan at Deep Creek Lake last year, and he died by her hand.

"Kate, her roommate said that that phone was brand new. And we checked the line. It's never been shut off." Rick's deep voice, thick with exhaustion, came through. I'd heard what he wasn't saying, loud and clear.

"I guess we're going to Vegas." I sighed, and threw my Jeep into reverse.

# CHAPTER 2
*Kate*

*A week later. ...*

VEGAS WAS A BUST. The dead hooker's roommate had no further information on the Yankee strip club connection, but forensics was able to trace Reggie's cell phone number to a motel outside Tulsa, Oklahoma. We moved in, but got there too late. We found a destroyed cell phone, along with another dead woman, with no I. D. We ran her fingerprints and picture through our facial recognition software, but so far, there had been no hits. We left Vegas feeling dejected, with nothing but more pieces to a freaking jigsaw puzzle.

I gripped my pink and black polka dot carry-on, and wheeled it through the jetway, eager to get my space. My five foot, five-inch frame could fit into most spaces pretty comfortably; however, even I had issues being in the middle seat, next to two three-hundred pound, unwashed gorillas. Despite what the TV shows always portrayed, there were no private planes for this chick. Hell, the only time I got to ride on those luxury birds was when I flew with one of the big men in charge. I heaved a sigh of relief when I exited Baltimore-Washington International Airport, and headed toward the long-term parking. There was nothing more I wanted to do than to take a shower, eat some dinner, and sleep for a week. Megan and Shane's wedding was the first day I'd had off in over ten months, and my brain was fried. Not to mention, my body was dragging with each step.

I hefted my bag into the back of the Jeep, texted my brother that I was on my way, and started the fifteen-minute drive to his place. Truly, I picked the house of least resistance, as the trek to my parents' house was only ten minutes longer. Being clucked over by my mom would've been amazing, but I knew she started her shift at the diner before the crack of dawn. And while it was not officially *my* bedroom, most of my clothes and personal crap were at Cole's. I second-guessed the decision the minute I drove down Holiday Street. The street was lined up and down with random vehicles, and my spot in the driveway was taken by a jacked up black Chevy truck. I groaned and slammed my hand into the wheel. *Are you fucking kidding me?*

I pulled in behind Cole's blue truck, and wrestled with the exhaustion threatening to overtake me. Hopefully, the jokers would roll out soon so I could get some sleep. I got out, slamming the door harder than necessary, and grabbed my bags. Easing the door open, my eyes widened at the scene. Every available seat in the small living room was taken up by big guys, glued to the Ravens-Steelers Thursday night game on the 60" TV above the mantel. The shouts were so loud, that my entrance into the house went unnoticed, until Jax, Cole's brown brindle Pitbull, barked his welcome.

"Hey, sis," Cole called from his spot on the brown leather recliner, his eyes returning to the game. "There's pizza and beer in the kitchen."

I nodded, and dragged my bag down the hall, flicking on the lights as I closed the door behind me. The volume penetrated the thin walls, and I groaned in frustration. I looked longingly at my bed, but the shouts from the living room told me that there was no chance of going to sleep anytime soon, so I headed into the attached bathroom. As the hot water heated, I stared into the mirror, horrified at what I saw. The bags under my eyes, and unusually pale skin tone showed the stress I'd been under. The damn case had been my life for so fucking long, it was all knew anymore.

Something needed to change. The case needed to

come to a close before I fucking cracked.

I stepped into the shower and let the hot water wash away the airplane funk, the travel dust, and some of the tension from my shoulders. After twenty minutes, and using up all the hot water, I finally emerged from the steam-filled room. I quickly got dressed in a pair of yoga pants, sports bra, and my favorite gray hoodie, to beat the chill in the air. I was detangling my chestnut locks when the door knob started to rattle.

"What?" I called, but no one responded. *Probably some poor slob looking for the bathroom.* But the door knob rattled again. "You've got to be joking," I muttered, and stormed across the room, flinging open the door.

"Hey, girl. You're missing the party." Bleary-eyed and drooling, the man was a mess. Not only because he was wearing a Steeler's jersey with pizza sauce and nacho cheese stains on his beer gut, but just in general. The loser's words slurred with every syllable as he leaned against the doorframe for support.

"Yeah, no thanks." I put my hands on his chest, intending to push him back gently, when he grabbed my left wrist and pulled me into a wet, sloppy kiss. *Oh, fuck this.* With my free hand, I landed a swift, hard punch to his groin. He immediately released my left hand, and that was all I needed to turn around and kick him in his kidneys, causing him to shriek in agony. Our commotion finally broke through the sounds of the game, and Cole and Sketch came running down the hall.

"Pat, what the hell did you do?" Sketch pulled up the drunk man. Cole touched my elbow, making sure I was okay. I pushed him away, annoyed that I even had to deal with the asshole in the first place.

"That fucking bitch! I'm gonna stomp the shit out of her," he grumbled.

Sketch threw the guy against the wall. "You're fucking lucky you're my cousin, bro, because I'd stomp *your* ass for even trying to step up to her. Now get the fuck out." He tossed his cousin down in disgust, then turned to me. "Sorry about that, Tink."

I shrugged my shoulders. "Whatever." I walked through the living room and into the kitchen, pushing through the crowd to get to the fridge. I reached in and grabbed the last remaining bottle of Fat Tire, then searched the littered countertop for an opener amongst the half-empty beer bottles, plates of pizza, chip crumbs...*Everything but the frigging opener.* Then someone put a plastic green bottle opener in my hand.

"Thanks..." I started to say, then froze. The letters spelling out *Miami, Florida* were faded from use, but I recognized the tacky souvenir anywhere. It came from a night of playing tourist, and ended with the best sex of my life. I sucked in a breath and turned around.

"Noah," I breathed, flicking the top of my bottle. Dressed in a black zippered sweatshirt, dark jeans and boots, I almost didn't recognize him. His *Ominous* ball cap was pulled down low over his dark, chocolate brown eyes, but that smirk—oh my Lord, that smirk. It was my undoing. I tipped my beer to my lips, waiting for him to say something…anything.

"Hey, Kate. It's good to see you again." *Ah hell, that voice.* My insides quaked as his gaze ran over my body like a hot iron, searing me with heat. *Act cool, Kate.*

"You, too. Mind telling me what you're doing in my house?" I asked, like it was no big deal that my walking sex dream was in my kitchen, talking to me.

"Sketch is an old friend of mine."

"Really? Funny, he's never mentioned you before," I stated, taking another swig.

"Yeah, well, he's never mentioned you, either." The fire in his gaze was contagious. The conversation was throwing me off-balance, and I needed to reassess the situation.

"What brings you up north?"

"Family. My folks live out near Chesapeake Beach," he said with a drawl. He took a swig of his beer, holding my gaze the entire time. The knowledge of how close he'd been to me the whole time didn't help the flush in my face. I raised my eyebrows at the revelation.

*Live, as in present tense. As in, currently living only thirty minutes away? I'm so screwed.*

"Great. Maybe I'll see you around sometime," I said with a smirk of my own. He opened his mouth to reply, but was cut off by a roar of cheers. I used the distraction to slip away, and hurried to my room. *It's not like he doesn't know where you went, you moron!* I groaned to myself in frustration as I shut my door. I could fight off drunk guys. I could shoot at people and not flinch. I could run a mile in under nine minutes. I kicked ass and took names. *So why the hell am I losing my cool around him?* Not sure what had changed, I wasn't liking the way the butterflies were making a mess out of my stomach. Everything that happened in Miami was just casual, because it wasn't real. It was an act. *If it was such an act, why is he having such an effect on me?*

"Kate." Without knocking, or asking to come in, Noah walked into my room and shut my door. I stood there, stupid and tongue-tied, then internally shook the cobwebs from my head and walked toward the door to lead him back out.

"Noah, look, it's great seeing you, really. But do you mind if we catch up another time? I'm beat. I've been away…" I didn't make it far when he grabbed my arm and pulled me into him.

"I know you've been away. Do you know how long

I've been waiting for you?" he whispered, walking me backward, until my back was against the wall. My breath hitched as he pressed into me, his arousal nudging my belly. "When you left me in Miami, I didn't think I'd see you again." He rested his arm above my head and leaned in, tracing my jawline with his nose, inhaling me. My jaw clenched to prevent a moan, a whimper...hell, any sound from escaping. "Imagine my surprise when I see your picture on the wall at Sketch's gym. I got hard instantly, just remembering that night, having my thick cock inside that tight pussy."

I couldn't help it. My lips parted, and a breathy sigh escaped. His large hand cupped my face as he buried his face in my neck. The feel of his breath sent electric shocks right down to my core.

"You're remembering that too, aren't you? Remembering how I feel. How I taste." All those memories flooded back, and my panties were drenched. Everything else went away. All that was left was Noah, and how he was making me feel. Dimly, I heard his name shouted.

"I've been waiting a long time for you to come home, Kate. So I'll definitely be seeing you around." And with a smirk, he turned and left. My body screamed for him to return, and my heart pounded.

"Argh!" I groaned in frustration. He can NOT be

here right now. I slammed the door behind him and stomped over to my bed, ripping off the blankets. Echoes from the game filtered through the walls. I sat on my bed, fuming. My body's response to Noah was not what I needed.

My time with him in Florida was an *escape*. I could be a different person, and more carefree. When I was with him, the Cartel issues slowly faded into the back of my mind. No one questioning why I went out at all hours of the night, or why my appearance changed suddenly. *And more importantly, no one got hurt.* After seeing the turmoil and heartache that Megan and Shane had gone through because of the Cartel, and seeing how quickly their relationship changed because of Shane's lies and Meg's worries, I couldn't do that to someone I loved. I didn't want someone worried so much for my safety that they'd risk their own just to save me. I wouldn't have that hanging over my head.

With Noah, there were no strings, and no relationship drama. We knew where we stood. Sex, pure and simple. *Really good sex.* Mind-blowing, toe curling, multiple orgasm sex. Desire ached low in my belly, and I rubbed my legs together to quell the ache, but that only increased the need.

*Oh, to hell with it.* I pulled open the nightstand drawer and reached for my blue battery operated friend, the only thing that had been able to relieve any sort of sexual frustration. Flicking the knob, the familiar, pulsating hum of my high-powered toy sent shivers down my spine with anticipation. My eyes closed on their own, and it was like I could feel Noah with me. His rough, callused hands gripping my thighs. His magic tongue, slipping inside me. My insides trembled as I rubbed the vibrating tip onto my sensitive nub. A groan escaped before I realized what was happening, and my pressure increased. The orgasm built quickly, as the toy escalated me to the top…

And then, nothing.

"Are you fucking kidding me?" I growled, frantically flipping the switch on and off. *Nothing. Mental head smack.* I completely forgot to charge my flipping vibrator. *Argh!* I dug through the box of toys hidden in the nightstand drawer. Sadly, yes, I had a box of goodies. *What other sexually frustrated single woman doesn't?* All dead. I threw myself back onto the bed in disgust.

*This is all Noah's fault.* Granted, I had been using my toys whilst thinking about him, so I guess it wasn't technically his fault. But the fact that he got me all worked up by doing something as simple as just looking at me? Well, that was his fault, dammit. I thought, after leaving Florida, I'd get him out of my system. I craved separation in my life, keeping my job and FBI political bullshit isolated from my personal life. But damn, if they weren't swirling around together. Just one touch, one freaking whiff of that leather, citrus and soap scented man, and I was done.

If it only took five minutes for me to become a mumbling, horny school girl, then how the hell was I supposed to cope if he was there all the time?

*I'm so screwed.*

# CHAPTER 3
## Noah

I WALKED OUT OF HER BEDROOM, even as my hardened cock screamed at me to go back, to finally claim the woman that I had been looking for. *Keep it together, man.* I caught Cole's evil eye as I walked toward him. Hell, I couldn't fault the man. If my sister looked half as good as Kate did, I'd knock a joker out. But being on the other side of the coin, I knew I had to play it cool. I couldn't flaunt the fact that I knew his sister in the most carnal of ways. I wanted to be able to continue to get to know her.

"Noah." His tone was one of warning, a tone I'd heard before. I reached out my hand, and his own gripped mine in warning. "That's my sister. Don't fuck with her. You're like a brother to me, dude, but I won't hesitate to drop your ass where you stand."

I nodded, and gave him a hard stare. "I can respect that, so I'm only going to say this once. Your sister is a big girl, and can handle herself. What happens between us is our business. But trust me when I say, hurting your sister is the last thing I will ever do."

Cole met my stare, then raised his chin. "As long as you know that." He released the death grip on my hand and slapped me on the shoulder, harder than necessary. "Why don't you come by the gym tomorrow? We can see what you're really worth, or we'll find out if you're still the same pussy from when we were in BUD/S together."

I shook my head. "Let me see what I can do. I'll catch you later." I grabbed my leather jacket from the back of the couch and headed out the door, making my way to the truck where Sketch leaned against the hood, smoking a cigarette, while his cousin Pat puked his guts out by the tailgate. I raised my chin at Sketch, my intent clear as a bell. He gave a slight nod, which was good, because I was going to do it with or without his okay. I reached Pat, and my fist cocked back and hit his jaw faster than he could blink.

"Damn, man, what the fuck is that shit for?" he whined, holding his fat jowls with his meaty hand.

"That's for even breathing in her direction." I pulled back and hit him again, knocking his drunk ass clean out. "That's for putting your fucking hands on her."

"Shit. You're helping me get him into the backseat." Sketch stubbed out his cigarette and made his way over to the lump that was his cousin. I was half-tempted to leave the fat bastard there, but I knew that wouldn't go over too well with Cole and Kate, so we hauled him into the backseat of my Chevy, then I drove the twenty-five minutes to my place in Edgewater. I was on autopilot. My mind, my thoughts, were filled with her.

Seeing her today was a shock to my system. I knew it would only be a matter of time before we ran into each other. I wanted to find her the second I realized the connection between her and my best friend, when I saw her picture in Sketch's office. She was in a group shot with Sketch, Cole, and two other people that I knew were Shane and Megan. Her brown hair was shorter, lighter, and her body was leaner, but damn those eyes— those crystal blue eyes. The urge to go and find her was strong, but Sketch held me off, said that she was dealing with a lot of shit, and it was her story to tell. Because, obviously, she wasn't the Kate Parker from Toledo, Ohio, that I met in Miami. Too bad I already knew who she was. I knew who she was the minute she moved into our apartment building.

I pulled up to the place I bought only a few months ago on Bayside Drive and cut the engine. "You crashing here?" I asked, getting out of the truck.

Sketch shrugged. "Nah, I got to get this fat bastard home." He got out and I followed. He cupped his hands and lit another cigarette. "So…Kate, huh? You better know what you're doing."

I'd never been able to lie to him. He'd seen me at my worst. He knew the shit I'd been through and still, despite everything, had had my back since we were sophomores at Northern High School. When I'd first asked him about her, the first time I was at his gym, he didn't tell me a thing, just said that there was some bad shit going down, that she was in deep, and that I needed to back off. That sure as hell wasn't happening, so I pressed and asked questions. Pissed him off to the point that he threw me into a submission move that I was unable to get out of, until I gave him my word that I wouldn't fuck with her, unless whatever drama she was in settled down. And doing that was hard enough. But luckily, my own life was messed up enough that it took my mind off of her, or at least, put her behind everything else, temporarily. Thankfully, it was something that only reached a plateau in recent weeks.

I shrugged my shoulders. "I can't not talk to her, bro. Something is there, a connection between us. I feel it. And I think she does too."

Sketch nodded. "You both have a lot of baggage. But

if anyone can get past the bullshit, it's you. But you have to tell her, dude." He gave me the hard look. I knew exactly what he meant.

Pat had snorted from inside the car, and I threw him a disgusted look. "Yeah, I know." I threw open the door and smacked Pat upside his bald head. "Wake up, fucker. Your stench is soaking into the car." With Sketch's help, we'd managed to haul his cousin into the back of Sketch's pickup truck. I slapped him on his back. "I'm picking Aubrey up on Sunday, so I'll see you then."

I walked into the dark house and flipped on the lights as I went. My orange and white tabby, Harley, greeted me in the kitchen. "What's up, fat boy?" I scratched him behind his ear and opened up the fridge. Nothing but beer, two-week-old pizza, and a bottle of ketchup. My plane from Miami had just landed that afternoon, and I hadn't had time to get to the store yet, so I grabbed the beer and made my way into the living room.

I'd been in the most extravagant mansions, and the most desperate of hovels, and nothing had felt more like home than this. Even that apartment the military had rented for me down in Miami wasn't home. This was a place I could raise my family—where I *would* be raising my family. The little three bedroom beach cottage had plenty of space for Harley, my daughter, and me.

Damn. I had a daughter. It still took me by surprise when I said it. One minute I was in the jungles of Bolivia, and the next minute I was on a plane, back to my parents' house, with a brand new life. I didn't find out about her until earlier this year. I'd missed her birth, and the first three months of her life. Who the hell knew how much more I would have missed, had the police not raided the house her mother was staying in. I gripped the neck of the beer tighter, remembering the night my mom had called me, her controlled voice my only clue that something was up. My gut immediately tightened, thinking it was my old man and his heart again.

But no, it was more life-changing. I had a three-month-old daughter, and her mother, my former girlfriend, otherwise known as Sketch's sister Jennie, was arrested for child abuse, neglect, endangerment, along with a whole host of other charges like possession of narcotics, and intent to distribute. She was high as a fucking kite when they busted down that door, where she had left Aubrey covered in waste, and screaming in the back room. The only bright side was that Jennie was coherent enough to give her mother's name as her emergency point of contact. Within hours, she was granted emergency custody. The scary thing? No one had seen Jennie in quite some time, and her family had no clue she had even been pregnant, much less who the father was. But Ana took one look at Aubrey and knew exactly who she belonged to.

I'd come as soon as I could, and there was no question in my mind that Aubrey was mine. She had my brown eyes, and her mother's blonde curls. From the moment I'd held that baby in my arms, she had me hooked. My priorities changed. But I couldn't leave my team behind, so I made the commute. I went back home as often as I could, spending as much time with my daughter as possible, and doing as much work as I could remotely. But I always had to make that trek south.

Miami was only supposed to be temporary. Everything about Miami was temporary. Except for Harley, I didn't expect to bring anything back. Hell, my targets weren't even supposed to make it back to the area. They were supposed to meet their maker in the Florida Everglades. And I was proud to say that most of them did, just not the main one. In my team, it was ingrained from the very beginning; don't leave a trail, cover your tracks, and never let your brothers down.

The prep work I'd done on the case encompassed three years of my life—learning their movements, hacking our way into their network, planting someone within their lower ranks—taking a massive amount of manpower and a shit ton of money. But damn if we didn't get close. So close, I almost tasted it. We'd planned for every possible contingency.

But I hadn't planned for Kate. The moment I saw her in the gym at our apartment building, I was hooked. Hell, I wasn't stupid. I'd checked her out in our database as soon as I got wind that the agent on the Cartel Task Force was coming our way. I knew who she really was, what her true purpose was for being down in Florida. But I didn't want to show my hand. Our missions were aligned, but mine was on a much grander scale. Separation between the two was an unfortunate necessity. I had to live for the mission. Pussy was great, but I couldn't have a relationship, not when so many things were up in the air. I didn't need a stage five clinger when I had to be on the move at a moment's notice. Thankfully, she had the same mindset, which made her perfect. A hot ass woman like her, with her own life and career, who was happy with no strings attached sex? *Sign me right up*. And it stayed that way, for a while. I did my thing, she did hers, but somehow, her no-nonsense attitude, contagious smile, and juvenile sense of humor wore me down. And damn, that body rocked me.

But she was getting too close. She was fishing around in waters that shouldn't have been, and I knew that soon, our two cases would combust together. The Cruz Cartel were basically the middlemen for the Syndicate, and the more Kate poked her nose around it, the more she'd find about the Syndicate, and that was not something that she needed to get involved in. We had too much riding on our case, too much effort and money invested, so she had to go. I knew her boss, Rapoles, was a complete dick, and wanted her out of Miami. She once tore him a new asshole because he couldn't—or more likely, wouldn't—see that Tommy Greene was their mole. So I made a judgement call. Looking back, maybe it wasn't the best idea, but I did what I had to do and called in a favor. Rapoles owed me from the time I saved his son's ass in a raid up in Michigan. It may have been a dick move, but it got her out of Florida. I didn't expect her to stick around after getting an earful from the higher-ups. That was one thing Kate didn't do, was stay where she wasn't wanted.

I'd thought I could let her go. One more night of beyond amazing sex would be all it would take to get her out of my system. But after round one, I couldn't let her go. She'd felt so right in my arms, like she belonged there. The decision to send her back to wherever Rapoles was sending her made my stomach feel like lead. I knew I'd thrown her off when I'd asked her to stay the night. But the thought of not being inside her, not having her in my arms one more night, angered the beast within. She was the calm, the relief from dealing with the scum of the earth. I'd started to need her more than I needed air to breathe, which had scared the shit out of me. I had never been that way, until she walked her pert little ass into the gym.

I drained my bottle. Checking my phone, I knew I had to go to bed, or there would be hell to pay tomorrow. Running a business alone is a ridiculous amount of work, but to put that on top of the work I was doing with the DEA and my team? Luckily, the bar ran itself, and Josh was pretty chill about what was going on. With our cousin and third partner, Jason, finishing up his season with the Tampa Bay Rays, I didn't feel bad leaving the bar and restaurant in his hands.

I tugged my clothes off and left them on the floor in my wake, all the while stepping over a baby rattle, Harley's catnip toy, and a used, empty bottle. *Fuck it, I'll clean tomorrow, along with the million other things I have to do.*

I climbed into the bed, my mind instantly going to Kate in her bedroom. She smelled so clean, her coconut and lime scent so ingrained in me, and it took everything I had not to push her onto the bed and go to town. My cock hardened at the memory, and I groaned, taking it into my hand. The fragrance, the touch of her silky smooth skin, the suction of her mouth—all memories that I'd kept handy for times like these, when I wanted nothing more than to sink my cock into her slick heat. To bring her to the edge, but to keep that orgasm at bay until she begged for it. My strokes got quicker, and I finally came with a grunt, coating my stomach. No matter how fantastic the memories were, I wouldn't be satisfied until I had her in my arms. And that would happen soon.

# CHAPTER 4
*Kate*

*G*OD HELP THOSE WHO GET IN *my way today.*
With only three hours of sleep, I was in no mood to go to work. But knowing my accounting and reports needed to be submitted, I trudged over to my closet to get ready. I threw on a pair of black skinny jeans, a purple oversized cowl-neck sweater, and my three inch booties, all the while thanking the powers that be for casual Fridays. After I ran the flat iron through my hair and applied my makeup, I was somewhat prepared to face the crazies of the world.

I headed into the kitchen, thankful that Cole had had the decency to start the coffee maker after his morning workout.

"Well, good morning, sunshine," Cole quipped as I

walked in. I gave him the evil eye as I maneuvered my way around him for my travel mug, then filled it with the precious brew.

"Did we keep you up?" he asked, cutting up peppers and mushrooms for his omelet.

"Nah, between travel and this case, I don't sleep very well." Which wasn't technically a lie. I sure as hell didn't want to say, "*Your buddy left me too frustrated, and my vibrator's battery died!*" I didn't think that would go over too well. I grabbed the milk and cereal, and sat down at the counter with my Cocoa Krispies.

"What's the plan for this weekend?" he asked, flipping his breakfast.

Shoot, I had no clue. The days had been running together. I pulled out my Galaxy S7 and checked my calendar. "I have no clue. Probably try and catch up on my sleep. Why?"

He looked up from the pan, and his brown eyes glinted with mischief. "Sleep when you're dead, and take Monday off. We're going up to Deep Creek for some riding, and one last party before the snow comes in."

I shrugged. "Wait, can Megan even ride? I mean, I know she's doing better and all with the hip injury, but what's Shane gonna do? Sit her at the campsite while we go off and have fun?"

Cole flicked a pepper at me. "Look at you, trying to stir up some drama. Do you honestly think that Shane would leave Megan? After all the shit they've been through? Cut the man a little slack. They've cleared it with the doctor, and she's good to go. She'll be a little sore, but Shane's already planned for a huge cabin with a hot tub. Plus, it's not like she's going to be alone. Everyone's coming up."

I snorted. "Deep Creek Lake? Even with all the shit that went down at Tommy's house, Megan's ready to go back?"

Cole shrugged. "Their therapist said it would be good for them to face that part of their past together. They're going up there this afternoon, get a lay of the land, before we come in and crash their solitude." I nodded. That made sense.

Hmm. A weekend in the woods, with my closest friends and family? That was exactly what I needed.

I grinned. "Sounds good. I'll stop by the store on my way home from work and pick up provisions."

"Good. I'll grab Karla on the way out tomorrow morning, so we'll head out early."

*This is surprising.* Normally, Cole was the love 'em and leave 'em type, but for some odd reason, he'd been keeping this one around. Karla was a gym bunny, flirting when she should be working out, and loving up on all the guys, trying to be their friend or bed buddy, and had apparently taken quite the shine to Cole. She was okay, in small doses. Not someone I'd want to be around for an entire weekend, though. Granted, I'd never been the easiest person to get along with. I'd been known to be a little on the cold side, but this girl drove me bananas. Everything was so happy and cheerful, and...*ugh*. Gag me with a freaking spoon. She was so fake. That, and everything Cole did was brilliant. I knew my brother. We'd been family for twenty years, and he didn't need a damn cheerleader. But, Cole liked her. And I was staying at his house, which he was letting me crash in rent free. So I'd ignored her loud shrieks of pleasure when she'd come over. Thankfully, it was an infrequent occurrence, so her joining us on the trip was something big for Cole.

I got up, put my bowl in the sink, and grabbed my bags. "Sounds like a plan. I'll grab the earplugs too. There's only so much of *'Oh Cole, you manly man you'* I can take," I mocked, dodging the dish towel he threw at me. I couldn't help it. Mocking my brother made my day.

I was still chuckling as I pulled into my office building thirty minutes later. Thankfully, I was assigned to the Baltimore field office. Distance was definitely better, because of less pressure, less formality, and supposed less political bullshit. Unfortunately, it wasn't far enough. Thanks to Tommy's emergence as the next cartel badass, the political weight on my team, and my supervising agents, had increased tenfold. Not only was that an embarrassment to the federal government, but the leadership we were under.

My partner and I had had a feeling something was up, and we'd tracked as many leads down as we could, before Tommy was able to slip through our fingers. We'd broached the possibility of a wiretap and surveillance, but were denied repeatedly. *Well, we proved them wrong, didn't we?* It took photographic evidence, and Tommy holding Megan hostage before they'd finally took me seriously. And even then, they were like, "We didn't have enough information to make a formal complaint." That was pure and utter bullshit. The Special Agent in Charge, as well as his bosses, couldn't even think of their golden boy doing any wrong.

I got off at the tenth floor and worked my way through the maze of cubicles, hoping to get to my own little slice of real estate before Special Agent in Charge Rapoles realized I was in. I passed by his darkened office and heaved a sigh of relief when no one stopped me, and headed into my team's cluster of desks, located in a big corner office.

Affectionately known as the Romper Room, the

room was the command center for anything Cruz Cartel related. Ten of us sat in the hideaway, far more people than OSHA recommended, I was sure. Thanks to the immediate fallout, we were able to add to our ranks and bolster our efforts. But, as the months went on, that fell by the wayside. Now, it was like we were the red-headed stepchildren. Tolerated, and given a bone or two, but in the end, not really looked upon with pride, just with disdain.

I sat my stuff down and logged onto the computer, waiting impatiently as the antiquated system churned and loaded. As usual, I was one of the last people in, and the office was already bustling with a flurry of activity. Printers whirled, phones rang, and the scent of our tech expert's wife's famous blueberry muffins wafted through the air. I had a feeling that if it weren't for her, we would be stuck on fast food and energy drinks. I drained the last of the coffee from my travel mug, then moved to the table in the back of the room to refill it.

"Morning, Parker," Rick mumbled as he moved past me to get to the printer situated behind the door.

"Morning, Simms. Did we get anything back on that phone?" I added my favorite coconut milk creamer to my cup and got back to my seat.

"Nothing."

"Has forensics gotten any prints off it?" I pulled up my email while Rick responded.

"Yeah, it's not looking good.  Not only did we find the hooker's print, we also found a partial thumb for an unknown. We're running that through missing persons, and all the other databases now, but I doubt we'll come up with anything. But, on the bright side, the hooker in the hotel has a name."

"Yeah? Someone local?"

"Melodye Jensen. She has all the same traits as the other girl, Elle Freeman. Early twenties.  Lived in Cherry Hill. Estranged from family and friends, so no one noticed when they were gone. There's no record of them getting on a flight; however, that's not saying much. They could have easily been driven to Vegas, or gotten on one of those private flights if they had a rich enough john. Both had marks from the same gun, a Smith and Wesson M&P 45. Both had massive quantities of heroin in their systems."

"Shit. Are there any markers?" Certain drug dealers would cut heroin with different materials, such baking soda, flour, rat poison, or quinine. They tended to use the same amounts of the same material. Not only to increase their quantity of product, but to keep that edge so people needed to keep buying more.

"No, that's the thing. This shit was pure, uncut. It

was like it was straight from the plant."

I groaned. "Just like Rachel Morrison." Rachel was yet another victim of the Cruz Cartel. She'd been a friend of Megan's, the former girlfriend of Shane's best friend Adrian, and the sister of one of the Cartel's former dealers. They'd killed her earlier this year with enough smack to kill three men, then they set her, along with the vehicle she was in on fire, in the park close to Megan's house.

"You got it. We need the find the bastard that's selling the shit, and find the route he's using to bring it in." Rick threw his pen in frustration.

I thought about it for a minute, mulling over any suspect possibilities. "What do our guys at DEA say? I mean, they're involved with this as much as we are."

Rick scoffed at the idea. "We sent over the report this morning, but they're working on the pipeline, so they're just as clueless as we are. We're lucky we have Shane's info, because without that, we wouldn't have gotten this far."

"I think we've picked all the info out of Shane that we could, but I can try and see if he has any other insights."

"You do that. I'm going to try and see what I can get on that new business in Baltimore, the one that took over Yankee's."

"Same type of business?" I sipped my coffee and

pulled up the travel accounting database.

"Pretty much. They slapped some paint on the walls and changed its name, but a whorehouse will always be a whorehouse. Doesn't matter whose name is on the lease, because what goes on behind those doors is the same thing. Just with a higher class of pussy."

I chuckled at Rick's frank assessment of the business. "And you're the one to check out the product being sold?"

Rick threw his hands up. "Hey, I can't help it if my job requires me to sample the goods."

"Uh-huh. Just make sure that you don't bring any crumbs home. You know how Baltimore ranked number one in crabs. And we're not talking blue crabs, either," I choked out, wiping up the coffee that I spat out.

"You got that right."

We worked in silence for the rest of the morning, as I prepared my report and spent way too long inputting my travel accounting. I pulled my peanut butter and jelly sandwich from the fridge when Rick came back into the Romper Room.

"So, the new tenant for the Yankee's building is called, coincidentally enough, Ravenous. The permit was pulled for a private entertainment establishment, cigar and scotch bar. Membership range from a three-hundred-dollar hourly guest pass, to a multi-month for an easy one thousand dollar fee. The permit puller is listed as Griffin and Associates. Looking deeper, it's an investment firm with similar clubs in Vegas, L.A., and Miami."

"Do we know the major players?" I asked, my mouth full of peanut butter goodness.

"The firm lists a Nicholas Santori as Chairman of the Board. No priors, clean record." Rick handed me a copy of the permits pulled, their approved liquor license, and a copy of the most recent health inspection. The signature of the manager listed had me raising my eyebrows.

"Did you see who signed off on this?" I said with a grin, showing him the form.

"Yeah, Paulette Sinclair. Who is that?" Rick asked with a snort.

I rolled my eyes. "For someone who is single and into Baltimore's nightlife, I'm surprised you don't know who this chick is. Three years ago, before I joined this case, a certain congressman was being blackmailed by some asshole in the city. There were pictures of him and Paulette Sinclair, only she's known as Madam Sin on the streets. She's a dominatrix."

Rick snorted. "Yeah, no thanks. I like the experience, but I sure as hell don't want some chick whipping me with a riding crop." He typed in her name to view her file and whistled. "She's pretty hot, though."

"Keep it in your pants, Casanova. You can't handle that shit." I looked over his shoulder to view any pending warrants or arrests, and much to my disappointment, she was in the clear. "Madam Sin is smart, toes the line. Her legit business is 'relationship and intimacy consulting.' Her clients pay a high price for the privilege to work with her and the privacy she secures. It's a very few and select assortment of people, and after that whole issue with the congressman, it's even more so. Her business is top-notch, so why is she signing for permits at a scotch and cigar joint? This doesn't make any sense."

Rick's upper lip curled into a smirk. "And how well do you know her business?"

I smacked him upside his head. "Focus, Sims. Some asshole client of hers got smart with a video camera and recorded the congressman's sessions with the Madam, tried to blackmail the guy for a cool three million. We were able to get ahold of the jerk and the camera feed before anything came to light. They were both grateful, but Madam Sin owes me a favor."

"We can always swing by there, say hello?" Rick gave me a wink.

"And get a drink to go?" I joked, then sat back down at my desk. "No, we'll swing by her office near the

Charles Center. I'll get ahold of her."

After the congressman debacle, Madam Sin gave me a special number and code to use, if I ever needed to call in the favor. Not sure I wanted to call in my favor before I truly needed it, but I wanted to get a feel of the new establishment, the owner. I pulled the black matte card from my desk drawer, listing the address and phone number of her professional offices, and dialed the number.

"Dr. Sinclair's office," a formal male voice sounded over the phone.

"I'd like to speak with Dr. Sinclair, please."

"She's with a client, so I can take a message."

"My name is…" I checked the name on the back of the card, "Tatiana Nym."

There was a pause, as the receptionist comprehended my name; the unspoken code. "Just a minute, please."

After a brief moment of silence, the voice came back on the line. "Dr. Sinclair is not available to meet with you; however, she did allow me to pass along that she will be at Marcone's tonight after eight o'clock. Your name will be on the guest list."

"Thank you." I hung up the phone with a grin. An invite to a private, exclusive restaurant always piqued my interest. Invites were hard to come by, and any sort of gossip was even harder. Marcone's was where all the congressmen went with their mistresses, where deals were hammered out with archrivals, and where more often than not, someone was cashing in on a bribe.

"So, are we hitting the club?" Rick asked, his brown eyes expectant.

"No. But we are going to have drinks at Marcone's." I checked my accounting to ensure it had been submitted properly, then logged off my computer.

"Shit, Parker. You know the finance folks are going to have a cow when they read that expense report." He tossed the remnants of his lunch into the trash. "Remind me not to go to that deli around the corner," he said with a wince, rubbing his chest.

"Why the hell do you eat that shit?" I asked, throwing him a bottle of acid relief.

"Same reason why I pick up pussy at bars, because it's what I want," he shot back, tossing back the pill with some Mountain Dew.

"Uh-huh. And that's when your ass is going to catch something. Better watch yourself, Simms." I picked up my purse and grabbed my leather jacket. "I'm taking some personal time. Pick me up at seven...and wear your suit!"

I climbed into my Jeep, cranked up my satellite radio, and headed to Annapolis Mall. I hadn't been to a place like Marcone's in forever. A little bit of retail therapy, and a new hair color would do me some good. After sitting down with my colorist, Julia, for an hour, I walked the lengthy mall, wandering in and out of stores, letting my mind zone out. I found a sexy, sleeveless, little black dress with a deep V-neck that would go perfectly with the raspberry, peep toe Jimmy Choo's I'd scored from a consignment shop in Miami.

After checking my watch, I knew I should get home soon and get ready, so I made my way toward the parking lot. I was paying more attention to my phone than I was watching where I was going, so it was no surprise when I bumped into someone right outside my Jeep.

"Oh, I'm so sorry…" My voice trailed off when the guy looked down at me. My eyes immediately got lost in his brown ones, and my breath caught. His scent of citrus and sea air, mixed with the smell of his leather jacket, formed an intoxicating aroma that sent my heart racing and my pussy clenching.

"Was wondering when I was going to run into you again." His southern drawl had my stomach in knots.

"Oh. Hey, Noah." I tucked my phone into my purse and brushed a newly black-cherry strand of hair behind my ears, and tried my best to look like I didn't want to drag him into the dressing room and have my way with him.

"Where you off to in such a hurry?" He trailed his finger down my arm, then entwined my fingers with his. The simple act of intimacy unnerved me.

"I have things to do, places to go," I said, as I gently removed my hand and held up my bags from Nordstrom's and Victoria's Secret. "What about you? What drags you up this way?"

"Had to pick up a few things. What are you doing tonight?" He stepped into my personal space as a car passed us, overwhelming my senses with his closeness.

"Got a work thing," I replied vaguely. Sketch wouldn't have told him much about what I did for a living, because if he had, Noah wouldn't have been so eager to talk with me if he knew I had been lying to him for the last year.

"Yeah? Meet up with me after that," he said in a low voice, brushing a stray hair off my forehead.

I chuckled. "Are you asking me, or are you telling me?"

He smirked. "Whatever you want to think, Princess."

I flirted back, despite what my brain was yelling at me to do. "What if I already had plans afterward? You don't know, I may be seeing someone."

Noah's full lips turned upward into a big grin. "Because, Princess, if that were the case, your pulse wouldn't be racing right now." He lightly ran a finger over the pulse point in my neck, then cupped the back of my neck. "And if you are, it doesn't matter anyway. You're mine now." He lowered his head, and his lips grazed mine.

I stepped back from his grasp, before it went any further. It was time to nip this in the bud. "Noah, I'm not anyone's. We had a fling, that's all there was." It hurt to do it, but knowing my luck with relationships, and the stresses of my job, there was no way in hell that anything good could come out of it.

"Okay, we'll see about that." His eyes darkened to the color of melted chocolate, and he smiled mischievously before he walked away. My insides fluttered. Noah loved a challenge, and I didn't think he would give up so easily.

I hopped into the Jeep and maneuvered my way down Interstate 97 toward Odenton, when my phone rang. Clicking on the Bluetooth, I answered.

"Parker?"

"What's up, Rick?" I asked, passing a minivan.

"I'm calling in the second string. Lunch caught up with me. I think I have food poisoning."

I busted into laughter. "Are you serious?"

Rick groaned. It must be serious if he was passing up drinks at a fancy, exclusive place. "Do you honestly think I'd pass up a government expensed trip to

Marcone's? That's, like, the holy grail, a trip to the Super Bowl, and the fountain of whisky all wrapped into one box. The only shit that comes out of that place are the reviews for food, and those steaks are supposed to be second to none."

I chuckled again. "All right, I hear ya. Too bad I can't bring any samples home for you. Who's my backup?"

"Evan Sarcozi. I'll text you a picture."

I started to say more, just as Rick groaned, then gave a strangled, "Gotta go." I felt bad for my partner, truly I did. But I couldn't help but take a little joy from of his discomfort.

I pulled into the driveway and headed in, set on getting ready. Jax waited, dancing at the door for me.

"Hey, buddy, what's going on?" I put my bags on the sofa and gave him a good belly rub. "Where's Cole?"

"Right here," Cole announced, walking into the room. "Did you go to the store yet?"

*Crap. I needed to get groceries.* "Nope. Totally slipped my mind."

He picked up a lock of my newly colored hair. "Yeah, okay. You remembered to color your hair, though."

I shrugged. "I needed a change. What time are we leaving in the morning?"

Cole leaned against the doorframe to the kitchen. "As early as possible. I'm hooking the bikes up onto the trailers once Sketch gets here with his."

I nodded. "That works. I'll swing by the store on my way home. I have a meeting with a dominatrix at eight."

Cole shook his head. "I don't want to know. There are some things a brother doesn't need to hear about his baby sister." I chuckled as I took my bags into my bedroom, and threw them onto the bed. After a quick shower to shave my legs and freshen up, I got dressed. The dress hugged what little curves I had, and it's V was so deep that I couldn't wear a bra. Luckily, I was blessed with small boobs, and some breast lift tape to fix that problem. I left my hair down, the black and cherry colored locks gently framed my face and made my bright blue eyes pop. A little mascara and blush, and I was ready to go. I slipped on my shoes, grabbed my black trench coat, and my purse, and headed toward the living room.

"Cole, I'm heading out. What do I need to grab from the store for tomorrow?" I slipped on my coat. No answer. "Cole?" *Must be getting the bikes ready.* I grabbed my keys and walked out to my Jeep. I didn't see Sketch's Camaro, but a black, jacked up truck sat in my side yard with a trailer hitched to it. I sent Cole a quick text, hopped in, and took off.

# CHAPTER 5
*Kate*

MARCONE'S WAS LOCATED IN a posh area in Baltimore, in the heart of the Capital Tower district on the top level of an otherwise ordinary office building. There was no sign indicating its presence, but then again, it didn't need the advertisement. Word of mouth alone from area power players kept the place in business. I gave my keys to the valet, and made my way into the posh lobby to the waiting host in front of the doors.

"May I have your name, Miss?" The British accent gave the air of importance and elegance, but the bulge at his hip told me that he meant business.

"Tatiana Nym."

"Of course. Thank you. Right this way." He led me into the small, dark paneled elevator and pressed the button for the fourteenth floor.

The doors opened to an elegant corridor. As I had expected, security was tight, with large men in suits stationed throughout the hallway. I checked my coat and slipped into the bar area, glancing around for my date for the night. It was after eight, so he should have already shown up. Thinking a drink would do me well, I claimed a seat at the mahogany wood bar and ordered a glass of Prosecco. I took a sip as I glanced around me, taking note of the exit points, the people, and the servers.

All the pretty people were there. The finest the city had to offer, dressed to the nines, sipping champagne and consorting with those who only wanted what they could take. It made me wonder what Paulette Sinclair had to offer. My thoughts were interrupted when a sexy stranger stepped up to the bar. I took him in while he asked the bartender for a scotch on the rocks. Black hair, on the longish side, with a dimple in his strong chin. No facial hair. I could tell the man was built like a tank because of the way his shirt stretched across his shoulders. I snuck a quick look at his taut ass and nodded slightly. *It doesn't take much to get me to notice you.*

"Hello." The smooth tenor of his voice was enough to send shivers down my spine, but I played it off.

"Hello."

"Evan," he tried again, sticking out his hand. *Ah, my backup.*

"Tatiana," I replied with an eyebrow raised, and extended my hand.

"Tatiana." The name rolled off his tongue like pure sex. I gripped my glass, just a smidge tighter, imaging what else he could do with that tongue. "It's nice to meet you. Have you ever been in a more pretentious room?" he asked, sipping his scotch.

I couldn't help it, a chuckle bubbled up. "I have, unfortunately, more than once."

Evan shook his head. His gray eyes pierced mine. "It's truly a traumatic experience, isn't it?"

I nodded slowly before spying the Madam, making her way into the room. Our eyes caught for a brief second, then she turned and walked toward the restroom. She captured the men's attentions, as they followed her sensuous figure, clad in a high-waisted, black pencil skirt and tight, white button-down blouse, with their eyes. "Sadly, it is. Excuse me for a moment." Giving Evan a slight smile, I followed the Madam to the luxurious bathroom.

"Thank you for meeting me, Doctor," I said politely, after checking the stalls for any guests.

"I can't say it's a pleasure, Agent Parker. So please, tell me what you need from me." Her green eyes scanned herself in the floor to ceiling mirror.

*Right to the point, I see.* I gave the Madam a slight smile.

"I wanted to check in with you, see how your latest business ventures are going."

She pursed her ruby red lips. "I see. Apparently, nothing goes unnoticed by the Feds."

"I noticed your signature on the Ravenous permits. Given the history of that location, I was curious as to what a successful relationship consultant was doing with a scotch and cigar bar," I said nonchalantly, looking her in the eyes.

Madam sighed. "Would it matter if I told you that I consider it an investment, and my partnership with Griffin and Associates is nothing more than a simple business strategy?"

"Your investments are your business, Madam. I simply want to ensure that there are no other...*obstacles* that could prevent you from succeeding."

"Agent Parker, exactly what do you want fr
om me?" The annoyance in her eyes flashed a warning at me, but it did nothing to keep me from holding my tongue.

"I'm simply interested in the type of clientele that Ravenous is catering to."

Madam nodded. "Of the dangerous variety, I

assume."

"Primarily, yes, unless there are other sorts I should know about?" I smiled at her.

"Agent Parker, Mr. Griffin came to me with a proposition over three months ago, to provide consenting entertainment and company to the members of his club. I've been looking into expanding my brand to a more lucrative business model."

I nodded, but I didn't quite believe her. Her gaze was steady, but a shift in her eyes revealed a glimmer of fear.

"And what sort of business model are we speaking about?"

The Madam's gaze turned into an icy stare. "Why, Agent Parker, I do believe I'll plead the Fifth. You're more than welcome to apply for a membership and find out for yourself." She leaned over, and artfully applied another coat of red lipstick to her already plump lips. "Is that all, Agent?"

*Obviously, we're done here.* I went to the door, but turned around before opening it.

"Dr. Sinclair, I truly apologize for any intrusion. Please know that if I can be of any assistance, you can call me, no matter what. I hope I can say the same for you," I offered, my voice low.

"Of course, Agent Parker. Anything I can do to help

the Feds." The sincerity in her voice was fake, along with the smile she gave. Nevertheless, I passed her a business card with only the number to my cell on it and left the room. Whether she kept the card or tossed it, I didn't care. Something was up with the Madam, and I was going to find out what it was.

I paused at the coat check, handing over the ticket to the clerk, when Evan came to my side.

"Tatiana, I told you to wait for me at the bar," he said, in a seductive tone. I glanced at him, and immediately stiffened as he put his arm around me, and lowered his lips to my neck. "Security, at your three o'clock," he whispered in my ear.

I plastered a wide grin on my face, and tucked my face into his embrace. "Mics?"

He emitted a quick, low chuckle. "You got it. Mics and cameras everywhere."

I looked up into his startling gray eyes, with what I'd hoped was an adoring smile. "Ready to go?" He just smiled at me, and helped me with my jacket. Our hands entwined as we strolled down to the elevator, as if nothing was wrong. All the while, our eyes discreetly scanned for any threats.

Once we exited the building, I gave the valet the card for my Jeep and we waited. No words were spoken. After we got inside and pulled away, he typed something on his phone, then showed it to me.

*Stay quiet.*

I nodded. First thing we needed to do was ensure we weren't being followed, then we needed to ensure the car wasn't bugged. Overreaction? Possibly. However, our group was keen on being overzealous with our security measures ever since Tommy hit the wind. Evan pulled out a small device, fitted with a radio sensor to determine if there was a frequency transmitting a signal. After a few seconds, the indicator light turned blue, meaning it was clear to talk.

"Well, that was fun," I quipped, taking the exit for the interstate. "I'm Kate, by the way. But I guess you already knew that."

"Nice to meet you, Kate," he said easily, watching the side mirrors for any cars changing lanes.

"So what was the deal back there?" I switched lanes and sped up, taking the next exit, leading back into the city.

"I don't think they were watching you as much as they were watching out for her. There was a heavier amount of security in that hallway than in any other part of the room."

"A protection detail," I confirmed.

"Exactly. Now, the question is why she needs so much muscle. There were six guys watching her when you walked in."

I mentally scolded myself. I'd only counted the four.

He shook his head. "There's no way you could have seen all of them. Two were in the alcove, out of your line of sight." *And this, folks, is the reason to have backup.*

"Was I the threat?"

Evan shook his head again, his black hair falling into his eyes. "Possibly. Because you're a woman, they didn't take you as seriously as they should have. Plus, there's no way you could have been hiding a weapon in that dress," he said with a chuckle.

I joined in, relieved that the tension was over.

"How are we doing?" I asked a few minutes later.

"We're good. Go ahead and drop me at Pickles. I have a car waiting for me."

I turned back on to Pratt street, headed toward the stadiums, and in no time, we were in front of Pickles Pub, a game day favorite hangout.

"Hey, thanks for covering me today," I said with a smile.

"No worries. Tell Rick he owes me. I missed out on dinner with my wife."

"Will do." And with that, his imposing figure exited my Jeep. I did a quick U-turn and headed toward home. I immediately put the phone to my ear and called Lucy, my go-to for finding dirt on anyone. She was always on point, and could fly under the radar at work. Most people loved taking credit for their work, but Lucy was happier working in the background.

"What's up, Wonder Woman?" Her nickname for me never failed to make me smile.

"I got a job for you, Luce."

"Of course you do. Why else would you call me at nine thirty on a Friday night?"

I chuckled, knowing that she was right. We hadn't been out on the town in forever. Lucy was one of only a few girls I could call a friend outside of work. Like me, Lucy kept to herself, but once we got her out of her shell, she rocked the town.

"We'll go out soon. I'm hoping that next week will be easier."

"Hey now, don't worry about me. I'm happy staying on my butt at home. Last time I went out with you, I ended up with a hickey on my tit from some dude with an eyebrow ring, and I couldn't find my damn phone for a week. I think I'm okay with once a year."

I let out a snort of laughter. "I promise, next time you'll remember. I swear! But back to business. I need you to find all the info you can on a Dr. Paulette Sinclair, especially financials."

"On it.  Need it now?"

"No, that's okay. I'm going out of town this weekend.

Whatever we find can wait until I get in on Tuesday."

"Got it, Wonder Woman. Have a great night."

We disconnected, and I tossed my phone onto the passenger seat. Whatever Madam Sin was hiding, Lucy would find it.

I stopped at the light at route 301 and Waugh Chapel, and a huge yawn escaped. Not feeling much like shopping, but knowing my brother would give me hell if I didn't, I pulled into the nearest grocery store to stock up on food. With Shane's and my brother's appetites, we'd end up having to hit the store before going home, so I overloaded my grocery cart. I left the store with a lighter wallet and aching calves. *Note to self, don't wear four-inch Jimmy Choo's to the grocery store.*

I pulled up to the house, only to find that my spot in the driveway was taken by the same large black truck that was there when I'd left. *Are you for real?* The urge to lay on my horn was strong, but I didn't want to be the douche that woke everyone up at ten o'clock at night. And knowing my brother and his boys, they wouldn't hear it anyway.

"If I can't have my spot, then they're bringing the damn bags in," I muttered, stalking up the driveway. I resisted the temptation to key the black monstrosity. I opened the door to Jax's welcoming, and the loud voices of juvenile men playing video games. *I seriously need my own place.*

"Hey! If you want to eat this weekend, I suggest you get your asses out to my Jeep and bring in the food," I shouted, turning my back to them as I removed my trench coat to hang in the jacket cupboard. All of a sudden, the room went quiet, with only the video game sound effects filling the air. I turned around slowly to find three faces staring back at me.

"What?" *What the hell is going on?* I frantically checked my dress, but everything was in place. "What the hell is your problem?"

"You…ahem…look great, Kate," coughed Adrian, and quickly averted his gaze. I rolled my eyes as Cole smacked him upside his head. "What!"

"That's my sister, dumbass." Cole turned to me and gave me a pointed look. "You need our help?"

"Yeah, so get your minions together and bring it in. Some asshat decided to take my spot."

"I guess I'm the asshat." A low chuckle came from the recliner. With the back toward me, I couldn't see who laughed at my expense, but a knowing feeling came over me and my stomach dropped. The chuckler stood up and stretched his long, muscular arms over his head. His dark green Henley creeped up over his sculpted abs, giving me a peek of the Japanese dragon on his lower left side. My eyes widened, then I quickly composed my face.

"So, you're the one with the jacked up truck? What, your old ass Challenger couldn't hang?" I said, moving away from the door so Cole and the rest of the guys could get to the Jeep. I stepped out of my heels, and without waiting for his comment, I headed to my bedroom. I felt his presence behind me, but I ignored him. I grabbed a pair of yoga pants and a gray thermal shirt and went into the bathroom, locking the door behind me. I couldn't help the bitchiness bubbling out. I knew he didn't deserve it, but it was either be the ice-princess I was known to be, or turn into a melted pile of butter at his feet.  I mean, hell, how could he not know how badly his presence was messing me up?

"What's up with all the grouchiness, Princess?"  His voice came through the door, low and clear as a bell.

"I'm just not feeling like chatting right now. Is that an issue?" I said loudly, pulling my shirt over my head. I stood on my toes, trying to stretch out the kinks in my calves, but it just made the pain worse. After washing my face, I opened the door, brushing past him as I walked to the kitchen to help put away the groceries that were sitting on the counter. Sounds of the guys in the basement playing pool filtered up the stairs. *Thanks for dropping them off and running, boys!*

"No, Kate. That's not an issue because I don't plan

on chatting for long." He grabbed the gallon of orange juice and put it in the fridge.

"Not happening, Noah," I muttered, throwing him a tight smile as I put the cereal and pancake mix in the box that we were taking with us.

"Tell me why, then. Why is it so different up here than down in Miami? What changed?" He stood close to me and folded his arms across his chest.

*Because you were an escape from everything up here!* I wanted to say so badly, but the words faltered at my lips. He tried to dip his head for a kiss, but I ducked and moved back. I couldn't let him get close. Time to nip this shit in the bud.

"Because it is. It's complicated. My life is too stressful right now to deal with this. But I'm always down for more friends."

Noah smirked. "If that's what it's going to take to make you realize you're meant to be with me, then sure. Friends it is."

I sighed, and flashed him a fake smile. "Great. If you're crashing in the basement, there's towels, blankets, and pillows in the back. Cole can set you up. Good night."

I moved to walk out of the kitchen, when he caught my elbow and yanked me back into him. He crushed his lips to mine, capturing the slight gasp I let out. His tongue swept in, and heat hurtled through my body. He cupped the back of my head; his long fingers tangled in my hair as he deepened the kiss. Then, without warning, he broke it off.  My eyes flew open and I stared at him, panting.

"But I guarantee that we won't be 'just friends' for long. Good night, Princess." He adjusted the bulge in his jeans, gave me a cocky grin, then headed out of the kitchen. I heard him chuckling as he took the stairs to the basement. *Damn, it's going to be a long weekend.*

# CHAPTER 6
*Kate*

Thanks to Noah and a fully charged battery operated friend, I didn't get as much sleep as I had hoped. As much as I had said I didn't want him, the fact that he didn't come upstairs to see me had me slightly disappointed. So needless to say, I wasn't in a friendly sort of mood.

After my shower, I stuffed clothes into my duffle bag, threw in some toiletries, and grabbed one of my many hoodies from the closet. Since we were going to be all muddy, and with no one to impress, there was no reason to worry about what I was going to wear. I put my gun case and duffle bag in the backseat of Cole's truck, then headed back inside for coffee.

The guys slowly ambled their way upstairs, and

by looking at the recycling bin, they were having a rough morning. My smart-ass self was dying to bring out the cymbals to make them cringe, but my brother was all about the paybacks. And Lord knew, I had been subjected to those more than once. Instead, I did the nice sister routine and made sure the coffee was fresh and the donuts I hid away last night were open for all to see. At six in the morning, it was only going to get worse. Hopefully, we'd stop for breakfast.

"Mornin' fellas," I chirped cheerfully, much to their disdain. Their grumbles were loud and clear, and I just grinned at their discomfort. Cole finally left his bedroom thirty minutes later, dressed and bag in hand. While the guys made sure the four-wheelers were strapped on tightly, I packed the rest of the food into the coolers for the three and half-hour drive.

"Morning, Princess. How'd you sleep?" Noah asked, taking my coffee mug from my hands and taking a sip. *Oh, this boy doesn't realize that's the ultimate sin. Nothing comes between me and my coffee.* Seeing as how it was his first offense ever, I let it slide.

"Like a baby. How about you?" I lied through my teeth. I'd slept like shit again, and it was his fault. Was it wrong of me to hope he didn't sleep at all?

"The same. Ready to get a little muddy, *friend?*" He turned his Baltimore Orioles cap backwards and pulled on his black leather jacket.

"Abso-fucking-lutley." I whistled for Jax, grabbed my purse, and headed out the door. Jax ran around like a lunatic, happy to be outside with the guys. Sketch and Adrian climbed up into the black truck that was taking my place in the driveway, and I went over to Cole's blue truck to let Jax in.

"Oh...hey, sis. I need you to ride with the guys."

"Wait, what? Why?"

"Because I'm picking up Karla on our way, and the girl likes to get a little freaky on road trips."

I scoffed and rolled my eyes. "Are you fucking kidding me? Are you that hard up that you can't wait three and half hours for some pussy?"

"I can't help it. She's pretty talented." His dark green eyes pleaded with me to understand, so I threw up my hands in surrender.

"Fine. You're taking your stinky ass dog, though." I grabbed my purse and bags, then stomped over to the truck. Sketch's shoulders were shaking with laughter.

I climbed into the backseat, next to Sketch, and smacked his arm.

"That's for laughing like the hyena you are." I pulled my phone and headphones out of my purse and plugged them in. The sexy country drawl of Brantley Gilbert filled my ears. I caught Noah's watchful brown eyes in the rearview mirror, so I gave a tight smile, then settled in for the long ride. My exhaustion from the past six months had finally pulled me in, and I surrendered to its grasp.

A gentle caress on my cheek, and a sexy southern drawl woke me later.

"Wake up, Princess. We're here."

My eyes popped open and I took in the gorgeous, chiseled jaw covered in scruff, his full bottom lip, and his soulful brown eyes. My heart did a little leap, and I groaned softly at how my heart did its little dance. But just as swiftly, I averted my gaze and discreetly wiped the drool from my mouth. I climbed out of the truck and surveyed the area and our weekend home. The two-story log cabin looked like it came from a storybook, with the pine trees surrounding it and Deep Creek Lake shimmering behind it. From the noises around back, the guys were getting the four-wheelers set up.

"Where's Cole's truck?" I slid my sunglasses onto my face, guarding my eyes from his.

Noah's lips twisted into a smirk. "They're about thirty minutes behind us. Something about taking in nature."

*Nature, my ass. I'm sure they stopped off for a quick romp in the woods.* I grabbed my purse from the seat, slammed the door, and headed for the spacious front porch. The screen door did little to stop the sounds of Aerosmith from floating outside, bringing a little rock to the tranquility of the lake. I popped open the door and shouted my presence.

"You're finally here!" squealed Megan, as she made her way over to me. Her gait was smoother than when I'd last saw her at her wedding, and her limp wasn't as noticeable. But it shouldn't have surprised me. Megan, despite her graciousness, kindness, and adorableness, was a fighter. And I was glad that we'd gotten to be as close as we were.

"Hey, momma. How's it going? You're looking great!" I wrapped my arms around her and squeezed her tight.

"I'm good, I'm good. How are you, stranger?" she asked, her brown eyes shining. I pulled back and searched her face for any sign of distress or conflict, but her porcelain features were calm.

"I'm good, and ready for this weekend. I need to just veg for a moment, not have to worry about my phone or next shift, or flying off to God-knows-where." I gave her a tired smile, and she squeezed my hand.

"I completely understand. And you totally deserve it, too. You've been going nonstop since I've met you!" Her eyes glinted with a hint of mischief. "So, go stake out your sanctuary. No one else has picked their room yet, so you may want to grab yours before the savages try to stake their claim." She waved her hands to the wooden staircase.

"Thanks, chick. I'll only be a minute." I picked up my bags and walked up the beautiful staircase.

With knotted pine panels, exquisite skylight, and a stone fireplace, the house was the epitome of what a log cabin should be. I scoped out the three other rooms in question and planned my strategy. My hope was that I was the farthest away from Cole and Karla. I planned to sleep, and I sure as hell didn't need Karla's porn star moans and bed squeaking to keep me awake. I bypassed the room with the dual set of bunkbeds because the boys could sleep there, and took the room that faced the back of the house. With a fluffy down comforter and a blue gingham quilt on the brass full-size bed, and a spectacular view of the glistening lake, I knew I'd found my sanctuary. I dropped my bag on the wooden bench next to the closet and unpacked my gear. Extra ammo for my Glock went into the nightstand, clothes went into the dresser, and my toiletries went into the shared bathroom. *Six people to one bathroom? Just like college.* I rolled my eyes at the thought, then headed back downstairs to the massive kitchen.

Megan looked at home, rolling out dough and singing along with the radio. I took the glass of water with cucumber and lemon that she put on the counter for me, and turned to look out the back. Adrian, Sketch, Noah, and Shane were messing around with the ATV's, making sure everything was in working order for the afternoon. I sipped my water and looked over at Meg. Even with her front covered in flour, she looked in her element.

"What the heck are you making?" I sat down at the kitchen island, where she was messing with the dough.

"We had leftover chicken from the other night, so I'm making a couple chicken pot pies for dinner tonight." She rolled out another circle of dough and I shook my head.

"Megan Turner, you better not stay in the kitchen this weekend. This is a time for us to hang out and relax, not bathe yourself in dough and meat," I scolded gently. She didn't know how to relax, but then again, who was I to say anything?

She stuck her tongue out at me. "I promise, I'll be social. I just don't want to have to worry about dinner once we get back."

"Trust me, we won't starve. Cole has the cooler, and it's filled to the brim with meats and junk food."

Megan chuckled and placed the dough strips across the top of the two pie dishes full of vegetables, chicken, and creamy sauce. "So, what's been going on? How's work?"

"It's going all right. It seems like there's a dead end at every corner. We chased down a lead in Vegas this week, but we're not any closer. Tommy went ghost, and no one seems to know where the hell he went," I bit out. Between losing funding, and our best assets to other cases, and the lack of leads on *anything*, frustration on the case was mounting.

"Could someone have already taken care of him?" she asked, moving to the sink to wash her hands.

I fiddled with the red checkered placemat in front of me. "It's possible. For all I know, another heir to the Cartel could have risen up to take control. We don't know much about Christian Cruz's family life. He had one illegitimate son. Who knows if there are more."

Megan slid the pies into the fridge and started to clean up. "Not that I care about him, but whatever happened to Tommy's mom, his sisters? Did they get rolled up in all this mess?"

I snorted. "His mom and her husband lawyered up before we even got to their brownstone in Manhattan. So far, nothing has come from their camp, aside from their lame attempt of disavowal."

Megan rolled her eyes. From what she'd told me, Mr. and Mrs. Greene were nothing but rude and nasty to her while her and Tommy were engaged. She opened her mouth, but was interrupted when Shane walked in. At six-foot-two, two hundred thirty pounds, and former hockey player that just missed the pros, Shane was larger than life. With brown hair shaved close to his head, penetrating hazel eyes, and a body full of tattoos and piercings, he epitomized the alpha bad boy that girls read about in those smutty books. Fortunately for Megan, he'd only had eyes for her since the day they first met when she was sixteen.

Shane went right for Megan, ignoring the flour dusted on her hands and shirt, and wrapped her into a passionate kiss. I pretended to gag. As much as I adored the two of them, there was only so much PDA I could stand. *Especially when I'm not getting any myself.*

"Sorry, Kate. Didn't see you there," Shane joked with a shit-eating grin.

"Uh-huh. Take her to the bedroom, perv. We don't need to see that," I shot back, covering my eyes playfully.

"Good idea. Fix us some lunch, why don't ya. We'll need to refuel." He picked her up like she was nothing but air, bridal style. "Oh yeah, Cole just pulled up." And without a backward glance, he carried a giggling Megan off to the master bedroom down the hall.

*If I wasn't already used to their tendency to hump like rabbits, I might be slightly uncomfortable.* I shook my head at the two lovebirds and wandered out to the front porch. Cole and Adrian were messing with the the gear, while Karla leaned against his truck, twiddling with her phone. The rest of the gear, including coolers, helmets, and their bags, all sat on the ground, waiting to be brought in. I groaned, my irritation level with the princess act at an all-time high. I stomped down to the truck and hefted the soft cooler strap over my shoulder, and grasped the larger blue one by the handles.

"Yeah, this place doesn't have a bellhop. Unless you want spiders and shit getting in your bags, I'd suggest you bring them in," I said dryly, then headed back into the house. Apparently, that snapped her out of whatever spell the phone had her under, and she looked up at me with her doe eyes.

"Oh my gosh! I'm so sorry, Kate. I was trying to get ahold of my friend, Cami, who has a place down here, and wouldn't you know it, they're down here too. We were thinking we could get everyone together and…" she said in one breath, huffing and puffing under the weight of her luggage. I knew it was hers because Cole's standard issue luggage was not pink and purple floral print. I ignored the babbling and brought the coolers into the kitchen.

"Where should I put my bag? I really need to take a nap. The trip was exhausting." I rolled my eyes. *I'm sure it was. Your head must have been doing a lot of work.*

"Upstairs, first door on the right," I called over my shoulder, and set to work on unpacking the perishables.

Twenty minutes later, I yelled to the boys outside that the food was ready. A stack of sandwiches made with Megan's mom's roast beef was piled high on the table, along with four bags of chips, potato salad, and coleslaw and broccoli salad I picked up from the deli last night. The thunder of feet on the porch outside and the barking of two dogs had me staking out a chair quickly. I knew better than to get in between the guys and their meal. Megan and Shane ambled out, with the post-coital glow on their faces. I didn't bother yelling for Karla. If she hadn't heard me the first time, she would get the leftovers.

Somehow, I got stuck between Noah and Adrian, so I moved closer than necessary to Adrian, and away from Noah, practically sitting on Adrian's lap. The smirk on Noah's face said it all. He knew I was avoiding all physical contact with him. And hell, if I could do it the entire weekend, I would.

Everyone was digging into their food, when Megan finally asked, "Weren't you supposed to bring someone? Was that Karla?"

I choked on my sandwich as Cole looked around the table. "She said the trip up was *exhausting,* Cole. What did you do to that poor girl?" I asked with a snicker.

He gave me an arrogant smile. "Definitely made the trip worthwhile, I'll tell you that much."

Megan stifled a gag. "She must mean something if Cole brought her up here. Is she your girl, Cole?" Her face was a mask of innocence, as that simple statement gave Cole hell for being whipped by a gym skank. Cole's face turned bright red and he shook his head. He opened his mouth to answer, when Karla walked down the stairs and entered the fray. She took in the seating arrangement and plopped down right next to Cole, and leaned into his shoulder.

"You didn't come upstairs, baby. I was waiting for ya," she said in a breathy voice. I snorted and received a glare from Karla. Cole, as usual, wasn't fazed.

"We were busy." He shot her an annoyed glance and continued eating. Feeling the sting of rejection, she looked over at everyone and the spread.

"I can't eat this. There's nothing but fat and carbs. I'm really watching my figure. Is there anything else?" she asked, her voice full of phoniness. My inner spring of a temper coiled tightly, and I curbed the urge to drop my plate in her lap.

"Oh, let me find…" Megan started, and I held my hand out to her to get her to sit down.

"No, she's fine," I said to Megan, then turned to Karla. "Help yourself to whatever's in the fridge. If there's anything special you need, the store is about 10 miles up the road." Everyone became intent on their food, so they missed the glare I received from Ms. Happy-go-lucky. *Well then, the gym slut has a temper, does she?* I raised my eyebrow and gave her the universal look, telling her to bring it. She rolled her eyes and looked away.

After we finished up lunch, everyone went to change into their gear. I pulled on a pair of my oldest riding jeans, a tank top, a thin lined shirt, and my *Carhart* hoodie on top. I laced up my riding boots over my ankle and grabbed my purple helmet. As I was about to walk down the stairs, Karla joined me. With her skinny jeans and tank top that showed ample cleavage, along with a cotton jacket, she was nowhere near prepared for the trip.

"Are you going with us?" I asked incredulously, going down the stairs.

"Yep. I can't wait to feel that baby between my legs. I bet it'll get Cole hard as a rock," she quipped, slipping on a pair of canvas tennis shoes.

"Ew. I didn't need to hear that." I fought the bile rising in my throat and changed the subject. "But unless you're planning on changing into something that's a little more suitable for riding, you're not going." We may have joked around and acted like fools, but safety was always our main priority. We never rode when we were drinking, and we sure as hell didn't ride without the proper gear.

Karla actually stomped her foot in protest. "What the hell is wrong with what I'm wearing?"

"You're going to freeze. We're in the freaking mountains, and the temp is dropping rapidly. And you'll more than likely get your foot ripped off because you need a heel to stay on the pegs. Didn't Cole tell you any of this?"

She flipped her dirty blonde hair out of her eyes and snarled at me. "I'm fine. What the hell do you know, anyway?"

I put up my hands in surrender. "If you want to freeze your fake tits off, that's fine by me, but don't come crying to my brother when you can't freaking walk because you wore the wrong fucking shoes." I walked outside to the rest of the group, fuming.

"Cole, you better check your girl. She seems to think that riding is like a fucking fashion show." He groaned and ambled back into the house, while I climbed onto my Polaris RZR White Lightening and turned the ignition. The rumble of the engine instantly centered me, but the trails were calling me. I looked around. Shane was helping Megan onto his Kawasaki. Adrian, Sketch, and Noah were also geared up and ready to go. The only ones we were missing were Cole and Karla.

Shane's phone alerted him to an incoming text. "Let's roll out. Cole's staying here." *Of course he is.* I fumed at the audacity that that chick had. I pulled my helmet over my head and adjusted my goggles. We had about four more hours of daylight left, and I intended to make the most of them. We followed the map, leading us into Garret County National Forest. The views going up the mountain trails were nothing short of spectacular. The autumn colors shone throughout the valley. One by one, we crisscrossed the mountain trails, going through streams and mud. We didn't top more than thirty miles per hour, but I felt like I was flying. Nothing to focus on but the trail in front of me, and the sky above me.

We rode for three hours, finally racing each other back to the house, and totally covered in mud.

"I totally smoked your ass!" Adrian shouted out, pulling into the driveway.

Sketch skidded to a stop behind him. "Whatever, man. Not my fault a deer ran out in front of me."

I shook my head as the boys squabbled like children and rolled my ATV over to Cole's truck. The third gear was sticking, and Cole would have to look at it before we headed back out tomorrow.

"Was that your third gear messing up back there?" The southern drawl of his voice caused my stomach to tighten. He hadn't spoken a single word to me since we arrived. Granted, I hadn't been the most approachable, either.

"Yeah, it's sticking." I took my helmet off and set it on the seat. "I'll get Cole to look at it tomorrow, before we go back out."

Noah gave me a crooked grin. "You could always ride with me."

I smirked at his innuendo. "I'm sure I could. But that doesn't help me on the trail."

He grabbed me by my waist and yanked me toward him. "Who says it won't?" Pressed against him, even through the layers of clothes between us, I swore he could feel my heart pounding.

"So what are you saying? We have a quick fuck and you'll let me ride your bike?" I teased.

His brown eyes hardened and his grip tightened. "When have I ever been quick, Princess? It hasn't been that long. Do I need to give you a reminder?"

*Reminder...like I need one.* Memories were the only things that helped me late at night, with my vibrator in hand.

"As much as I would like to revisit old times, I'm going to head on in." I gently pushed his chest back for him to let me go, but his arms remained around my waist.

"Princess, when are you going to let me in?" he

whispered, his brown eyes searching mine.

The rare light of vulnerability in his gaze weakened my resolve. Loneliness was a bitch, and the craving for that connection with someone started to bloom in my chest. But I pushed those feelings down and steeled my nerves.

"You don't know me, Noah. Trust me, this isn't what you want." I pushed on his chest again, and with a sigh, he let me go.

# CHAPTER 7

*Kate*

I QUICKLY WALKED TO the front porch and pushed open the front door. Cole was in the kitchen, drinking a soda.

"Why didn't you come out?" I asked as I toed off my mud covered hiking boots, leaving them by the door.

He smirked. "Karla had other plans for me."

I rolled my eyes. "Since when do you let pussy dictate what you do?"

Cole's brown eyes threw daggers at me. "Since when are you so worried about what I'm doing?"

I shrugged. "Whatever. It's your business. You came up to ride, not to bang some gym slut." *Damn, my bitchiness is in full force.* "Okay, that wasn't right. Sorry, Cole."

He waved me off. "You need to get more sleep or get laid, because you're grouchy as hell."

*No kidding.* Seeing as how I didn't plan on getting laid any time soon, a shower and a nap sounded heavenly. I climbed the stairs, my bones weary from riding, grabbed a set of clothes, and went into the bathroom I would be sharing with the guys. Thankfully, I got to it first, because I'd camped with Adrian and Sketch before. For such masculine guys, they sure did take a long time in the shower.

I turned the hot water on as high as I could stand it, and stood under the rainfall spray. As much as I wanted to clear my mind, his whispered words haunted me. *Why don't you let me in?* The better question was why would I? I'd been burned too many times to trust anyone to the point of letting them in. Too many times I'd been let down. Too many times they'd left me high and dry. Too many times I had fallen apart and been left alone to pick up the pieces of myself. I didn't need that bullshit in my life. Plus…say I was to get close with someone. That was a weakness, a vulnerability that I couldn't have. In my line of work, I had a lot of enemies—enemies that would use anything and anyone against me.

I shook my head. It was better this way. I poured body wash into my hands and washed my body, letting the lime and coconut scent wash away my stress. My eyes closed as I caressed the flat planes of my stomach, then went lower. For a moment, I let the power of memories wash over me. The touch of his calloused hands gripping my hips when I rode him. The taste of his kiss when he pushed me up against the wall. My breath hitched and I leaned against the cool river rock wall. I rubbed the little nub with my thumb, while my other hand pinched my pebbled nipple. A small cry escaped my lips as the crescendo of arousal rose.

"God damn, that's so fucking sexy."

I didn't have to look to recognize the husky voice. My eyes opened slowly, taking in a very naked, very aroused Noah, standing outside the shower door, stroking his long, thick cock. All of my common sense went right out of the room. I opened the door and grabbed his hand, pulling him inside the steam shower. Primal need took over. He crushed his lips over mine, sweeping them with his tongue. I moaned, and his tongue plunged in. He ran his hands down my body, ending right under my ass. Gripping it, he pushed me up against the wall. My legs locked around him, with his cock pressed right at my entrance.

"Look at me, Princess. I want to see those pretty blues when you come." He teased my clit with the head of his cock. I writhed against him, needing him inside me before I exploded.

"Noah, please!" I begged.

"I love to hear you beg," he growled, and thrusted into me. I let out a cry as he moved.  My eyes locked onto his, matching his thrusts with my own. The steam thickened the air, but all I needed to breathe was him. I pulled his head to me and dominated his mouth, mimicking my tongue with his thrusts. It didn't take much time before my world exploded. I closed my eyes as I teetered on the ledge.

"Oh God, Noah!" I cried out.

"You're mine, Kate. I'm the only one that's going to fill this pussy. This is my pussy."

My eyes closed in ecstasy, and I dropped my head to his shoulder. Just as quickly, I fell off the ledge again. My pussy clamped around his cock, taking everything he could give me.

"Mine!" he roared, pulling out quickly and emptying onto my stomach, marking me as his.

With our chests heaving, he pressed his lips against mine. The kiss was unlike the earlier one. It had less urgency. It felt more loving, more intimate. It shook me more than anything else. He let me down gently onto my trembling legs, and grabbed the soap. With a heated gaze, he washed my body. Caressing and gentle, his touch sent electric tingles through my core. I took the soap from him and followed his motions, my eyes traveling over the cords and ripples of his muscular frame. The phoenix, the quotes, and side piece glistened brightly in the water, the colors becoming more pronounced. My eyes landed on a new piece of ink. When we were together in Miami, he didn't have the name *Aubrey* etched over his heart. I inhaled deeply as my stomach ached. For all his talk of how I was his, apparently, some other woman had made such an impression that she'd left a permanent mark on him.

I rinsed him off, gave him a fake smile, and moved quickly out of the shower. I made fast work of drying off and changing into my clothes, and was out the door before he even turned off the water. I mentally chastised myself for being so weak, for trusting someone who had no intention of telling me the truth. In my room, I ran my comb through my hair and pulled on a clean hoodie. *Whatever. It doesn't have to mean anything.* There was no reason why everything had to be so freaking complicated, why I had to make it a bigger deal than it needed to be. It was an itch that needed to be scratched. No big fucking deal. I pushed the nagging tinge of loneliness aside and padded down the stairs.

# CHAPTER 8
*Kate*

S HANE AND MEGAN WERE in the kitchen, getting dinner ready. The ever-present Xbox blared the latest shoot 'em up game with Cole, Adrian, and Sketch at the controllers with new arrivals, Ryan and Sean. After giving them shit about showing up only for dinner, I looked around, but Karla seemed to be missing from the ruckus.

I lifted my chin. "Where's your girl, Cole?"

"Her friend came by and picked her up. Said something about a spa, or whatever. They'll be back later," he answered, not bothering to look up from his game.

Whatever. The less time I had to pretend to like her, the better. I walked over to the counter and inhaled the savory aroma of chicken pot pie.

"What can I do?" I asked, hating the fact that once again, Megan was taking care of the group.

"Yo, we asked if we could help, but Megan threatened to hit us with a spatula if we bothered her," Adrian interjected from his spot on the couch.

I snorted and stole a tomato from the salad, then wandered over to the sectional sofa, wedging myself in between Ryan's muscular torso and Adrian's massive frame.

"You want in, Kate?"  Sketch asked, his fingers rapidly pressing the buttons.

"Yeah, no thanks. I don't need a video game to tell me that I'm a badass. I already know I am," I replied, tucking my feet underneath me. A noise from the stairs had me looking up as Noah walked in. Dressed in a pair of sweat pants, and a long sleeve *Ominous* brand T-shirt, he looked relaxed, like he didn't have a care in the world. That he wasn't worrying about what just happened in the shower.  If he didn't care, why should I?

"About time you bastards showed up. How the hell are you doing?" Miraculously, they paused the game so Noah could give them one of those weird half hug/ handshake things. I just watched him interact with guys that I'd known for a while, and found it extremely funny that no one had mentioned him before. How the hell did they know each other?

The conversation turned to topics of cars and the goings-on at Adrian's shop, where Ryan and Sean worked, along with Shane. Not interested in hearing about the latest bike mod, I got up to allow the boys to have their time. Of course, Noah picked the same time to move into my seat. We did that awkward dance, not able to get out of each other's way.  After two missteps, he picked me up by my waist and moved me out of the way. I won't lie, the touch of his fingers on my waist sent electric shocks through my body. His gaze held mine for a second longer than was necessary, searching for God knew what. He must not have seen what he was looking for, because he sat me down without another glance.

I brushed off an uneasy feeling and went into the kitchen to open a couple bottles of wine. My favorite brand of Prosecco was chilled and waiting for me, thanks to Megan's thoughtfulness. I had taken a big sip of the fruity, bubbly goodness, when the large front door was thrown open. Karla burst in, followed by the rest of the gym sluts, Jessica, Andrea, and PJ, or as I liked to call them, the Barbie trifecta. With their fake ass blonde hair and boobs to match, their claim to fame had nothing to do with fitness or fighting, but who could get on their knees the fastest.  Their squeals of arrival did nothing to improve my mood, and I raised my eyebrow at Megan.

"Seriously? Who let the skanks out of their cage? Karla's all right by herself, but as a trio, they're an absolute mess."

Megan shook her head. "We have six single, sexy men out there. They'll leave us alone." She handed me a plate of food and grabbed the bottle of wine. "The guys can have the sluts, we're going outside."

I carried my food out to the wooden planked table and turned on the outdoor heat lamps that surrounded the table and seating area. With the sun setting, the night chill had set in. Megan set down the wine and her plate, with Shane right behind her.

"You're not eating with the boys?" I motioned to the crew still playing Xbox, while the girls lounged over the brown leather sofas, trying to draw their attentions.

Shane scoffed. "Why would I eat in there, when I have the view of the most amazing stars right here?" He pulled Megan into his arms and gave her a lingering kiss.

I rolled my eyes good-naturedly at the lovebirds and dug into my dinner. The tender chicken and flaky crust melted in my mouth, and I let out a tiny moan of delight. After weeks of fast food, pizza, and protein bars, it was exactly what the doctor had ordered. And so was the conversation. It felt good to talk about things other than the case, like I had a life outside of my FBI persona. To feel like a person again.

Shane started a fire in the pit, while Megan and I took the plates inside. She set about making her special, super-secret adult hot chocolate, with Baily's Irish Cream and vanilla vodka, while I grabbed the fixings for s'mores. We moved with the stealth of ninjas, but it wouldn't have mattered. The skanks were too busy fawning over the boys, pretending to be enthralled with whatever video game they were playing. I shook my head at the ridiculousness of it all and followed Megan outside, our arms laden with mugs, thermoses, and marshmallow goodness.

The fire crackled brightly against the starry night sky. The absence of any real development in the area allowed the millions of stars to shine brightly. I leaned back in my Adirondack chair, and inhaled a deep, cleansing breath.

"I'm so glad you came out here with us," Megan said warmly, handing me a mug, filled to the brim with her specialty. I took a sip and nodded.

"I'm glad Cole dragged me out with you guys. This is exactly what I needed."

Shane stood up and kissed Megan on her forehead. "Hot chocolate isn't going to do it for me, so I'm going to let you guys get your chick talk in. I'll keep the rest of the heathens at bay for as long as possible."

"Thanks, babe." Megan shifted in her chair, tucking her legs underneath her and faced me. "We do need to talk."

*Shit. Here comes the inquisition.* I mimicked her movements and faced her. "About?"

She raised her dark brown eyebrow at me with skepticism. "About a certain six foot, three-inch-tall sexy man with gorgeous brown eyes that can't seem to stop looking at you."

I looked over my shoulder to see who was nearby, then shook my head.

"Oh, hell no. You can't go all quiet on me now. Especially since you weren't exactly silent when you were in the shower."

My eyes bugged out and my face burned bright, and not from the heat of the fire. I buried my head in the crook of my arm and moaned. "Please tell me you're joking."

She giggled and sipped her drink. "I'm just messing with you. You weren't *that* loud. I was putting something away in the bathroom, and came in when you had…your grand finale. The bathroom ducts must be connected."

I groaned with embarrassment, but Megan wouldn't let up. "You have to tell me everything. This isn't the first time you've met him, is it?

I sighed in resignation. Megan was relentless when

it came to love stories, and knowing her, she wouldn't give up. So I gave her the edited version—how we met, the lies, the way we found each other at my house. Her eyes widened at his claim of how I was his.

"What do you think changed his attitude? Because you said he wasn't like this in Miami, right?"

I shrugged, wondering the same thing. "I have no clue. It's not like I did anything to change his mind."

"Maybe you're just that good," she said with a laugh.

"Well, yeah, I know I am. But damn, I'd have my own entourage of men if that were the case," I joked, sipping more of the chocolaty goodness.

"Maybe it has to do with…" she started to say, but a whore's cackle penetrated the conversation. Male voices drifted out, and I knew our chat was over. Despite my intense sisterly bond with Megan, some things didn't need to be discussed in-depth. Hashing it out with Megan made me uncomfortable, and I was thankful for the interruption. Whatever was going on with me and Noah, I'd deal with it later.

"Great, the skanks found us," I muttered. Shane walked up, carrying two folded blankets, another thermos, and his own bottle of 'shine.

"They caught me sneaking out," he said sheepishly, handing me a blanket. I immediately shucked off my sneakers and tucked my legs underneath me, with the blanket over me.

"They're fine." Megan waved her hands toward the empty chairs around us. "Have a seat!"

I threw her a pointed look, then settled back into my chair. Shane and Sketch grabbed sticks to roast marshmallows for the s'mores, while someone hooked up their portable Bluetooth speakers to their phone. Florida-Georgia Line flowed through the speakers, pushing the quiet vibe out the way, replacing it with a more party-like atmosphere. The girls kept the boys entertained by dancing seductively with each other to the music. The guys were hypnotized by the swaying hips, grinding of pelvises, and roaming hands. Drinks were passed around; 'shine and Fireball poured through their veins like water. I chuckled to myself...*these boys are in for a hurtin' tomorrow.*

My eyes caught hold of the sexy, chocolate brown eyes I had been searching for and raised my eyebrows, as if to convey, *Seriously, this gets you turned on?* He lifted his chin and gave me a sexy smirk, that *Come here if you want it* grin. I knew his game, though. His challenge was clear. He wanted me to make a move, to pursue him, to make a claim. Too bad I didn't play those games. I always took what I wanted, when I wanted it. He could have the little sex show in front of him. If I wanted him bad enough, I'd have him.

# CHAPTER 9
## *Kate*

ESPITE MY BEST EFFORTS, my internal alarm clock woke me up early the next morning. I threw on my clothes and sneakers, then tiptoed through the house, trying not to disturb anyone. But with the way the guys drank last night, it would take a freight train running through the house to wake them up. The view from the stairs into the living room proved that. With Sketch and Adrian sprawled out on the two sofas, and Ryan propped up in the recliner, the only place left for Cole and Sean to crash was on the floor. Bottles of booze and bags of chips were scattered everywhere. I looked at the mess in disgust, then nudged my brother's leg. After a few times, and what were going to be a few nice bruises, he finally woke up from his stupor.

"What the fuck, Kate?" he grumbled, holding his head for dear life. I snorted, then nudged him again with my sneaker.

"You boys trashed this living room, and I'll be damned if Megan's going to clean this shit up. Get up and get moving. If this isn't done by the time I get back, you are all going to be sorry."

Cole groaned and rolled onto his back, then looked up at me, bleary-eyed. "Where the hell are you going?"

"I'm perfectly fine this morning, so I'm going to enjoy the cold mountain air. I mean it, Cole. Megan and Shane come out to this mess, I'm totally kicking y'all's asses."

He grumbled under his breath as he shielded his eyes. I didn't hear exactly what he said, just fragments, of something along the lines of "epic, raging bitch." I smiled sweetly at him and blew him kisses as I walked out the front door.

I inhaled the crisp, fall air. The cleansing affect was instant. I stretched my calves and hit the trail that circled the lake. I purposely left my earbuds at the cabin, so the sound of the morning was my playlist.

I jogged at a nice pace for a good while, until pounding of feet on the trail behind me caused me to increase my stride. Like clockwork, my mind took stock of my location, exit points, and any possible additional getaways. But outwardly, my cool remained in check, and I casually looked to the side, only to find Noah running side by side with me. With his aviator glasses on and his earbuds in, he barely acknowledged my presence, with the exception of a slight nod. I exhaled and rolled my eyes, and increased my pace. Unfortunately, he kept matching my speed until I was all out sprinting for the last quarter mile of the trail, leading to the end of the trail.

"I beat you." My chest heaved as I desperately sucked in some much needed oxygen.

"Not a chance, Princess. I did the gentlemanly thing and let you win." He chugged his bottle of water and tossed it into a trash can.

"Whatever helps you sleep at night, Noah." I guzzled my own bottle of water and let my eyes travel the scenery below. The trail we ran climbed up the side of the mountain, overlooking the beautiful lake. My gaze landed on the sexy specimen next to me. The drenched shirt clung to his broad shoulders and narrow waist. The urge to lick the sweat from his sculpted abs was almost overwhelming, but I looked away and wiped my brow with my sleeve. *It's just the endorphins from the run...You are* not *some hormonal teenager, Kate. Get it together.*

"No, what would help me sleep at night would be your tight, naked body, completely sated, and curled up next to me," he replied nonchalantly. I looked up and caught his smoldering gaze. I wasn't sure what unnerved me more, the fact that he was dead serious, or the fact that my heart skipped a little beat when he said it. Apparently, my heart and my head were on two different paths.

"Not going to happen, so get that out of your head right now," I grumbled.

He chuckled. "You keep saying that, but you'll see. My bed is where you belong. Mine, and no one else's."

"Since when are you into sleeping together?" I scoffed and raised my brow. "When we first started this…whatever the hell you want to call it, we were on the same page. No overnights. No feelings. No strings. Why the hell are you changing the rules?"

"Life happened," he said simply, with no other explanation. I threw up my hands and shook my head.

"Life happens all the time, so I'm not sure what the hell happened to you that would make 'claiming me' something to consider. I don't want a relationship. I don't need to be claimed. I'm not anyone's property, and I'm sure as hell not yours." I pushed past him and headed down the trail.

*That big jerk. What the hell does he think he's doing, bringing feelings and commitments into this? What happened to just sex? To satisfying a damn need? That's all I wanted.*

The running commentary in my head distracted me, and for the first time in a long time, with my mind preoccupied, I wasn't focused on my surroundings. So I completely missed the copperhead snake that crossed my path until I was almost on top of it. With a yelp, I leapt to the side, off the trail, stumbling over exposed tree roots and rocks. I tumbled to the ground with my arms flaying, rolling down the hill. My arms protected my head as I rolled, until I finally came to a stop.

My eyes popped open, and a moan escaped my lips. I heard my name shouted from above, but my voice couldn't answer. I laid still, taking stock of my limbs before trying to sit up.

"Stay down, Kate. Don't move." The shout from above me filtered through the trees, and I grimaced at the panic I heard in his voice. Pain shot through my shoulder and arm, and I ground my teeth together to keep in my scream of agony. After what felt like forever, Noah finally came to a stop next to my head.

"What's the story, Princess. Where does it hurt?" His gentle southern drawl threatened to let loose the tears of pain building up. I exhaled deeply and clenched my jaw.

"Lower body is fine, I think. Right shoulder is dislocated."

"How's the head? Feeling faint? Nauseous?" He moved his fingers gently around my scalp, looking for cuts and bumps. I winced when he moved over a particularly sensitive area. Frown lines appeared on his tanned face, and he caught my eye.

"Relax, the Ranger is on his way."

*Oh, fuck no.* I didn't want to be the damsel in distress, and leave the woods on a fucking stretcher. I groaned at his words and held out my left hand for him to pull me up.

"Why don't you stay put? You took a pretty good tumble."

"Help me up, Noah. I'm fine." He sighed and shook his head, until he finally relented and held out his hand, pulling me up. The forest spun around me, so I leaned against him for support.

"You're not looking so hot."

"Fine time to be commenting on my appearance, jerk," I gritted out, trying desperately to relieve the tension in the situation. I tried to straighten, then immediately toppled over.

He muttered a curse, then swept me up into his arms. "We'll meet the Ranger at the trail head."

"I can walk. I just need to use your arm," I bit out, my teeth gnashing together.

"Yeah, you can use more than my arm, Princess. But for now, kindly shut up and let me hold you. There's no way we'd make it to the trail head by sundown if I let you walk."

I sighed in resignation, knowing he was right, and wrapped my left arm around his neck. We walked in silence for a while, with each step jarring my sore body, but I held it in. Sweat dripped from my brow as I focused my breathing, and tried not to think about the pain. It took everything I had not to cry out, but I refused. We made it to the parking lot of the trail, where a Ranger with a modified ATV waited to take us back to the cabin. He offered to take us to the local hospital, but I refused. The last thing I needed was the attention of an ambulance ride.

"Don't be bullheaded, Kate. You're going to the hospital," Noah demanded.

"Screw off, Noah. I'm fine. I just need to wrap my wrist, then have Cole pop my shoulder back in," I said with finality. My wishes went unheard, and as soon as we got to the house, he carried and sat me in the front seat of his truck. When I voiced my protests, he threw in his wild card.

"Do you really want Megan fussing over you, when she should be relaxing?"

*Oh, you pull out the big guns, huh?* The jerk knew I wanted Megan and Shane to enjoy their trip, and if I didn't go to the doctor, she would spend the rest of the time trying to take care of me. I shot him the middle finger and closed my eyes.

Three-freaking-hours later, we emerged from the hospital with a concussion, a badly bruised ankle, and a fixed shoulder. And drugs, of course. Good stuff.

"The pain reliever they gave her should be setting in now. It's pretty potent, so make sure she doesn't do anything by herself until the effects wear off. No operating heavy machinery, driving, using sharp utensils. She'll need to be watched carefully."

"Ma'am, I have no intention of letting this one out of my sight," he said with a wide smile. In my weakened state, I couldn't do much but give him the finger, in case he needed to be reminded of my feelings toward him. That earned another giggle from the flirting nurse. I must have dozed off, because the next thing I knew, he had me in his arms and we were almost to the front door of the cabin. My nose was burrowed into his neck, breathing in his scent.

"How can you smell like the water when you're here in the mountains?" I mumbled.

He chuckled softly. "I think the drugs have definitely hit your system."

I shook my head, then winced at the pain.

"Just rest, Princess. I got you."

# CHAPTER 10
## Noah

ITEXTED EVERYONE WHILE we were at the hospital so they were aware of what had happened. Thankfully, everyone was out or in their rooms when we made it back. Her pride was wounded more than anything else, and I could tell she hated people seeing her at her weakest moments. I made my way upstairs, and pushed into her bedroom. With as much gentleness as I could muster, I laid her on the bed, careful not to disturb her wrist, ankle, or shoulder.

"Hey, how is she?" Megan whispered from behind me. I shrugged and turned back to look at the angel laid out in front of me.

"She's a survivor. Just minor injuries. Lots of scrapes and bruises. She'll be hurting for the next day or so."

"I'm glad, and I'm glad you were with her. It could have been a lot worse," Megan said softly, then handed me a bowl full of warm water and a washcloth. "I figured she couldn't take a shower until later, but this may help her feel more human."

"Thanks, Megs. Sorry we busted up your trip and everything," I said, taking the bowl from her and setting it on the nightstand.

"Noah, this is our new normal. The fact that there hasn't been any gun fights or car chases, means it's been a good day." She giggled softly, then put her hand on my arm. "Just don't hurt her. She's been through hell."

I knew she didn't mean while I was wiping her down, but in general. The warning was clear.

"I can't say I won't fuck up, Megan. Because I am far from perfect, and there is so much she doesn't know. But one thing's for damn certain, no one will be more cherished or loved than she will be," I promised her best friend.

"Good. Because whether she knows it or not, you're good for her, Noah." I bent down and accepted her kiss on my cheek and watched her leave the room.

Winning Kate's heart wasn't going to be easy, and if the past few days were any indication, I had a long way to go. But having her best friend on my side, it may just end up working after all.

After I managed to take off her clothes, I took a moment to gaze at her battered body. Underneath the bruises and scrapes, her skin pebbled against the cool air. Her small, taut frame made me catch my breath, and it took everything I had not to press my face to the curve of her breast.

With a sigh, I squeezed the water from the washcloth and started wiping away the sweat and dirt. Her breathing never changed, and she never stirred, the drugs were that strong. My gaze lingered on a sight I'd never seen before. The words, "Always A Part of Me" with the Roman numerals for March eighteenth underneath it, in the smallest, yet most elegant piece of calligraphy I'd ever seen, were etched onto her ribs. I sat back on my heels, confused. Because of the amount of time I'd spent with her in the past year, memorizing her beautiful body, I knew the ink was new.

I wondered what the significance was, but then filed it away for later. I had my own new ink to explain, and the sight of her eyes catching hold of it in the shower made my stomach hurt. The hurt in her eyes killed any post-orgasm buzz, and her walls immediately went back up. I had to explain it to her soon, before she came to any crazy conclusions. I covered her naked body with the down blanket and made sure she was breathing before I hit the shower myself.

I threw on a pair of jeans, my favorite gray T-shirt, and shook the water droplets from my hair before padding downstairs. My stomach growled at the aroma of steaks and chicken on the grill. Megan had the kitchen counters packed with appetizers and snacks, and I grabbed a chicken skewer before I joined the guys on the back deck.

"Hey, man. Welcome back!" Shane said, clapping me on the back. "She asleep?"

I nodded, my mouth full of spicy chicken. I took the beer he handed me and washed it down before replying. "Yeah, they gave her some good shit. She's going to be hurting for the next few days, though."

Cole nodded and tipped his own beer back. "But she won't show it, will she?" He nudged Shane, and they both shook their heads.

"No, her stubbornness runs in the damn family," Megan said, smacking Shane in the stomach.

I chuckled along with everyone else. Cole never said much about his stepsister's life before she came to live with him and his family, but that his own mom passed away from cancer when his sister was only two years old. A year later, Kate and her mom, Cathy, entered their lives, and had been there ever since. Kate knew that family didn't always equal blood. I hoped she remember that when she met my family. *If she meets them.* The worry and guilt began to eat at my stomach again. Once she was clearheaded, and not in a drug-induced haze, I'd tell her about Aubrey. *And hope to God she understands.*

After shooting the shit with the guys and Megan, my body became heavy with fatigue. I drained the last of my beer and tossed it in the trash.

"Megan, thanks again for a wonderful dinner. I'm going to have to do extra time at TR when we get back."

She nodded. "Yeah, I think you lost an ab muscle or two."

I laughed heartily, knowing full well my eight pack abs were intact. "I'm crushed."

She surprised me then, by wrapping her arms around my waist and squeezing me tight.

"I know you're going to be great for her. Be yourself, and be honest. And let her see what a great guy you are. You're already in her head. Get yourself in her heart. And if you break it, I'll kill you."

"Yes, ma'am." I kissed her on the head, just as Shane came in from outside.

"You might want to remove your hands from my girl, asshat."

"Sorry, bro. She can't seem to keep her hands off me!" I dodged the punch he threw in jest. But knowing Shane's strength, there would have been some serious power behind that punch.

I made a couple peanut butter and jelly sandwiches, grabbed a couple bottles of water, and went back upstairs.

"Noah, hold up." Cole came up the stairs behind me, as I paused in front of his sister's room. *Well, this is slightly awkward.*

"Look, bro. I have no clue what your intentions are with my sister, but I know you were there for her today. And I see the way you look at her. If you can get through her defenses, I wish you nothing but the best. But if she gets hurt in any way, you're in for a world of hurt."

I nodded. "Dude, I know. Megan already told me. Y'all will kill me. Trust me, I have no intentions of hurting your sister."

Cole smirked. "It's not us that'll hurt you. She'll kick your ass. We won't have anything to do with it."

"Duly noted. 'Night."

I opened the door quietly and set the food down. Kate's beautiful blue eyes popped open, and she went to sit up.

"Oh no, Princess. I got you...easy does it." I helped her sit up, just as the sheet covering her chest fell to her waist.

"Why am I naked?" Her voice sounded so damn sexy, even though it was thick with sleep.

"I got most of the dirt and mud off you, since you can't take a shower yet. And because I'm a pervert, and just wanted to see your sexy body."

She nodded her head. "I always figured you were a perv. I can't walk out there naked, so give me your shirt."  I happily obliged. The 2XL shirt dwarfed her small frame, but having something of me, having my scent on her, made my heart pound. A primal urge rose from within me.

She couldn't walk without my assistance, and despite her feeble protests, I helped her use the bathroom and wash up. After cajoling her to eat a sandwich and drink a bottle a water for her pill, she finally fell back to sleep. I felt her body relax in my arms, and I finally sighed in relief. The head trauma she suffered, along with her bruised bones, had me worried. I knew from my field medical training that the head bleeds were the worst, but nothing could have prepared me for seeing her dark hair saturated with blood. My arms tightened around her at the memory, and I pressed my lips to her temple.

"I got you, Princess. And I'm not letting you go."

# CHAPTER 11
*Kate*

I'M NOT SURE WHAT WOKE me first, the throbbing pain radiating throughout my body, or the hundred-degree heating pad draped over me. I used my left hand to lift his hand, only to have him pull me closer, his nose nuzzling my neck. I breathed deeply, inhaling his scent.

"What are you doing, Noah?" I mumbled, closing my eyes. His fingers grazed the side of my stomach, inching closer to my hips.

"Holding you." *Well, thank you, Captain Obvious.*

"Yes, I know that. Why?" I asked with a sigh.

"So you'll go back to sleep. You're nicer when you're asleep."

"I'm always nice to you," I said indignantly, my eyes flying open.

"The only time you let me hold you is when you're sleeping, so shut up and let me hold you, woman."

I gave him a sharp nudge in the chest with my elbow, and to my satisfaction, he let go with a grunt.

"You're grouchy in the morning," he grumbled, rubbing his chest.

I flipped him the bird with my left hand, then gingerly swung my legs around. I caught a good look at my body and groaned. My right wrist was all scraped up, which went perfect with the bumps and bruises all down my legs.

"You've got to be kidding me," I muttered. *How the hell am I supposed to work like this? How am I supposed to shower?* My gaze landed on a familiar looking teal and polka dot cane, just as a sharp pain shot through my ankle.

"Why is Megan's cane up here?"

Noah climbed out of bed, his black jersey shorts hanging low, and showcasing that delectable V-shaped muscle that always drew my eye. I shifted my gaze and looked into his beautiful brown ones instead.

"She said you can use it until you get your own, since the doc said you can use a bandage."

I nodded slowly, formulating my plan of attack, but before I could do anything, he quickly reached down and swept me up, and into his arms.

"What the hell? What are you doing? I can do this myself!" I shouted. I didn't need his help at all. If I could get over to the bathroom...

"Trust me, it's for the whole house's benefit that I get you cleaned up, and quick. You're kinda fragrant," he joked as he walked me into the bathroom. He set me on the toilet and carefully removed his shirt from my body, then turned on the showerhead.

"Before you get too comfortable in here, can I have bit of privacy please? I'd like to pee alone," I grumbled.

Noah rolled his eyes, and muttered something under his breath, before he said, "I'll wait outside. Don't even think about getting in that shower without help. I'll be back in sixty seconds."  And sure enough, sixty seconds later, he was back in the bathroom, just as I was finishing up. He carefully unwrapped my bandages, then gently placed me on the tiled seat in the shower.

I sat there and let the water wash over me, acclimating myself to the needlelike pricks of the water. My sore and bruised skin tightened with each drop. I gritted my teeth. I turned my head to look for the soap, only to stare directly at a ten inch, semi-hard cock jutting out at me. My mouth dropped open, and I couldn't help but stare.

"Don't look at me like that. Being in here with you is already a struggle, Princess. That mouth is driving me nuts, but I'm trying to be good here," he swore softly.

He motioned for me to bow my head forward. "I can't wash your hair, but we can rinse out some of the blood."

I licked my lips and nodded. My eyes closed as his hands lightly massaged my scalp, and I moaned softly as each touch of his fingers electrified my core. The pain slowly dissipated, only to be replaced by building desire. After a minute, he lifted my head up with his finger, then took a soap covered washcloth and gently scrubbed my body, taking special care around my cuts and bruises. The scent of coconut and lime from the body wash swirled around us, and my breath quickened. His hands moved in between my legs, lingering over my most sensitive areas. My core ached, and my legs trembled with need.

I looked up, and instantly caught his intense stare; his brown eyes darkened with hunger. I focused my eyes on his engorged length, only inches away from my mouth, and did what any red-blooded woman would do. With my left hand, I pulled him closer, because one didn't let a perfectly exceptional cock in the face go to waste. I licked the pre-cum that beaded at the tip, circling my tongue around the swollen girth, then gently gripped his thick length , adding pressure with each stroke. His fingers tightened in my hair as I slid my hands over his cock, slowly squeezing.

His hips started thrusting slowly, and his groans

echoed against the stone tiles. My thighs clenched, my own need throbbing with want. With only one hand, I could either touch myself, or continue touching him. There was no question. My left hand moved on its own, cupping his sac. I could feel his release moments away, so when he tried to pull back, I didn't let go.

"I'm gonna...oh God!" His cock pulsed over my breasts, spilling his creamy seed in between them. He gazed down at me, desire flashing in his eyes. "My turn."

Without a second to spare, he dropped to his knees and sucked in my throbbing clit, as he plunged two of his fingers deep inside of me. I gasped at the onslaught, my hips thrusting in time with him. My left hand gripped his hair, pushing him closer, my thighs clenched to his head. My inner walls clenched around his fingers; using them, milking them. The rise to the ledge was swift, and the moment he curled his two fingers and flicked my clit with his tongue, I soared.

Noah rose from his knees, and crushed his lips to mine, tangling our tongues. Our flavors mingled, and he lifted me into his arms, then pressed me against the wall of the shower. The pressure against my bruised and sore body was too much, and a cry of pain escaped.

"Shit, Princess. I'm sorry," he said, pulling back. He put me back on the bench, then shut off the water.

He grabbed the white, fluffy bath towel, and wrapped it around my shoulders, then toweled himself off. I watched him, as his gentle hands took extra care around my wounds and bruises. Pieces of my wall crumbled, and I wasn't sure how I felt about that. His tenderness unnerved me, so much so, that I began to rethink everything.

The knock on the door interrupted my thoughts.

"Yo! Some of us would like to get a shower sometime this century!" Adrian's voice bellowed. Noah smiled widely. He swung me into his arms, then maneuvered me out into the hallway. Adrian's mouth dropped open at the sight of me in Noah's arms, and I ducked my head into Noah's chest.

"Well, it's about time, bro. About time," he muttered, shutting the door behind him.

Noah took me into my room and laid me on the bed before climbing in next to me, and pulled me into his arms.

"I should get dressed," I said, struggling to sit up. His grip tightened around my shoulders, until I finally gave up and sank into his embrace.

"You need to keep that sexy little body right here next me," he murmured, pulling the white comforter over us.

"Noah, I'm not an invalid. I can get up and walk

around," I muttered, but I didn't make any further attempt to get up. His arms were comforting, and solid around me. Protective. It had been a while since I felt something like that—a long, long while. Feelings I thought had vanished slowly trickled back, and I wasn't sure if I liked it.

"Kate, just…stay. Stay with me. Here."

I closed my eyes and turned my head, pressing my nose against the side of his pectoral muscles. "What are you doing to me, Noah? What are we doing?" I whispered. The room was silent, and I knew he heard each word I said.

"I couldn't get you out of my mind when we were in Miami. And when you left that morning, I didn't know what to do. I thought it didn't mean anything. That I could fuck anything I could, just to get you out of my system, but hell, it only made me want you more. You were the first thing I thought of when I woke up, and your name was on my lips every time I took my dick in my hand. Being without you, for this long, has been hell."

I swallowed the lump building in my throat, and told the butterflies fluttering around in my stomach to calm the fuck down. "What happened to no strings?"

"You've had me by the strings ever since the day I met you in the gym. I just didn't realize it until you left."

His fingers trailed lazily up and down, over my goose bump covered arms. I didn't say anything, just let his words wash over me. "Kate?" he pressed his lips to my forehead.

"You don't know me, Noah. You really don't," I protested.

"I know more than you think."

I craned my head to stare in to his eyes. "What do you think you know?"

He gave me a little smile. "I know you're hot as hell. And you're funny, smart, and pretty damn talented in bed. You're a badass in the gym, on the trails, and pretty much whatever I've seen you do. What more do I need to know?"

*What more? How about I carry a gun for a living. Or that I put my life in danger every time I go on assignment. Oh, and I have trust issues.* I sighed and pushed myself into a sitting position.

"What did I say?" he asked, concern filling his voice.

"No, it's nothing you said. I don't do the whole 'relationship' thing. You're amazing, truly. And yeah, the sex is off the charts. Just believe me when I say it's all me." I scooted to the edge of the bed and reached for the wrap. Noah sat up and took it from of my hands, then securely wrapped my ankle.

"What are you scared of?" he asked quietly. He kept

the hold he had on my ankle, as if trying to hold onto me.

I shook my head slowly and met his gaze. "You," I whispered.

I removed my ankle from his grasp and limped over to the dresser. After finagling clothes onto my body, I threw my hair up into a messy knot, trying not to show my pain. I slipped on the protective wrap  and grabbed the cane Megan so kindly left behind.  He stopped me at the door, and cupped my face with his hands.

"At some point, Princess, I'm going to break down those walls. And you're going to realize what you've been missing." His brown eyes speared my own, and my breath hitched. Noah's lips brushed against mine, and then he walked out the door.

I touched my lips and replayed his words in my head. *I'm going to break down those walls.*

That was exactly what I was afraid of.

# CHAPTER 12
*Noah*

I STALKED BACK TO MY ROOM—frustration boiling under my skin—just as Adrian was coming out. The behemoth African-American and American Indian man stood in the doorway, looking at me expectantly.

"What?"

Adrian shook his head and smiled. "Never thought I'd see Kate look so…dependent on someone. It's good man, real good. A woman like that—" *Yeah, fuck that. He's not going to tell me about my woman.*

"Not going there with you, Ad. I know you mean well, but what goes on with me and Kate is our business," I replied dryly. I pushed past him and headed to the bunk where I stowed my bag. I pulled on a pair of cargo shorts over my boxer briefs, a T-shirt, and a hooded sweatshirt over top of that, then headed back down the stairs. That damn princess had my head all confused. I needed to get out. I needed to breathe fresh air and clear my head, not inhale the coconut scent that drifted from her bedroom. I wanted to be done with her fucking games, but she was an addiction—a drug I couldn't shake.

I shoved my feet into my boots and headed out to the bikes. Fixing Kate's bike would be the distraction I needed, so I grabbed my toolbox from the back of the truck and got to work. An hour later, I was elbow deep in transmission parts, when AC/DC's *Highway to Hell* broke my concentration. I just shook my head, knowing full well who was on the other end. I wiped my hands on a dirty rag, then answered the call.

"Where the fuck have you been?" I demanded, foregoing any pleasantries. The caller chuckled, amused at the tone of my voice. *Motherfucker's been gone for the last six months, and he has the balls to chuckle? Are you kidding me?*

"Knee deep in guns, pussy, and coke, motherfucker," he said. I could picture the shit-eating grin plastered on his face.

"Uh-huh, and how much of that shit is work related?" I tucked the phone in between my shoulder and ear, and picked up my wrench.

"Wouldn't you like to know? What? Are you missing the action?"

"Hardly. I'm getting plenty of action here." My mind immediately went to the blue-eyed brunette upstairs. Maybe not the type of action Torin Campanari was talking about, but it was enough for me.

"Yeah, you keep telling yourself that. You know damn well you're missing out on all the fun."

"'Cause getting shot at, diving in below freezing waters, and jumping out of planes is a real good time," I joked. But, in reality, I missed the adrenaline coursing through my veins, the thrill of the hunt, the feeling of satisfaction when taking down a particular gang of assholes. Yet, I didn't regret the choices I'd made. Coming home was not only my duty, responsibility, and my obligation, but it was my choice. I could have easily walked away from it all. But, after knowing the love I had now, I couldn't think of anywhere else I'd rather be.

"I know you didn't call me just to bust my balls, so why don't you tell me what's going on?"

"Getting straight to the point, as always, Russo. I gotcha," he said with a pause. Torin pausing was never a good thing. My gut clenched as I waited for whatever shoe to drop. "I wanted you to hear it from me first. Mac is gone."

I hissed out the breath I was holding. George "Mac"

Cleary was one of the other five guys on our six-man team. We were a tight-knit group. You had to be, living day in and day out with the same six guys. We weren't just a team, we were brothers.

"How?"

"Sniper took him out while he was doing recon in Mexico."

"Fuck." I rubbed my face and closed my eyes, remembering the last time I saw my friend. "How's Julie?" I asked, knowing that his new bride must be devastated. High school loves had finally tied the knot a while back, on the rugged shores of Ireland. My brothers and I were proud to stand for him, the first guy on our team to find his soul mate.

"She's a fighter, man. When they told her, she had to be sedated, but she's holding it together now." The catch in his voice told me that Torin was just as tore up about it as I was. "The funeral is Wednesday in Boston."

I mentally checked my calendar. Anything I had going on at the bar could be covered by my cousin, Josh. "Yeah, I'll be there. I'll fly out Tuesday."

"Good, I'll text you the info. Watch your six, bro."

I hung up with Torin, with anger and rage coursing through my veins. Mexico. Mac was in fucking Mexico. That was my area of expertise...that would have been my mission, to bring down a gang of mercenaries tied to the Syndicate. But then my life changed. I had to hand the reins over to Mac, my second in command. Had I stuck with it, stayed with the team, this wouldn't have happened.

This group is nothing but an international melting pot of the world's nastiest sons of bitches. We're talking Russian mobsters, heroin traffickers from Asia, human smugglers from Africa and South America, and good ol' coke dealers from Central America. It was a highly dangerous group of people. Most of the 'axis of evil' are represented, and surprisingly, they all worked well together. My team, Triton's Edge, Alpha One, had our connections within the organization. We got in, got the intel needed, and we were taking care of business. We were taking them down, doing what the international forces couldn't do.

And then, we got shut down. Word came down from people way above my paygrade, that they were pulling the plug on our mission, just as we were about to go in deeper. Words like 'political suicide' and 'international relations' were tossed around like beads at Mardi Gras. A bunch of bullshit if I'd ever heard. But we were pulled out of there and sent back to our command center in Miami to wait it out.

So we watched...and waited. Scratching my balls and looking stupid were two things I could've done on my own time, and I sure as hell hate doing it when I could've been, and should've been, doing what I did best. So after a while, we started going off the grid. We'd take out the boats and do some recon. We'd watch over the ports in the Bahamas, a common transit point for human traffickers and drugs. We saw evidence of the Syndicate doing their thing, but our hands were fucking tied.

So, like Seth always said, "It's better to ask forgiveness than beg for permission," so we took matters into our own hands. Without funding, without orders, and sure as hell without legal approval. Oh, they knew what we were doing, and they sure as hell didn't do much to stop us. But in the public eye, they had complete and total deniability, which was a good thing for them, I guess. A lot of bodies were left in our wake, but I doubt anyone cried for those soulless bastards.

But Mac—knowing what Julie and his parents were dealing with—brought me to my knees. The news of Mac's death was a punch to my gut, a reminder that despite all our training, our precision shots, our aim, it only took one bullet, one shot, and it would all be over. I'd never again be able to hear his ridiculous laugh, or his ongoing rants over anything political, or the way his green eyes would light up when talking about the love of his life. My best friend, gone before he even got to know his newborn son. Gone before he could have more kids. Fuck, gone before he hit thirty.

Emotions—rage, fury, sadness—swirled around in me. I turned and chucked the wrench I held onto with all my strength. The splash of my best tool landing in the water did nothing to satisfy the rage building inside of me. I knew that being around people would just frustrate the ever-loving fuck out of me. I palmed the keys to my ATV and jumped on; the keys were in the ignition before my ass hit the seat. But, before I could put it in gear, my name was screamed out over the sound of the engine. I ignored Kate's voice, and the way my hands itched to grab onto her and hold her tight. The urge to destroy everything in my path was strong, but not nearly as strong as the need to have her in my arms. Not fit to be around anyone, I stomped on the gas and clutch, and tore out of the yard.

Me, Mac, and our team came into this life, knowing the risks. Our line of work wasn't for the weak, wasn't for those who failed. It wasn't for those who wanted love, a family, or even normalcy. Hell, normal wasn't in our vocabulary. We kept our secrets; we kept our families away from the danger, separating work from personal as much as we could. But this…this hit my home. This hit my family. And I would avenge my family.

# CHAPTER 13

*Kate*

My stomach dropped when Noah left the yard. Not because he went too fast, but because of the vacant look on his face. The look of numbness. The look of a man who had been defeated. I'd seen that look before, on Shane, and that terrified the fuck out of me. I hobbled back inside and slammed the door behind me.

"What the fuck just happened to Noah?" I demanded from the slack-jawed group lounging in the open family room. Using Megan's cane, I made my way into the kitchen, where my cell phone was charging on the counter. I scrolled through my contacts and sent him a text message.

*"Come back."*

I looked around the room and raised my eyebrows.

"Seriously? No one?"

Cole shrugged. "No clue, sis. You were the last one with him. Maybe it was something you…"

I lifted up the cane to hit him, and he quickly backed off. "Hey, hey, hey, I'm kidding. Sheesh. You need to calm the fuck down there, killer. No one knows why your boyfriend took off like a bat out of hell. Damn."

I lowered the cane and gave him the finger instead. "He's not my boyfriend."

"If you make those moans with just your friends, why don't you and I…" Sean started, but Cole's hand was around his neck before I could blink.

"You wanna finish that sentence?" Cole seethed. Sean's face was beet red when he shook his head. "Good, didn't think so. I'm the only one who can talk shit, so don't even try."

I rolled my eyes and sat down with a huff. The conversation went on like nothing had happened, like their friend hadn't driven off like an idiot. I knew they were letting him cool down, or do whatever it was guys did when they got pissy, but this was ridiculous. Thirty minutes later, my phone buzzed in my hand, and my heart jumped when I saw his number.

*"Not yet."*

I threw my phone on the couch in disgust. *This is a perfect example of why I don't do relationships,* I thought.

*I don't have the patience or the desire to decipher cryptic messages like this. I deal with enough bullshit with the assholes I'm after. I sure as hell don't need this.* I wanted to push it aside, to not care about what had Noah so upset, but a nagging and persistent feeling in my gut told me that I needed to know, because I cared. I tried to shake off the feeling, but it didn't matter. Even with him gone, he still pulled me in.

"Fuck this."

I grabbed Cole's keys from the basket and ignored the group's protests as I hobbled out the door. Just as I started the engine, Noah's bike came roaring back down the driveway. I was off the bike and limping toward him before he even removed his helmet.

"Are you fucking insane? Who the hell goes flying off in the middle of nowhere by themselves? We were worried about you. You could have gotten hurt…" My rant was interrupted by his snort of laughter.

"Don't worry about it." The smile he gave me was beyond fake, and the haunted look in his dark brown eyes worried me. He grabbed the box that was strapped to the back of the seat behind him, and sauntered over to the house, like he didn't have a care in the world.

"What the fuck just happened?" I muttered to myself. I shook my head at the change in his demeanor, and slowly followed him inside. The loud roar of approval when he showed off his new purchase stopped me in my tracks.

"Fireworks? Are you for real? Is this going to be an episode of 'Hold my booze and watch this?'" I asked, my voice filled with acid, taking in the box of not-so-legal mortars.

"Don't get your panties in a twist, Princess. We're just gonna liven things up a bit," he said with a sneer. His eyes hardened, and I had to do a double take to make sure I saw it right.

"Hey, Dr. Jekyll, what's up with the attitude?" I shot back.

"No attitude, Princess. I'm just being me. Just believe it's all me." My words came back to haunt me.

I lifted my chin. "It's nice to finally meet the real you." I sat down, as gracefully as one could with a bandage wrapped around her foot, in between Sean and Ryan. Cole shot me a questioning glance, but I ignored him, turning my attention to Sean next to me.

"How the hell are you doing, Sean?" I asked pointedly. Sean had the common sense not to try and flirt, because the daggers that Noah was throwing could have killed him.

And that was how the rest of the day went. By the time dinner rolled around, I was emotionally drained. The shit Noah was throwing my way was numbing, and I was long past the point of giving a rat's ass about whatever was going on with him. If he chose to be a complete dickwad, that was his business. And it was probably better this way in the long run. But that didn't mean I had to sit there and accept the bullshit, either.

After dinner, the guys made their way out to the clearing, away from the house, to set off the fireworks. Megan and I ambled our way to the fire pit, with our thermoses of spiked hot chocolate and blankets. We watched the colorful display as we sat by the fire, with the lake right behind us. After the fireworks had been set off, the guys came back to the pit, along with the gym sluts. They must have multiplied, because I didn't recognize some of the new faces. But I didn't pay them any mind. The boys could have all the gym pussy they wanted. Didn't faze me one bit.

With the music blaring and the moonshine flowing, the party got going pretty quickly. Pretty soon, the girls were dancing with each other, grinding to the music. Sketch, Sean, and Adrian were getting their fill of the ladies. And low and behold, Noah was getting his own private showing from Ms. Karla herself. His hands were on her ass, while she ground away on his lap, her little denim skirt showing exactly what Victoria's secret was. And the whole time, his eyes were glued to mine.

I shook my head with a smirk. If this was breaking

down my walls, if this was what he meant by thinking of me, then he was definitely in for a rude awakening. I had no inclination to deal with this type of foolishness. I wasn't about to play those sort of games. I told myself that I didn't care what he did, or who he did it with. With the assistance of the cane, I rose to my feet and waved off any help.

"I'm good. I'm going to take some pills and head to bed," I said, giving Megan a kiss on her cheek. She glared over at the scene directly across the fire from us. Karla was still doing her overly-dramatic, porn-star-wannabe routine on his lap. And this time, he looked like he was really enjoying it. I waved good-bye to whoever in the group wasn't getting sex, regularly or oral, and headed back into the house.

I made it as far as the kitchen, when a hand grabbed my elbow.

"Can I help you to bed?" Ryan's short black hair and hazel eyes made his features striking. And if I didn't already know of his fascination with his girlfriend back home, I would have thought that he was hitting on me. But he only had eyes for one pretty lil' thing, and her name was Claire.

"Sure." He wrapped his arm around my waist, and I allowed him to pick me up. We only went up two stairs when a voice commanded him to stop.

"Get your fucking hands off my woman."

"Really? Your woman is out there, probably giving another man a lap dance right now. Why don't you go get your dick wet with the gym slut?" I shot back, irked that his presence made my stomach do flip-flops.

He ignored my comment and pulled me into his arms, like I was a rag doll. Ryan held his hands up in surrender, and allowed Noah to carry me up the stairs. Despite my protests, he placed me on the bed, then paced in front of me.

"How much have you drank tonight?" I asked wearily.

"Not enough, apparently," he muttered, rubbing his face.

"Just go back down, Noah. I don't need you here."

"That's the problem, Kate. You don't need anyone."

"What the fuck? Where did that come from?" I demanded, my face growing hot with anger.

"You don't ever need anyone, do you? You want everyone to think ice runs through your veins, that nothing affects you, but that's bullshit. You know how I know? Your clear blue eyes show the storm that's brewing. But you fight it. You don't want anyone to know that you have feelings, that you're human. You have these walls up so fucking high, that you can't even see over them yourself."

"You've had way too much to drink, so I suggest that you take your drunk ass downstairs before you say something else," I warned. I didn't address his comments, or the truth behind them. Admitting something like that to him would only further intensify his blabbering.

"The truth shall set you free, isn't that the quote? Because Kate, you know damn well that the truth will set you free. You need to stop living the life of someone you're not. You're not a coldhearted person. You're not this ice-princess that you're making everyone believe you are. You're not that person, so why can't you let people in?"

"Because people will use that against me. They'll use my kindness, my love, and my trust against me. Because that's all that ever happens to me. The only people I have let in, aside from my family, are the same ones that hurt me the most. And I will never feel like that again." My outburst surprised him. Hell, it surprised me.

"Who broke you?" he questioned, to which I let out a harsh laugh.

"Who broke me? No one broke me, Noah. I'm whole. I am a whole person. I keep things in, not because I want to isolate myself, but because I want to live my life the way I want to. I work undercover as an FBI agent, Noah. I keep secrets for a living. I chase crooked politicians, human traffickers, and drug dealers across the fucking country. I cannot have weaknesses. My weaknesses are those that I love because more often than not, they will be the ones hurt. They will be the ones used against me. So yes, I keep my walls up and my circle tight. I can't afford any more weaknesses."

"So that's what relationships are to you? A weakness?"

I growled, and threw my hands up. "Seriously. Out of all that, you get that relationships are weaknesses? Yes, they are, Noah. They twist your heart and tear out your soul, until you're only a shadow of what you once were. I've been down that road twice, and I'm sure as hell not going back."

"What the hell happened to you?" he cried out in frustration.

Seriously? Do I have to spell it out? *Oh hell, here we go.*

"Take your fucking pick, Noah. It was either the deadbeat dad that kept beating me and my mom until I was six years old, and she finally escaped the hell in Indiana. Or was it the mayor's son, who took my virginity at fifteen because he 'loved me,' then dumped me before the bed was cold, leaving me with a baby. Suffice to say, I have some freaking issues when it comes to relationships with men. I'm allowed to. Between that and my job, I don't need bullshit like this."

"You have a kid?" He barely controlled the tremor in his tone. *Fuck.* I did not mean for that to come out. Only my family knew about the baby. It wasn't something that I ever brought up in normal conversation. I mean... hell, what do you say? 'Oh yeah, when I was fifteen, I got knocked up because the most popular kid in school popped my cherry while we were drunk.' Because that would always go over well.

I sighed. "No. I don't have a kid. I gave birth to a beautiful seven pound, thirteen-ounce baby boy over ten years ago. His name is Jonathan, and he is the most kick-ass kid I've ever met. But I'm not his mother. He has a wonderful, gracious woman who stays at home, does carpool, and makes freaking cookies. And his dad is a lawyer that coaches Little League; not some overly presumptuous, entitled asshole who blasted it around about how easy I was, and basically made my life hell, to the point I dropped out of school."

Noah's face was stricken with guilt. "Kate, I didn't mean – "

I put my hand up to stop whatever placating bullshit he was about to spew. "I'm not interested in what you have to say right now, Noah. Truly I'm not. You wanted to know me, the real me? Well, there it is. I'm not hiding behind my walls. I'm not ashamed of who I am. I just don't want to put myself out there to get hurt again. I have enough people in my life that can accept who I am, as I am. I don't need someone telling me how to act around perfectly good strangers. If people don't like me because I'm blunt and honest, well then, fuck it. I don't need those people in my life. This is who I am, Noah. And if you can't handle this, then you can just go," I blasted, my chest heaving from exertion.

He moved quickly, faster than any drunk man should, and clenched me against his chest. "It's not that I can't handle you, Princess. You just have to let me," he said softly. He crushed his lips to mine, slipping his tongue inside. All resistance fell. My right hand let go of the cane and curled into his dark blond hair as I pulled him closer. My other hand gripped his shirt, running under the band of his cargo shorts, then trailed down his smooth skin, and encased his growing cock. Noah groaned, and arched his hips into me.

"Take these off," I ordered softly. Without moving his lips, he quickly unbuttoned his shorts, letting them pool around his ankles. My hand gripped the silky skin, stroking with added pressure. Noah's fingers slid under my own capris, and quickly plunged his fingers inside my already drenched folds. I gasped at the intrusion, my head falling back. Noah took that opportunity to trail his tongue down my neck, to the top of my chest.

"This needs to go," he growled, yanking my tank top over my head. His hand immediately went to my small breast, and he feasted on it like a starved man. He sucked and kneaded with just enough pain to be exquisite. My grip on his cock tightened, and my strokes quickened as I rode his other hand to find my impending release.

"That's it, Princess. Ride my hand like you ride my cock." I ground my pelvis over his hand, as his thumb strummed my clit with perfect precision. The dirty talk propelled me over the edge.

"Oh God, Noah," I moaned. My body went limp. He removed his hand and sucked my release off his fingers.

"You taste fucking amazing, Princess." Noah swept me into his arms and laid me on the bed, then carefully removed my cotton pants over my injured ankle. Leaving his shorts on the floor, he grabbed a condom from his pocket and whipped off his own shirt.

"Should I ask who that condom was for?" I teased, half-joking.

His smirk reached his brown eyes. "What? Were you jealous?"

I rolled my eyes, then moved to get up. "Yeah, we're not doing this."

Noah blocked me, putting his arms on either side of me. "I wanted to make you jealous. I wanted you to finally get so pissed, you would react and finally realize what you've been denying this whole time. But you're right. Enough of these games." He rolled the condom over his engorged shaft. "Because we both know the truth."

His gaze held mine, and in that moment, all my walls crumbled. I pulled him to me, as he pushed in. We both moaned.

"Your body was made for mine. Your pussy is mine," he breathed out.

"Yours, all yours," I admitted, as I arched my back to meet his thrusts. Noah grasped my left leg, wrapping it gently around his waist.

"Say it again, Princess. Tell me again."

"I'm yours, Noah."

"You're damn right, Kate. You're mine. All mine." His pace quickened, and soon I was at my peak, falling over. Our explosions came together, and I immediately felt peace. Whatever the hell this was, it was something I knew deep in my heart was inevitable. That this *relationship* was what I needed—what *we* needed.

We broke apart, panting. He rested his forehead on mine and closed his eyes. "God, you feel good in my arms."

I nodded, my throat tightening with emotion. This felt good. Almost too good. So good, that I knew it wouldn't end well. Because nothing so amazing ever ended well for me.

"What are you thinking about?" he whispered, his lips brushing against my skin.

I opened my mouth to speak, but before I got the words out, my cell phone rang. Not my personal one, either.

"Shit. That's the office." I untangled myself from him and reached for my phone. "This is Parker."

"Parker, we're going to need you here tomorrow." Sim's voice came across the line, and I groaned.

"Not that I don't enjoy seeing your smiling face, because I do, truly. But what's going on?"

"Forensics are back. We're having a recap tomorrow at two o'clock, then we're flying out to Miami at five. Pack your bags, preferably for the heat."

I looked down at the bandage on my ankle. *Well, this is going to suck.* "See you at two." And I disconnected the call. I looked over at Noah, and rolled my eyes at his arched eyebrow.

"You're going in?"

"Yeah." I reached for the cane and pulled myself up. I limped to the closet, pulled out my pack and started throwing clothes inside. Noah watched for a second, then got up, only to push me back onto the bed. I sat back and crossed my arms, as I let the caveman have his way.

"Sit. I got this." He packed my bags quickly, making sure to grab the extra ammo from the nightstand.

"You didn't have to do that. I could have done it just fine," I muttered, after he laid back down.

"Yes, I know you could have. But at some point, you're gonna to have to let other people help you," he said gently.

I shrugged. "I guess so. I'm going to have to accept help sooner or later. It's not like I can traipse all over Miami as quickly as I used to."

Noah's face turned to stone. "You're going back?"

I leaned back against the headboard and closed my eyes. *And so begins the explanations and dramas.* "Continuation of the Cartel case. There are a few leads that we need to track down."

"Don't you think you're going to need to take it easy? You just fell down a mountain, for Christ's sake."

Irritation bubbled within, and unfortunately for him, my filter disengaged. "See, this is exactly why I don't do relationships. This is my job. It wouldn't be the first time I've been injured and tracking down bad guys. Don't worry, I know what my body can handle and what it can't."

He gave me the "yeah, right" look, but I stood firm. I knew my limitations and my weaknesses. I may not like to admit them, but I knew when too much was too much.

"Whatever you say, Princess." He ran his hand down the length of my torso. "Now, tell me. Can your body handle me?" The heat in his eyes gleamed, as his fingers played with the barbell in my nipple.

I sighed, and gave him a cocky grin. "Oh, you? I can definitely handle you." And I proceeded to show him exactly how I could handle him.

\*\*\*

WE WOKE UP WITH THE next morning, and after giving a barely there explanation, we said our good-byes to the group. The guys loaded up the trailer with the bikes, and we threw our stuff inside the vehicles. We were on our way within minutes. The first half hour was silent. I knew he had a lot on his mind, we both did. There was something about returning to the land of civilization that was always a mood killer. After an hour of silence, he finally spoke up.

"So, tell me how you became this big, badass FBI agent," he said with a sidelong grin.

I shrugged. "There's not much to tell, really. I dropped out of school when I was pregnant, and ended up getting my GED as soon as I turned sixteen. I had my bachelor's degree in criminal justice by the time I turned nineteen, went through the police academy by twenty-one, and then I was accepted by Quantico when I turned twenty-two. I was working on task forces before I had even graduated the academy, because of my age. I was working drug cases as an undercover, making buys at college parties and whatnot."

Noah shook his head. "I'm not easily impressed, Princess, but you've thoroughly impressed me. What was your drive? I mean, hell, what made you decide to bust your ass like that?"

I stared out the window. "I don't know. I guess the fact that I didn't have much of a social life was one thing. After the sperm donor made my school life hell, I had no one to confide in. He turned everyone against me, to the point that I was threatened daily by his groupies. So I did the pussy thing and left."

"What is this douche's name?" he growled.

"Why, so you can defend my honor?" I teased, giving him a smile.

"Exactly. I want to beat his ass."

I shook my head and laughed. "Don't worry about it. He gave me the ambition I needed. I got off my ass and got shit accomplished. Who the hell knows if I would have had the drive to do all that, if everything in high school was all hunky-dory. I am who I am, despite all my issues. I'm okay with that."

"I'm pretty okay with that too," he said, bringing our entwined hands up to kiss my knuckles.

"It's my turn to ask a question."

He raised his eyebrows. "Okay, shoot."

"Who is Aubrey?"

# CHAPTER 14
*Noah*

It's not like I hadn't been expecting it. I wish I could have told her before she asked me, but either my cock was deep in her pussy, or I was a pussy myself, and couldn't bring up the subject.

"Aubrey is my daughter," I said carefully. I quickly glanced over at Kate, whose face remained blank and emotionless—the look I knew that was calculating and thinking. I knew I had to head her off before she made any wrong assumptions. "She was born last November."

"And the mother is…" her voice trailed off, but I knew what she wanted. This wasn't easy for me to explain, because the history was complicated. So fucking complicated.

"I grew up in North Beach, close to Sketch's parents'

place. In fact, we went to the same school together. Him, me—"

"And his sister, Jennie," she surmised. Kate turned to me, with the question in her eyes.

"Jennie is Aubrey's mom." I confirmed her suspicions, and immediately her eyes widened.

"You're Bree's dad?"

I grinned, thinking of my one proudest accomplishment. "Yep. That little angel is my pride and joy."

"I don't know all the details, but what the hell happened to Jennie? I heard she got mixed up in some bad shit."

My face went hard at the mention of my daughter's mother. "Jennie and I were together for a while, on and off since we were in high school. I joined the Marines and we lost touch. I would come back for home leave, and we'd hook up. When I'd leave again, it was over. My unit was based out of Florida, so it's not like we'd get a chance to see each other, especially with me traveling so much. But as I came home, I noticed she was hanging out with the wrong crew. They were bad news, like known drug dealers and gang bangers. It was pretty ironic because my unit was a Narco unit, working in conjunction with the Organized Crimes Division and the DEA, and yet the girl I was hooking up with had a drug problem."

"Did you know she was on drugs at the time?"

I rubbed the back of my neck. "Yes and no. She came to me at one point, and needed my help to get clean. I got her into an expensive, residential rehab facility in Miami, but I had to head out on a mission. Once I got back, she was nowhere to be found."

"Wait, you were with Triton's Edge?" she questioned.

I gave her my biggest smile. "Yep, darlin'. That would be me. I was Alpha One Captain for Triton's Edge."

"Holy shit. I worked with you guys before, while running the Cruz Cartel case. How did we not meet before this? Why didn't you tell me?" Her blue eyes were wide with surprise, and I choked on my next words.

"For the same reasons you didn't tell me you were FBI. We had to separate the two lives. And trust me, Princess, it killed me to do so. That shootout in Miami? My team was en route when we got the call that Megan went down. Our bird was in the sky, and then we were rerouted to track Tommy. They had him for a while, but then he went into a covered canal. That's where we lost him." My words had struck her silent as she processed the information.

"You said "they." Where were you?" she questioned.

"I didn't know Jennie had the baby until I got the

call from Sketch that her house was raided, and that there was an infant involved. The last time I'd seen her was last July. She came down, already pregnant. I asked whose baby she was carrying, and she said that it wasn't mine. She wanted help, wanted to get clean. I got her into rehab, but then I had to take off for another trip. She never told me who the father was. But when the baby was taken into custody by the Department of Social Services, they swabbed her for DNA, and voilà! I had a kid. I finished up my mission and made tracks for home. In fact, this was right after you left. Bought out half my cousin's shares of the Double J, and a little home for the two of us down over in Edgewater."

Kate took a deep breath, then nodded. "I met her once, at Sketch's house. It was comical to see him with a newborn. Scary man with tattoos, singing John Mayer songs to a squawking baby."

I snickered at the thought. "Yeah, she can't sleep without that CD playing. And without Sketch, his mom, and my folks, I wouldn't have had my baby girl. They were the ones to fight for me, when I was stuck in the jungles of Columbia. Without them, she would have wound up in the foster care system."

"Where's Jennie now?" she asked, circling the back of my hand with her thumb.

"Who knows. After she got out of jail, she vanished.

I haven't seen her in forever. She used to call, to get me to meet her somewhere with Bree, but she'd never show. And those calls stopped after a while. It's like she's a ghost."

Her eyes filled with sadness. "That sucks so much for Bree. But thankfully, she has your mom and Sketch's family. That's who she needs right now. Family isn't always about blood, it's about who you decide to share your love, your memories, and your life with."

If my heart could've been any fuller, it would've burst. I brought her hand to my lips again. "You don't know how happy that makes me to hear that," I said gratefully.

Kate gave me her winning smile, a smile that not too many people saw. A smile I fell for last year.

"To totally change the subject, let's talk about work. Since this is above my paygrade, obviously, is your team still involved with the Cruz Cartel case? Or did the Bureau cut the funding from that too?"

I snorted. "Alpha team got pulled and rerouted to the Syndicate case."

Her blue eyes widened. "Those are some scary dudes. I haven't worked specifically on that case, but there is a lot of similarities between the Cartel and the Syndicate. They're the suppliers, right?"

"Princess, they're the suppliers in everything the

underworld has to offer."

"Were they the reason you ran off yesterday?"

I nodded grimly. "I received word that a member from my team was taken out by a sniper."

She nodded. "And the Syndicate is responsible for that?"

"That's the going assumption. Mac was shot on the mission in Mexico, a mission I had been planning right before I left. But Torin is keeping me in the loop." I checked the time, and we had about another hour to go before we got home. I pulled her hand into mine, and we rode in comfortable silence for the rest of the trip, and before I knew it, we were pulling into her driveway. I looked over at her, and her head was against the window, sound asleep. I leaned over the console, and just took in her face. The stress and the pain weren't as prominently featured anymore, but I knew the toll this case was taking on her.

"Time to wake up, Sleeping Beauty," I said softly, as I ran my thumb down her jawline. Her eyes blinked open, showcasing those beautiful blues. I cupped the back of her head. "How are you feeling?"

"Good," she rasped, then cleared her throat. "I must have been more tired than I thought." I frowned at that. For someone who was injured and supposed to take it easy, I sure as hell didn't give her a chance to rest.

"Yeah, that's my fault. Look, we'll get you changed, and then I'll take you to the office." I knew she wasn't an invalid, and with the cane, she was able to get around. But I wasn't ready to let her go.

"I'll be fine, Noah," she replied, "I'm a big girl. I've taken care of myself for a while now. I think I can handle it."

I raised my eyebrows, and said, "Just work with me. I can't have you in my bed, so I'll take any time I can with you."

She rolled her eyes. "Before we do anything, why don't we put down some rules. Such as, I will drive my happy little self to work. This isn't the first time I've busted an ankle, or an arm, or a shoulder, or any other body part, okay? So let's dial down the caveman just a notch." She brushed her dark hair out of her eyes, revealing the dark bruise near her hairline. My eyes narrowed at the reminder of her injury, and I turned my focus to the house in front of me.

"Next?" I replied, placating her little rules.

She scoffed. "I may not have a lot of experience in relationships, Noah, but I'm not a fool. I'm not some submissive pushover who will let you walk all over her."

I chuckled. "No, Princess. You're not a fool. You are mine, though. And we're going to be spending quite a lot of time together. So you're gonna have to get used to me wanting to do things for you, with you, and to you." I brought her hand up to my lips, and kissed the underside of her wrist. "A relationship is all about the give and take. I promise, you won't be the only one giving. I plan to give you so much more." The thought of everything I wanted to do with her had my cock hardening. But then again, it didn't take much when it came to Kate. I could tell she felt the same by the faint flush across her tanned cheeks. Before I did something stupid, like haul her onto my lap and give her neighbors a show, I got out of the truck and went around to her side. After helping her inside, and hauling her luggage in, there wasn't much more for me to do, other than stand around and try not to be a horndog.

She threw some clothes into a polka dot suitcase, then changed her own outfit while I was in the bathroom. The little sneak purposely waited until I was distracted, because she knew full well that I wouldn't be able to help myself. And from the look of things, I didn't think she would have been able to, either.

"Seriously, I'm good, Noah. You need to leave. Don't you have to pick up Aubrey?" She urged me out the door, while adjusting her holster. The sight of her with the Glock tucked into her back holster had blood shooting to my cock. I adjusted the painful bulge and pulled her into my arms.

"All right, I'm leaving. Be safe down there, and watch your back." I crushed my lips to hers, taking in her sigh. My tongue swept against hers, memorizing the feel of her lips. We broke apart, panting. "Call me when you get home."

Kate snorted, then placed another quick kiss on my lips. "If that's your good-bye, I can't wait to see your welcome back."

I wiggled my eyebrows. "Oh, Princess, you won't be able to handle it." I palmed her tight ass in my hands and gave it a big squeeze. "Seriously, Kate. Call me if you need me. I can be down there in four hours."

Kate pushed me back. "Oh, for the love of God. Noah, just go. I'll be fine." I took the hint. Giving her one last look, I walked out to my truck. Before the key was in the ignition, I made the call.

"What's going on, Trey?" I asked, as I pulled out of Kate's driveway. I pictured the big thug looking jarhead, who was instrumental on my team. Trey Walker was the biggest enforcer on our crew. At six-five, and three hundred pounds of pure, homegrown muscle, Trey was my right-hand man. He was the muscle (no pun in intended), and my second in command. I only trusted a few people with my life, and Trey was one of them.

"Not much, brother." I heard the familiar sounds of

his Dodge Charger in the background. The garage and the gun range were the only two places you'd find Trey when he was taking a rare break. "How's life?"

"Good, man. Hey, I know you're probably going to Boston for Mac's funeral, but I need eyes on my girl while she's down there."

"Ah, you finally cracked, huh? Kate's a good woman, bro. I'm glad you finally got your head out of your ass," Trey said with a laugh. Trey was the only one who had met Kate, when he came to our rescue when a romp in my Challenger turned into a dead battery. He gave me hell, and Kate joined in. That was when it really started to sink in. When a girl can hold her own with your juvenile delinquent of a friend, then she may be the one for you.

"Yeah. Whatever, dude. Look, she's flying tonight, working with the Cruz case. Do we have anyone down there that can help us out?"

"Yeah, we have Zeke working IT. He's been our eyes and ears on that front. I'll put a bug in his ear and have him join up." There was a slight pause, and then he continued. "The word on the street is that the Syndicate has some deeper pockets than originally thought. Their ties with the Cruz Cartel have only grown, and they're venturing into new territory."

My stomach tightened. "What are those sick

motherfuckers up to now?" I growled, my hands gripping the steering wheel.

"They've expanded their trade market. Young kids, barely out of diapers, are being sold for God knows what."

I spat out a curse. I knew it was only a matter of time before they cast their sights on the more innocent.

"How many?" I barked.

"We rescued thirteen between the ages of six and thirteen. Five boys, eight girls. Ethnicities vary, but it looks like they're Americans. All thirteen spoke American English."

"Location?"

"Out of the port in New Orleans. Information is being sent back as we speak. The Coast Guard boarded the ship on a whim this morning."

I grunted, knowing the full truth. "A whim, being our one and only source?"

"Yeah, we got the info last night and put a bug in the captain's ear."

"Do we know the buyer's location?" My mind was running a million miles a minute. Just because the ships were manifested to a singular location, didn't mean that the Syndicate didn't have someone waiting for them on the ship, to move them onto another ship.

"Buyer is unknown. The manifest had it going to

Europe, but who knows where they could have stopped along the way."

I slapped the steering wheel with my hand, and pressed my foot on the gas. The urge to get up and fly down to Miami to be a part of it was strong, but I had Aubrey to think about now. My days of getting dirty at a moment's notice were gone.

"Just keep me posted. If I need to, I can make the trip."

"Sit tight, Noah. We'll update you at Mac's wake." And with that, we disconnected. No formal good-byes, no small talk. My boys and I were one unit. We didn't need that fluffy shit.

I pulled into the parking lot of the Double J, the restaurant I owned. Well, partially owned. When my cousin Jason was called up to the major leagues to play for the Tampa Bay Ray's, I had just taken custody of Aubrey, and I needed something to do. Yeah, my retirement from the military was decent, but it would only pay so much, and damn, babies are expensive little things. The timing was right, so I bought out half of Jason's ownership shares in the place. His brother Josh owned the other fifty percent, which was fine with us. He was the chef in the family, and ran the place like clockwork. Jason and I were the investors, and I occasionally played bartender. I quickly checked in with Josh, grabbed a to-go container of our famous crab cakes for lunch, and rolled out. The five-mile drive to my house was too long, and before I even got to the main drag, I had already stuffed half of one in my mouth. Of course, that would be the time when the phone would ring.

"Mmmphf," I said in greeting, clicking on my Bluetooth.

"You better have some crab cakes for me. The only reason why we have that restaurant in the family is because your uncle only gave that recipe to Josh. How else would we get them?"

"Hi, Mom," I greeted her with a grin, swallowing the rest of the morsel. I looked hungrily at the other half as it sat there, taunting me.

"Hi, Noah. Are you on your way home?"

"Yeah, I'm about five minutes away," I said.

"Good, we're on our way."

I smiled, and thought of my baby girl. I hated not being around her now, missing her, even after a few days. Hell, the second I held her in my arms, she had me hooked. I pulled into the driveway and sat for a minute. My two lives were at odds with each other, each one wanting to take precedency over the other. But once my mom pulled in behind me, and I held that baby girl in my arms, I knew what I had to do.

Because I knew that if I didn't, no one else would.

And I would destroy anyone who even dare to think about harming them.

# CHAPTER 15
*Kate*

"WELCOME TO MIAMI. Enjoy your stay!" The sunny greeting was lost on me as I ignored the bubbly blonde flight attendant. We touched down at a private airfield outside of Miami for the third time in four weeks, and made our way to the Suburban waiting for us. Well, they made their way. I limped along with as much dignity as I could muster. I knew those bastards were making judgmental remarks, and it took everything in me not to snap a retort. But Special Agent in Charge Rapoles made it very clear on the plane that I was here by invitation, and he was determined to send me back to Maryland as soon as possible.

"Parker, you good for this? Do we need to get someone to fill in for you?" The steely eyes of my commanding officer snapped me to attention.

"No, sir. I'm fine," I muttered through gritted teeth. They tossed our luggage into the trunk, and then we were on our way to whatever crime scene that was waiting for us.

"So, bring us up to speed, Sims. What do we have?"

Sims handed out manila folders, filled with crime scene photos. The girls in the pictures didn't look familiar, but then again, I'd ran across those types of ladies all the time. I grimaced at the mutilated corpses. I saw them earlier, and seeing them again didn't make it any easier.

"Four females, found with deep throat lacerations, with markings of rape and assault. Victims' names are Lacey Blackstone, Stacey Menroe, Stefanie McGongel, and Natacha Hemsington. Medical examiner said they were still alive when they were set on fire." My stomach rolled at the thought of the horror those women went through, but I swallowed my discomfort and answered the questions.

"A homeless woman found them in the alley outside a strip club, near the Port of Everglades. Sir, their bodies were filled with heroin, but they didn't die from an overdose. Their injuries include deep throat lacerations, cut from ear to ear. The medical examiner said that the women were still alive when they were set ablaze," I advised, keeping my emotions in check.

Rapoles looked over the report. His sharp, angular jawline hardened. I couldn't read his expression in the worst of situations, the man had a poker face that could win the World Series of Poker. After flipping through the pictures again, he handed the file back to us.

"Suspects?"

Sims took over. "We have every reason to believe that the Cartel is still in the game, for the simple fact that all these women had cell phones in their possession that contained the number for a Reggie Cruz. And similar to the Melody case, their phones were brand new—as in, purchased the day before. No other service was ever listed."

"And where are we on the wiretap warrant?" Rapoles looked as if he was bored.

"Warrant has been obtained and executed. There's only been one outgoing phone call on one cell phone, and that was from Stacey Menroe to George "Mac" Cleary. Because that name is under the DOD directory, an order has been issued. We should hear about that shortly."

Rapoles nodded, and turned his head toward the window. "I knew Cleary. He was with Triton's Edge, the joint DEA and Special Forces Task Force out of MacDill Airforce Base. We'll be bringing them up to speed first thing tomorrow morning."

My ears instantly piqued at the mention of Triton's Edge, but I didn't react. "We've worked with that group before, when Megan Turner was captured."

Rapoles's body tightened, and I swore his hands clenched a little at the not-so-subtle jab I sent him. He was the main person that never believed me when I brought up Tommy's involvement. Because of him, we almost lost Megan. My respect for him had sorely diminished, and there was no love lost between us.

"You're correct. They had our eye in the sky, while you and the rest of your band of misfits let the biggest mole in the FBI escape."

Fire shot through my veins, and I wanted more than anything to throat punch the old ass prick. But my job and this case depended on me keeping my cool, so I bit my tongue.

"Unfortunately, Agent Rapoles, as you might remember, resources were scarce during that period," I interjected, the ice in my voice clearly evident.

Sims coughed to clear the air, and brought the attention back to him. "With the phone number, that's our only tie to the Cartel case. However, we did DNA samples of the matter and material under the victims' fingernails, and they came up with a positive hit for a Stas Alexeyev, a name not commonly found in conjunction with the Cartel. However, he's widely known."

"Stas Alexeyev is a Russian dealer from the Ukraine, known for weapons and narcotics." I leveled my gaze at Rapoles. "Who is he working for?"

"We have every reason to believe that Alexeyev is a runner for the Syndicate. A highly motivated, organized group of the world's worst..." Rapoles droned on, but my patience got the better of me.

"Sir, may I ask, is our focus going to be on both organizations? Is the Cruz Cartel working in conjunction with the Syndicate?" After hearing from Noah about the group and his case with the Syndicate, I had a pretty good idea of what Rapoles was going to say.

And the fucker didn't let me down.

"I'm not sure where you got your information, Parker, but yes, we have reason to believe that the Cruz Cartel is working with Syndicate. We believe that the Syndicate is providing the Cartel with the drugs to funnel their weapon sales. The Syndicate has embraced the Cartel into their faction with open arms. So, in answer to your question, we are primarily focusing on the Cartel, but if we take them down at the top, we'll be better off for it.

"Fuck." We knew it was a possibility. Hell, in this game, anything was a possibility.

"Hence the reason we're meeting up with the Joint

Task Force, Triton's Edge. We feel the situation will be better off, combining our efforts," Rapoles replied dryly.

*And a feather in your cap when we take them all down.* I wasn't a fool. The man only thought about himself. Lord knew, he'd do anything to get up into Assistant Director status.

"Does this mean that we'll be receiving more resources?" I asked.

"You should try using the resources you have more efficiently, Parker. You have the best in the business at your fingertips. Use them well."

The anger bubbled up inside of me, and it took everything in me to not shoot back with a nasty reply. But I played the good little agent and kept quiet. The SUV stopped in front of the Miami Field Office, and we headed inside, leaving our luggage with the administrative assistant, while we received our updates and made sure we were all on the same page with Triton's Edge.

After ensuring everyone was up to speed, we were dismissed. I hailed a cab to the hotel that was arranged for me. As we drove by the old apartment building, memories flooded back. The time spent in the gym, the times we hung out at the bars. Late night swims in the pool. And the sex. The mind-blowing sex. After everything that happened over the weekend, I thought

I could actually get used to having someone around full-time. Being in a relationship scared me; the trust factor alone was a huge issue. I had a tendency to let my heart go with the wrong people, to put my faith and trust in those who truly didn't deserve it. But Noah was different. I could feel it in my bones.

The next morning, after fueling myself with multiple cups of coffee and a Danish from the hotel restaurant, Sims picked me up in the Suburban. We drove through the industrial park in the lower end of Miami to a nondescript warehouse on the edge of town. We'd used the space before, as a planning area for raids. It was where I spent most of my time over the last few years. The wide open space was sectioned off into staging areas, with the weapons locked up in the second floor office. Two agents with guns were waiting for us, and we pulled into the open bay.

"Do you realize what we're getting into?" Sims asked quietly. Aside from a grunt greeting this morning, he hadn't spoken the entire car ride.

"We're going after the biggest badasses there are in the world. What more do we need to know?" I joked.

Sims scowled at my deflection, and I quickly got serious. "Yeah, I realize that we're in a whole other league now. But hell, this is what we've been waiting for. We got this, Sims. We're finally getting the resources we need to take the Cartel down, and in the process, potentially dismantling the biggest international organized crime group there is. The damage that we can inflict on the Syndicate and their subordinates is huge. And whatever we do will have a trickle-down effect, from everything to the cartels and gangs, to the teenagers selling crack on the sidewalks. This is a good thing," I replied in an even tone. We'd worked with other government agencies before, but the stakes were never this high.

Sims and I walked to the center of the room, where a group of metal chairs sat in a semicircle. Five big, burly men were waiting for us, each looking deadlier than the other. Dressed in cargo pants and T-shirts stretched across their shoulders, you could tell that they took their jobs as seriously as they did their fitness level. I wouldn't want to meet these guys in a dark alley. Introductions were made and we sat down, just as Rapoles and an older man walked toward the front.

"My name is Commander James Lewes, Triton Edge's Alpha. We've been following the Syndicate now for the last four years. My men know the Syndicate inside and out, and we have been tracking their movements. They'll be able to answer any questions you may have. Alpha team is on a mission, but the Bravo team will be the ones assisting you with Cruz." His steely gaze held us in. His 'no bullshit' attitude lacked the whiny, wimpy-assness that often came with being a government crony. I found that refreshing, and instantly liked the commander.

"Thank you, Commander. Let's bring everyone up to speed, shall we?" Rapoles took over from there, and we went over everything. And by everything, I meant *everything*. From the birth of Christian Cruz and his family lineage, to the involvement of Shane Turner, and Christian's son Tomas, otherwise known as the FBI plant, Tommy Greene.

"How did the Cartel come to the attention of the Syndicate?" I inquired. We had been at it for the last two hours, and my stomach grumbled.

"We figure it was several things. Christian Cruz had his fingers in everything the underworld has to offer, but when shit went down last year, starting from the situation in Maryland, that brought the Cartel up to a whole new level. But they really caught attention when Tomas was revealed as the plant. Having the son of a cartel planted within the FBI is a huge coup. It takes balls, and the Syndicate noticed."

Rapoles bristled at the mention of his incompetence, and I fought back the claim of victory. *In your face, Rapoles. This is all on you.*

"Were they even players before this incident?" I queried, popping open a soda that they graciously provided.

"Oh yeah, of course. Make no mistake about it. The Syndicate was going to use the Cartel at some point, but their value skyrocketed when they had an FBI agent in their midst. They had an in. An edge, if you will, that no one else had. That makes them invaluable assets," a man in glasses replied. Tall and lean, with his muscle definition showing through his shirt, the man leaned against the desk, taking in what we had written on the whiteboard moments earlier. Good looking, with dark hair and eyes, he almost reminded me of Noah.

"I'm Zeke, by the way." He reached out and I shook his hand.

"Nice to meet you. I'm Kate, and this is Rick, my partner."

"Glad you guys are here. I've been waiting to kick some cartel ass."

"Were you part of the crew that assisted with the takedown of Tommy last year?

Zeke grinned, his beautiful, straight teeth gleaming. "Hell yeah. Although, flying the birds aren't really my thing."

I nodded. I wasn't fond of flying the birds, either.

"Wells!" His name was called from across the room, and he quickly stood straighter.

"We'll catch up soon." And with that, he jogged over to where a bank of computers had been set up.

"What do you think so far?" Rick asked, his voice low.

I stacked the files in order and looked over at the crew talking amongst themselves. "So far so good, I guess. We just need to work out the details, but things seem to be in motion. If anything, we'll get the resources we need. As long as shit doesn't hit the fan, we should be golden."

"I think so, too." He motioned over to the other side of the warehouse. "Wells has something to show us." Sims led the way over to the computer bank. Zeke had several screens up at once, with various pictures and video.

"Who is this?" I asked, leaning over his shoulder and pointing at a tall, bad man in a suit.

"That is Stas Alexeyev, weapons and drug runner for the Syndicate. His address is a vacant parking lot in the crappiest part of Miami."

"Are his prints the ones we found on the women's phones?" I inquired, nodding to Rick.

"His prints, as well as another partial set. We're working through Interpol now to determine if we've missed anyone," Zeke nodded.

"We have our link to the Cartel," Rick said grimly. Very rarely did emotion come through the normally stoic man's face, but damned if I didn't see a hint of victory in his eyes.

"That's not all you have." Zeke pressed a few keys and a new picture popped up. "These are his brothers. Moriz is on the right, Anton is on the left. They are the weapon purchasers. No weapons deal goes through the Syndicate without their approval." The grainy image was taken by stealth, as they were on the move. The three brothers were next to a boat, looking like they were ready to board. All three were big, bulky, and bald.

"Where was this taken?"

"Yesterday, at Port of Everglades. Time stamp is five-thirty in the evening," Zeke replied.

"What was the time of death?" I asked Rick, but as usual, he was one step ahead of me. He had the coroner's report on his phone.

"Time of death was estimated to be circa five pm. Their bodies were discovered at seventeen thirty."

"Puts them at the scene. Do we know where they are now?" I asked the master behind the monitor.

"His ship manifest states that he's supposed to be docking in the Grand Caymans, but we haven't seen the yacht he was on." Zeke paused. "We can pinpoint the coordinates with the GPS system on his boat, try to find it that way. But I can almost guarantee that they've already disconnected it." Zeke's gaze remained firmly on the screen in front of him.

"Do we have an in with the U.S. Coast Guard?" I mentally went through my rolodex, searching through all the contacts I'd made so far.

"We have one better," Zeke answered, his voice low. His bespectacled brown eyes searched the area around us, making sure we weren't going to be overheard. "We have a contact within the Syndicate. We're just waiting for the call."

"Is this source reliable?" I questioned quietly.

"Extremely. They should be making contact within the next two hours." He nodded to the disposable phone sitting next to him. "They'll call me on that. "

"Sounds good. Keep us in the loop." I straightened up. "In the meantime, we'll head out to the Port, see if there's anything we missed."

We made our way out of the warehouse, to where they had several cars waiting for us, and made our way up I-95, to Hollywood, Florida. The crime scene team were still in place, so I hoped they had more clues for us. Forty minutes later, we arrived, just as the afternoon sun had made it hotter than hell. We walked over to the active scene, flashing our credentials, and going beyond the crime scene tape.

"Wanna tell me why the hell the Feds are up in my case?" an angry Hispanic man bellowed, and walked over. Tall, and built like a tank, the man appeared to be in charge.

"Agents Parker and Sims, Baltimore Field Office." I showed him my badge, but the detective wasn't having it.

"I don't give a rat's ass who the hell you are. You're not taking this over. Your buddies already took over the last few cases of mine. I mean, seriously, what the fuck does the FBI want with a bunch of dead hookers?" he demanded. The spittle flew out of his mouth, and his eyes flared with anger. I shot a questioning look to Rick, before turning back.

"And who might you be?" Rick asked, his chin jutting out.

"Mike Perez, Special Victim's Unit. We run cases with the Feds all the time, so imagine my surprise when I get this hotheaded, punk ass bitch, calling claim to the many cases that affect this area. I get that the Port is a special interest area, but you people are pissing me the fuck off."

"Detective, have there been other instances of dead prostitutes in these parts?" I asked pointedly.

Mike rubbed his face in aggravation. "Does one nut not sit next to the other in the same sac? Seriously? I had one of your guys out three nights ago, taking over a case of two dead women. They literally arrived five minutes after we did, and called an audible."

Rick's face turned to stone. "Detective, have you not been brought up to speed on what's been going on in your district?" It was protocol to bring the local police, or at least their special crimes unit, into what was going on. They wouldn't get all the information, but on the same point, it was always good to give people a heads-up. My gut filled with lead, and I had a feeling I knew where this was going.

"What the hell do you think?" Mike scoffed. Well, that answered that.

"Who was the agent that took over that night?" I questioned.

"Special Agent Jessica Knowles. Her and this arrogant prick. They harassed my techs, and wouldn't let us onto the scene until they were done."

My gut was right. I shot a look at Rick, and glanced around at the team working busily around us, collecting any trace of evidence they could find. Jessica Knowles was one of the few that had unfettered access to Tommy Greene while he was still with the Bureau. After the investigation into his team, her name was bounced around as a possible plant. The evidence against her was scarce, but my instinct was that she was a part of it. She was cleared of any wrongful acts, and allowed to resume full duties on the Cartel case. I should have been surprised that she got through all the bullshit, but I wasn't. Evidence or not, I didn't trust the woman. With her sniffing around, I could only bet that Tommy was right behind her.

I scrolled through the images on my phone and pulled up an image of Tommy.

"Was this the agent that was with her?" I asked, showing Mike the picture.

"Yeah, that's him. They just fucked my crime scene over like a whore at church."

*Shit.* "Call it in," I muttered to Sims. An APB needed to be put out on Agent Knowles. This cemented my case against her. With Mike's testimony, the chick was as good as in jail. Sims moved off to the side, out of earshot from the rest of us.

"You see either of these two again, you need to call me directly. Is that clear?" I ordered, piercing my gaze into his deep brown eyes.

"What's going on here, Agent?" Mike asked, his brows raised.

"This Agent is no longer with the FBI, Detective. In fact, this guy is wanted for treason, aiding and abetting a drug cartel, abduction, trafficking, and a whole laundry list of charges." I scrolled through my contacts in my phone, searching for my liaison with the Miami PD. "This your boss?" I showed him the name on my phone, and he grunted his affirmation. "I'm going to send him all the details, but we're going to get you in contact with someone on my team. They'll be able to stay in contact after we roll out of here. The MO of this case is similar to others, and to tell you the truth, Mike, this has all the markings of the Cruz Cartel. So, I'm going to need your help. I'm not going to be like the others, and try to take over your cases. Truly I'm not. But I do need you to work with me on this. This Cartel is responsible for killing a lot of people up in Maryland. This is personal for me. I really need your help," I said in a low voice. I normally didn't plead for help, but something told me that Detective Perez wouldn't let me down.

"I got you." I breathed out a sigh of a relief when he didn't ask any more questions. The dude was legit. I could tell he had a decent head on his shoulders, and he knew what was going on. We ran through the evidence that they'd collected, along with possible timelines, body counts, and scenes where other victims were found. Thirty minutes later, Rick came running over.

"Rapoles wants a report within the next hour. We have to roll," Rick announced, putting away his phone. His eyes surveyed the scene in front of us. "What's the verdict?"

"We're going to need someone to stay down here and run point with Mike. I'm not trusting locals right now, no more than I'm trusting the field office here," I replied in a low voice.

"Think there's another inside track?" he muttered, folding his arms across his chest.

"More than likely." I sent off a quick text to Lucy, asking her to run down the latest on Jessica Knowles.

"Let's move. I'll send a couple of our analysts out here to keep the locals on track." We made our way over to Mike and his team, and reinforced our appreciation. Mike knew the stakes. You could tell from his eyes that he knew things were about to get messy, and I needed to be able to trust someone.

We sped back to the warehouse to give Rapoles the latest update. My gut instinct was right on the money. There hadn't been any FBI files or cases opened in regards to Mike's stolen cases. The missing dead women put a stain on Rapoles' joint venture with the Special Forces team; fury didn't even begin to describe his demeanor when we arrived back at the warehouse. A warrant was issued for Knowles' arrest, in connection with the murders of those women, and the evidence that Mike's team had gathered from the crime scene was sent back to the labs at Quantico for processing. As we searched through the evidence, the trail back to the Cartel grew colder. We spent days combing through evidence and following up on leads, only to end up with ghost trails and more dead ends. To say that we were frustrated would have been an understatement. Tempers flared, and patience was at an all-time low.

We'd been in Miami for over two weeks, with no end in sight. We hadn't seen hide nor hair of the Cartel's dealings since the death of the four women. We finally released their bodies to their next of kin, all from the same area in Michigan. The toxicology screens came back positive for heroin, oxycodone, and high amounts of cocaine. According to their parents, the women weren't known for their drug use or partying ways. They came to Miami for a bachelorette party two weeks ago, hoping to live it up with their friends for the weekend. But they never even made it to the hotel. From what we gathered from the security footage, a cab was called from the airport, and then they vanished. After that, there was no sign of them. Based on the amount of drugs in their systems, and the bruises on their bodies, we could only guess the worst case scenario.

"I'm sticking behind," Rick said grimly, as he finished up his report. We had done all we could in Miami for the time being, and we were redirected to head back to Baltimore. He shared my distrust over the local office, and I was glad he was staying behind. I needed someone who knew what the hell they were doing, someone I could count on.

"Sounds like a plan. Keep me updated." I packed

up my files and placed them in my messenger bag. A snort of laughter came from behind me, and I rolled my eyes. I knew who the pigheaded asshole was. He had been eye fucking me over the past few days, and it was seriously getting on my last nerve.

"So what, you got enough of his dick, now you get to run back home?" The large, bull of a man with a shaved head and jagged scar going down from his eye to his angled jawline, leaned in one of the metal chairs, his long legs stretched out, as if he didn't have a care in the world.

"I'm sorry, but I don't seem to remember your name. I'm Agent Kate Parker." I held out my hand, only to have him rebuff my attempts to be socially polite.

"I know who you are. Most of us know who you are."

"Well, I don't know you, but you seem to have already formed an opinion of me, so why don't you explain," I replied dryly, folding my arms across my chest.

He flicked his eyes over my body, glancing at me from head to toe, and I groaned inwardly. Just another meathead, trying to get his rocks off with the newbie.

"Oh, your reputation precedes you, all right. Question is, will it live up to the real thing?"

My patience was shot. "Tell me, soldier, what the

fuck are you talking about?"

"We heard all about you. How you originally got kicked off this case because you couldn't keep your legs together, and suddenly you're back." The snide comment plucked that last nerve that I had, the only one holding my sanity together.

"Do you want to run that by me again, slick? I didn't quite understand what you were saying," I replied, my jaw clenched. My previous detail down in Miami was not discussed in the briefing, so there was no way he would have known.

"Tell me, Agent Parker. Whose dick did you have to suck to get back onto the case? And what did your boyfriend say? I mean, he's the one that got you off the case and out of here, didn't he? So what did you do to get yourself back in their good graces?"

Fury raged through me, and I took a step closer, before Sims came up and pushed me back.

"Those lips look mighty plump. Maybe I should try them out myself." The fucker had the nerve to goad me even more. The urge to pound the hell out of his face was fierce.

"Leave it, Parker," Sims said in a low voice. I turned my gaze sharply to him, and I unclenched my fists.

"I'm not sure where you got your misinformation, soldier, but I can assure you, that I'm here entirely on merit. You've been trailing these Syndicate jokers for the last two years? Good for you. I've been on the Cruz Cartel case for the last three, and I know what the hell I'm talking about. This is my case, asshat. You need my crew just as much as we need yours."

He spat on the ground. "Fuck you, you stupid whore. Just because you're good at sucking dick, doesn't mean the rest of us have to bow down—"

"Finish that sentence, motherfucker, and I'll let her go," Rick warned, as he struggled to hold me back. I just wanted one swing. One swing, that was all I needed to take the clown out.

"Martinez! Is there an issue here?" Commander Lewes stalked over, the tick in his jaw obvious.

"No, sir," he replied. The Commander didn't believe him, but frankly, I didn't care. I wasn't going to be a snitch. It was bad enough that people thought my position within my group was based on sex, that I slept with whoever I could to get to where I was today. I sure as hell wasn't going to be a snitch.

"You good?" Sims whispered.

"Yeah, I got this," I replied, jutting my chin out at Martinez. I waited for the commander to leave the area before I shot Martinez an icy stare. "Take that pencil-dick out of your ass and listen to me. I don't know who the hell you've been talking to, but I sure as hell don't need to screw a man just to get ahead. And while my skills in the bedroom are amazing, you'll never know. Because I only open my legs for real men, not some steroid using, pill-popping, penis pump using jackass like yourself." I pushed off Rick and grabbed my bag. "Keep me posted, Sims." I walked out of the warehouse with my head held high, but inside, I was fuming. What the hell was Martinez talking about? What boyfriend? They weren't talking about Noah...were they? I pushed away any uncertainty and focused on the drive to the airport. I'd get to the bottom of it when I got home. The only thing I needed now was a bottle of wine and a long, hot bath.  However, I settled for the window seat, and ordered a Jack and Coke from the stewardess.

Three hours after I got home, the doorbell rang. Only two guesses as to who it could be, and the first one didn't count. I spied his truck from the window, and wordlessly answered the door, my face set in stone.

"You didn't call me when you got home, Princess," he drawled as he followed me in.

"I didn't realize you had me on such a short leash, Noah." I walked the short way into the kitchen. The need to have my hands full, clenching something other than a fist, was strong. I picked up the knife I had been using to chop vegetables for my stir-fry, and tested the weight of the handle, briefly wondering if throwing it at his feet accidentally would get my point across, or if that would be a little crazy. *Meh, let's not do crazy.*

"I didn't realize you were into that BDSM type of kink, Princess. But I'm game if you are," he said, smirking. I ignored his comment and continued with my chopping.

"You need to go, Noah. I'm really not in the mood to deal with you at the moment," I warned, as he put his arms around my waist from behind. His scent whirled around me, and I struggled to maintain my façade. My emotions flipped from anger and rage, to disappointment and sadness. This is the exact reason why relationships didn't work, why I had always put my career and family first, so I wouldn't break any further.

"What's going on, Princess?" His lips brushed the spot under my ear, flipping the bitch switch. I elbowed him sharply in the gut, taking him by surprise.

"Tell me something, Noah. Did you have Rapoles remove me from the Cartel case back in January?" I demanded. The slightest flicker of emotion crossed his blank face, and I knew the truth. He did. I pulled back my fist and punched him in the face with a right hook.

"What the actual fuck is wrong with you?" he yelled, holding his cheek.

"You prick! You're the one that went to Rapoles and

had me reassigned. You took me off the Cruz Cartel case last year!" I shouted. He had the audacity to look guilty, but I didn't care. I pushed him in his chest, making him move back.

"Okay, you're right. I did. But I did it for your own safety, Kate!"

"That's fucking bullshit and you know it, Noah. You fucked me over, and because of you, my case and my career took a hit!" I pushed him again, toward the door.

"Wait, back up. Tell me what's going on," he pleaded.

"I had a series of very informative meetings down in Miami. Your crew, along with General Lewes, gave us the rundown of their current mission. The phone number of your teammate, Mac, made it to the phone of a dead woman, with ties to the Cruz Cartel. So needless to say, we started digging."

"Hold the fuck up. You said that Mac's number was in a dead girl's phone? Which dead girl?"

"A dead girl by the name of Stacey Menroe. The link between her and the Cruz Cartel? She had their unlisted phone number in her brand new phone. And there were three other dead women with her."

"What did the team say? How did that girl have Mac's number? He's…"

"I don't give a flying fuck what Mac was like. I don't

care why he had the number right now. Right now? You're my issue. Who the hell gave you the authority to direct me off the Cartel case?" I shouted.

"You were getting too close to the Syndicate case. We had too much riding on it for it to go south," he shouted back.

"And how well did that work out for you? Because my case is the one that got the shaft. Had I been able to stay in Miami and keep my damn job, I would have made the necessary connections to Tommy sooner. Lives could have been saved, Noah! Tommy would not have taken Megan, and their lives could have been easier. And my career, the one I've worked so fucking hard to get, would not have taken the hit!"

Noah rubbed his hands against his face in aggravation. "Look, I'm not proud of it."

I snorted in disbelief.

"You have to understand, Kate, it wasn't personal. Truly it wasn't. Me and you—that wasn't supposed to be anything more than an occasional thing, but something happened. We connected. And I didn't realize that until after you left. But dammit, I will not apologize for protecting you!"

"This is my fucking case, Noah! Mine! Just like you've been looking at the Syndicate case, I have been working my ass off on this case. I have lived, breathed, and almost died this case. This is mine. And you decided to come in on your steel horse and take away everything!"

"Kate, look, I'm sorry. I was doing the right thing at the time. The Syndicate was—is, a higher priority. Once you take them down, the Cartel will crumble with it." Noah's reasoning failed, and it was all I could do to not scream.

"Are you kidding me? Are you that delusional? Do you not understand that the Cruz Cartel are the cockroaches of the United States? That no matter what anyone else does, they'll keep on surviving until they've been completely eradicated? Their business and cartel survival has nothing to do with the Syndicate."

"You're wrong there, Princess. I've been watching and waiting for these Syndicate fuckers to make a move, to do the shit we know they're going to do. And when they do, we'll be the ones to take them down."

I shook my head in frustration. "You know what? I don't even care about the fucking case right now. You sold me out. You had Rapoles sent me out of state. You called in whatever favors you could. And not only did my case take a hit, but my reputation did too. Apparently, everyone knows that you are the one that got me kicked off the case, and that I must have sucked someone's dick to get back in."

Noah tensed. The fury in his eyes was evident. "Who the fuck said that?"

I waved my hand. "It doesn't matter." Noah tried to interrupt, but I put up my hand. "I have busted my ass for the FBI for the last four years. I do not need your protection, and I sure as fuck don't need you in my life right now. This was a mistake. I shouldn't have gotten involved with you."

"Kate, just calm down and see—" Oh shit. Big mistake.

"Get the fuck out of my house!"

"You can't be serious!" His beautiful eyes widened, and I choked back a sob. But this was it. This was how it was supposed to be.

"I can't be with someone who would go behind my back, just to further their own career."

"Kate, Princess, I'm sorry. I didn't mean..." He cupped my face and tried to press his lips against mine. I couldn't handle it though. I pushed him away, roughly.

"Now, Noah! I'm done. Just...done." I willed the tears to stay away as I glared at him.

"Fine, I'll go. But I'll be here when you finally realize what a mistake you've made." His eyes gazed at me sadly. I turned away, jumping when the door slammed.

It was only then that I let the tears flow.

# CHAPTER 16
*Noah*

I SLAMMED THE DOOR AS hard as I could, and stalked away from the door. It took everything I had not to run back inside and drag her into my arms. To fuck her into submission, to make her see things my way. Yes, it was a fucked up move, and I wasn't proud of what I'd done. But in all fairness, she would have done the same to me.

*Asshole, do you really think that?* Even I couldn't believe my own lie. I hauled myself into the truck, and using the hands-free set, I called Trey. Even though we had just seen each other yesterday, maybe he could help me get a read on the situation from Zeke.

"Did you miss me already?"

"Shut up and listen for a minute. Who the hell met with Kate's team on Tuesday?" I racked my brain, but couldn't figure out who or why someone would blabber like that.

"Bravo team. Zeke was there too. Why? What's going on?"

I ran through the list of Bravo team in my head, and couldn't think of anyone that damn stupid.

"Someone fucked with Kate, told her that I was the one to get her kicked off the Cartel case last year, and that she must have been sucking someone's dick in order to get back in."

Trey cursed loudly. "I'll talk to Zeke tonight. He's meeting with the plant later to switch out some of her tech gear."

"Good, keep me up-to-date with what's going on. What did the team have to say about the meeting?"

"Nothing so far. But you know how Commander Lewes, and the rest of the Bravo team are. They don't talk much, and they sure as hell won't share if anything bad went down."

"I figured as much. Let me know what you find out."

"Roger that."

I continued the drive from Kate's house to the restaurant. I told Josh that I would fill in for a sick bartender, but my mind wasn't in it. Hell, my heart wasn't in it, either. I made it an hour before I called in another employee to take over. I couldn't stop looking at my phone. Not to mention, going over every possible reason why someone would try and screw me over like that. I made it to the house, just as Mom was pulling in with Aubrey.

"Hey, baby girl." I pressed my lips against her forehead and breathed in her fresh scent. I hooked the diaper bag over my shoulder and headed into the house.

"You okay, Bub? You're looking stressed," Mom said with a drawl, as she put away the rest of Aubrey's bottles.

"Yeah. This case is getting the better of me," I replied wearily. I put Aubrey down into the jumper thing that made a ton of noise, and joined my mom in the kitchen.

She peered at me, my own brown eyes looking back at me. "No, it's not a case. What else is going on?"

Who the heck was I kidding? My mom knew me like the back of her hand, just like she knew my brother, Mason. She knew when we were in trouble, when we were up to no good, and hell, when we were trying our best to get away with anything.

"I screwed up with this girl," I muttered, going through the diaper bag and pulling out the dirty clothes.

"You didn't get her pregnant, did you?" she asked, the warning in her voice clear. Not that she minded being a Nana to Aubrey, she just preferred I did it the traditional way. *But little does she know...* the voice in the back of my head whispered, and I brushed it aside. No sense in getting into the details of drama now, especially when things were so messed up.

"No, Ma, I didn't get her pregnant," I scoffed, turning to face her and crossing my arms. "I got her kicked off a case a while back, and now it's come back to bite me in the ass."

"Good."

"What do you mean, good? She could have easily been killed, or taken down a case that I was working on, the one that had me working overtime to finish up."

"No, good that you're regretting what you did. It sounds like you have feelings for this girl." she reasoned, brushing back her wispy white-blonde hair.

"Whatever, Mom."

"I mean, she must be fragile as hell, if you wanted her off the case that badly."

"She's not fragile, she's strong and smart as hell, and sexy, and—" I protested, but she cut me off.

"See! What did I tell you? You have feelings for this girl. And not the sterile feelings you get for a victim. This girl actually makes you think!" Mom cried triumphantly.

"That isn't the point, Mom."

"Bullshit. You have never had regrets about what you've done, either in life or on a case. Let me ask you this. Does the feeling of being without her make you cold? Do you want to stop at nothing to protect her?"

I stayed quiet. I hated when my mom was right. And she was always right. Of course, my mother wouldn't see it from my point of view. As much as she loved my Pop, she never could understand the overprotectiveness that we Russo's developed over the ones we cared about. The ones we loved. *Love?* Yeah, I guess I loved her, which would make anything going forward that much harder.

"Crap. I need to go find her." I straightened myself up and ran my hands over my face.

"Give her a day to cool down. Leave her alone, let her collect her thoughts. You need to do the same. You rush in there like an overzealous caveman, and she's going to run in the opposite direction."

Right. *Okay, man, think this through.* I ran through outlines, strategies, and possible outcomes. I fucked up; I knew that. I'd overstepped my bounds. Once I explained what was going on, she'd have to understand. *Screw it!* I picked up my phone to text her, when it vibrated in my hands with an incoming call from an unknown number.

"Yeah?" No pleasantries. I needed to get this joker off the phone as soon as possible, so I could start making things right with Kate.

"Noah?" A breathy, soft voice came over the line, and my mouth dropped to the floor.

"Jennie." Her name came out as a snap, and my jaw tensed. Nothing good ever came from one of her calls. I hadn't talked to her in over six months, and I gave up trying to get her to see Aubrey.

"How are you? How's my daughter?" Her voice was slurred, and my fury grew.

"*My* daughter is doing fine. What do you need, Jennie?" I asked tightly, desperate to get her off the phone.

She paused, and I could hear the gears in her head grinding, trying to formulate the words.

"I need your help."

# CHAPTER 17
*Kate*

I WAS SO PISSED OFF, I couldn't finish making dinner, so I turned off the burner and threw the pan full of half-cooked chicken and vegetables into the sink with a satisfying crash. I knew I should have gone with my gut. I knew it. Apparently, I couldn't trust anyone. There was no point in letting one in if they were just going to tear you down.

*But maybe, truly, he was only trying to keep you safe.*

I brushed that thought aside. The walls he penetrated were cracking, and I couldn't help but feel hurt. I refused to be the damsel in distress, the one that needed constant saving. *I may have a vagina, but I sure as hell can fight like a girl.* I sank into kitchen table.

This was exactly why relationships never worked

out for me. Trust was the essence of everything, and if he couldn't trust me with his case, or with keeping myself out of the way, then how could he trust me with anything else? With his heart? With his daughter? And now, how the hell could I trust him?

My heart ached. But despite everything, I needed to see him. I needed to feel his arms around me. He had something I never realized I craved—safety, security, and love.

Whatever this bump in the road was, we could work it out. Trust was something you earned, but it could always be repaired...right?

The phone rang, making me jump.

"Agent Parker," I answered brusquely.

"Yes, Ms. Parker. I'd like to call in that favor now," a stern voice came over the line.

My interest piqued immediately. "Madam, I appreciate you calling me. What can I do for you?"

She coughed lightly into the phone before replying. "I'm ready to talk...and Agent? Bring the paperwork for a deal."

I picked up my keys and made my way to the door.

"I'm listening. Where can we meet?"

She gave me the name of a cheap motel off Crain Highway in Glen Burnie, a town on the outskirts of Baltimore. I hauled ass and got there within fifteen minutes. My game was on. I pushed aside any personal issues and focused on what was coming up. This was what I needed. All that relationship crap aside, I had this shit. I collected my thoughts, and scanned the empty parking lot, looking for any signs of deception or trouble. After a quick text to Lucy, telling her where I was, I made my way to the room number that she sent me and knocked on the door. Madam Sin opened the door. Her eyes were cautious, and her body tense.

"It's just me. I'm alone," I reassured her in a low voice. She stepped aside, letting me squeeze my small frame just inside the door, then shut it behind me. I surveyed the interior of the room, taking in the ugly, floral polyester bedding and the plastic, wooden table and chairs. A twenty-year-old TV was mounted and chained to the yellow stained walls. With my gun in hand, I checked the empty bathroom and closets, then stood and waited. The Madam's body was fraught with tension; anxiety rolled off her frame in waves.

"You wanted me here, so here I am. What's going on?"

She wrung her hands, looking nervous. "We're just waiting for her. She had to call her husband."

I held my hand up to stop her. "What the hell are you talking about, Madam? Who's coming?"

"One of my girls. I couldn't stand by anymore and

do nothing. I had to get her out of there." Her normally silky, professional voice heightened with hysteria. I placed my hand on her arm and guided her to sit at the small table.

"Why don't you tell me exactly what's going on? Start from the beginning." I pulled out my recorder to get it on record, so I wouldn't forget any of the details. The Madam took a deep breath and began.

"I'd hoped to never see you again. No offense or anything, but in my line of work, Feds aren't your friends," she said with a smirk.

"No offense taken. I get it."

"I wasn't always a Madam. I had dreams, goals. But life gets in the way." She heaved a heavy sigh, and continued on. "My father had great plans for me as well. He was a Senator, and got caught up in some illegal bullshit. Apparently, while he was still in office, they worked out a deal. They would move their drug trade out of his district, in exchange for certain laws being passed. It all worked out for a while, until my father's debts became too big. He couldn't pay."

My eyebrows raised. "What sort of debts did he have?"

Madam shook her head. "My father was a monster. He got his rocks off with the other perverts in the basement of an old office building downtown. His preferences for the unwilling made him an even better target. The Cartel provided what he needed to satisfy his...you know, and my father provided his legal backing to them. He reduced the budget for police, took away the safety and security cameras from the worst neighborhoods in his district, and turned a blind eye to the carnage that was going down. Sure, he spun some great media and used the appropriate buzz words, but he basically did anything he could for the Cartel."

"And how did no one else find out about this?" I questioned. Something this big, someone would have surely said something.

"Who's going to listen to a bunch of poor people, the majority of whom are addicted to the very thing the Cartel was selling? The Cartel has been around for decades, and their pull in the local and federal governments are huge. "

The situation was a lot uglier than I'd realized. I nodded, urging her to continue.

"So for a while, it was fine. I had my therapy practice, along with the escort side of the business. The Cartel would frequent as customers, as well as provide protection. In my line of work, you can't be too careful. When my father died, I thought our arrangement with the Cartel was over. But then Sebastian came by the house. He..."

"Wait, who is Sebastian? Is that the name of Christian Cruz's other son?" The name had been missing from all the notes and family lineages that we could find. Like Tommy, the name of the other son was a mystery, as were any photos or descriptions.

Her brow furrowed as she thought about the question. "I'm not sure, to be quite honest. We had so many guys coming and going, the family dynamics were not something I asked about. He was supposed to be one of the good ones. He always treated my girls with respect, and paid well. He came to me one day, about six months ago, right after Dad died. They wanted to extend an offer to me. I would get the girls and a handsome profit for the business, and they would have their girls filter through. I would train them for servicing at their other establishments. I would manage the girls, make sure they were clean and healthy, and knew what to do. Something I was already doing on my own, but with their added business, the money was pouring in. And I needed it too. My mother's nursing care is barely covered by insurance."

"What made you come to me? Why now?" I asked. If things were going so well, or as well as could be expected when dealing with hookers and a drug cartel, something big must have happened if she was finally coming to me.

She rubbed her face. "Because at first, the girls were fine. They were ones that I would have hired—clean, young, great bodies. They had no fears or issues with sleeping with men for money."

"But what happened, Madam?"

"All the best girls were sent to Vegas and Miami. The others, the ones with terror in their eyes and track marks on their arms, would vanish from the house. I would ask questions, but would never get an answer. Finally, I stopped asking questions."

"Why did you stop asking questions?" I demanded.

"Because I was scared of the answers," she whispered. Her hands shook as she wiped away the tear rolling down her cheek. "Because every time I asked questions, another girl would get hurt. Finally, Bash took me aside and told me that the next question would be my last, so I stopped. I couldn't go to the police because the Cartel would kill me. They already have me over a barrel with my mom's nursing home care. They would kill her, just as a warning."

"We can protect you both," I said calmly. "There's always witness protection—"

"Bullshit. I know what happens in that program. You get sent to live in the middle of nowhere with no protection, and the Cartel finds you anyway. Isn't that what they did with your friend?" she said with a sneer.

"How do you know about Shane?" I snapped.

"It's hard not to overhear things when the crew meets at your establishment for refreshments. They talked about how they had an inside track into the program, and how they knew at any given moment, who was where. And frankly, Agent Parker, I'd rather be dead."

That I understood.

"So, who is meeting us here?"

"They brought her to me about two weeks ago. At first, they wanted me to get her clean. She wasn't of any use to them high all the time. But, sometime after she arrived, they started using her. And not just for sex, but for testing drugs. They would go into the basement that we rarely used, and they would be down there for hours. I could hear their laughter over her screams of agony. I wanted to do something... anything, to get them to stop. But what could I do? I couldn't just pick up and leave, and I sure as fuck couldn't call the cops. But today, early this morning, they left her in the basement by herself. Told me that she was of no use to them, so we were to dispose of her. They didn't think she would make it. But one of our clients is a prominent doctor over at Johns Hopkins. I called him over and he was able to do whatever was needed to save her. He gave her that OD medicine, or something like that. I'm not sure. We were limited on what we could do, because I knew they would make sure that we didn't take her to the hospital, but I couldn't just leave her out there for the jackals. Once she was stable, and coherent, we brought her out to a park down the street and left her there.   I couldn't risk being associated with her, or risk helping her, so I just left her there. But I did call the cops, and watched until they picked her up."

My heart dropped. "Where is she now?"

"One of the guards at the desk has a favorite girl, so I keep him on retainer.   He said that she called her husband and was picked up by him about ten minutes ago, right before you got here. She should be here any minute. I got her husband's number from the guard and sent him a text with the directions. "

"What's her name?"

"Jennie Davis," she said, with a sad look on her face, just as a knock came on the door.

The name rang a bell in my mind, and once I saw her, I knew.  Despite the gaunt face with the dark circles under her eyes, lifeless blonde hair, and the flimsy excuse for a dress, Jennie Davis looked like she did in the pictures that hung on the wall of her brother's gym. Her dark blue eyes remained glassy and unfocused, and I had to reach out to steady her.

"Do I know you?" she asked, her words slurred. I

checked the crook of her arm, and found the track marks of needle pricks, common among heroin users.

"I'm Agent Parker with the FBI, Jennie. And I'm a family friend," I replied with a sigh. "We want to talk to you." I pushed her thin frame forward, keeping hold of her upper arm, which was nothing but skin and bones, and I thought back to the pictures. Her face was lively and rosy, her blue eyes glistened. She was a shell of her former self, I thought sadly, as I led her into the dark, musty room.

"Why does the FBI want to talk to me?" she slurred again, her voice weak.

"There's a few things we need to discuss. Is there anyone you need to call? I thought your husband was bringing you over," I said gently, as I squeezed her hand. The fog in her eyes had gradually begun to clear, and fear replaced it. When faced with fear, people had different flight or fight mechanisms. Would Jennie fight with us, or help us with what we needed?

"He wanted to make sure I got something to eat, so he dropped me off and went to get me food."

Anger grew inside of me. What kind of man leaves his drugged up wife in a motel room full of strangers? I needed more answers, and I needed to talk to Sketch. I knew he was looking for her. I hustled out of the room and stood in the corridor, where I dialed Sketch's number.

"What's up, Tink?"

"I found Jennie. She's alive."

Silence. The only way I knew he was still on the line was because the phone call didn't disconnect. "Sketch…I know this is a shock, but you have to listen. You need to come up here." I rattled off the name of the motel, and paused. "She was bailed out of jail, and there are a number of charges against her. But the Bureau needs to talk to her first—"

"No."

"Sketch, don't—" I warned, jumping at the edge in his voice.

"No fucking questions until I get there. I'll be there in twenty." With that, the line went dead.

*Well, fuck me.* I rubbed my eyes, and felt a nasty migraine coming on. I needed to push aside any personal feelings and think this through. I made a few phone calls, one being to Rapoles, and another to a public defender that I knew well. If anything, a plea deal would need to be made, and I couldn't risk bringing either of them into the field office for the proper procedures. *Protocol be damned*, I thought as I grabbed a soda from the antiquated vending machine.

Headlights swung into the parking lot. I slunk back into the room and closed the flimsy curtains. I motioned for Jennie and the Madam to move into the bathroom, and I pulled my Glock out, ready for anything.

The knock on the door came quietly, as did the low murmur of "It's just me." And before I could stop her, Jennie rushed forward and threw open the door.

"About fricking time," she shot at the person standing in the doorway.

"The drive-thru line was ridiculous." Oh God, that voice, the one I knew so well. The voice that made my heart jump, and the stupid fucking butterflies flutter was Jennie's husband. My heart grew heavy, so heavy it ached. I wanted to scream and hit something, but I kept my emotions in check. It wouldn't do anyone any good to be a heartbroken whiner.

"Noah. Glad to see you could join us." The ice in my voice was evident as I holstered my weapon. The resignation in his face was visible, almost as if he was defeated. Guilty that he was finally caught in a lie? Who the hell knew, and I couldn't care anymore. At least not right now.

"Now that everyone's here, let's get this done," I said, with as much professionalism as I could muster.

"Kate, listen. Can we talk? Let me explain…" Noah muttered, his calloused hands clasping around my elbow.

"No. It's Agent Parker, and explanations won't be

necessary," I replied in a hard tone. I shook off his hand and sat down across from Jennie, who was shoving food her into her mouth.

"Jennie, you should slow down. You're going to get sick," I warned her, but I received the middle finger in response. "Well, let's get started. Where did you bail her out from?" I directed my question to Noah, but couldn't bear to look at him.

"Baltimore Detention Center." He pushed the paperwork toward me, and I gave it a cursory glance. Lewd acts in public, public intoxication, disorderly conduct, assault on a police officer, trying to bribe a police officer, and solicitation. I made a mental note to call the public defender and put the paperwork aside.

"Jennie, as I stated before, my name is Agent Parker. I'm here to help you, but only if you want to help yourself."

"I want those charges dropped," she whispered, the food clearing the lingering fog in her head.

"That's understandable. We're going to try and make that happen, but only if you can help us out."

"What do you need to know?" She threw a worried glance over to the Madam, who put her hand over hers assuredly.

"How the Cartel came to find you?"

She gulped down her drink and wiped her mouth.

"I was with some friends, just hanging out, you know? They approached the guys to make a buy, then one of them was like, flirting with me and stuff. Promised me some good shit, ya know? So we started hanging out, and the next thing I know, I'm in some stank-ass basement, higher than I'd ever been."

"What happened while you were down there?" I questioned.

"The guys would take turns screwing me. They would keep me feeling good, though, until last week. Last week they gave me some strange stuff, something I've never had before." She shook her head at the memory. "It made me feel horrible. I hated it. It hurt. It made me see things that weren't there." She grabbed Noah's hand and gave a sad smile. "I wanted to give up. I wanted to die. But the face of our baby girl kept me going."

I swallowed the thick ball of emotion that had suddenly built up and cleared my throat.

"Did you receive medical care while at the detention center?"

Jennie shook her head. "No. I refused, so they kept me in the drunk tank."

"When was the last time they came to you?"

"This morning. They said that they'd be back tomorrow."

"We need to get a rape kit done. Would you be comfortable going to a private doctor? No one will know that you went," I assured her.

"No kit. There's no reason. They would use condoms, then spray me down with hot water after they took their turn. Besides, I just want to go home."

I turned to the Madam, and raised my eyebrows. "Are they expecting you to be back there tomorrow?"

She nodded. "I need to get back there tonight. Today was our slow day, and not much on the books in the way of appointments. A lot of girls had tonight off."

"Are both of you prepared to do whatever we ask, to get these guys off the streets?" My question was not normally asked as protocol. Too many people feigned forgetfulness when it came to testifying, or making a report. I wanted to ensure that not only did we get both of their statements on the books, but that they would be willing to go before a judge, or a panel with their stories.

Jennie nodded, and the Madam pursed her lips.

"Do you have any questions, Madam?" I snapped, ready for it all to be over with. I winced internally, even more pissed off that my emotions had gotten the better of me.

"How is our safety going to be ensured?" she asked. It was a valid question, and one I should have anticipated.

"I'm going to put something in place, possibly an undercover at your location.   We'll look into having someone watch your place, but it won't be set until tomorrow when I can talk to my boss. Do you have an extra phone? Possibly one of those pay-as-you go phones?" She nodded, and I gave her a small smile. "Good. Program my number into it, and use that to call me from now on. There's no telling what sort of pull the Cartel has with the phone company." With that settled, I turned to Jennie.

"Do you have a place to go?" She turned back to Noah, and raised her eyebrows.

"I don't know. Do I have a place to go?" she asked him softly, her hand still entwined with his.  My heart cracked even more, and I looked down at my notes.

"Yeah, we'll figure out something," he murmured. The heat from his stare penetrated my soul, and I knew I had to get out of there quickly.

"I think that's it for now." I rose from my seat, as my mind raced with questions and tasks that needed to be done.

"Noah, I'm trusting you to make sure that she's safe. The Cartel will be looking for her, so make sure she's secure. I have her statement recorded, but that's informal, and I need it in writing. She's the catalyst we need."

"I understand that, Kat—I mean, Agent Parker. This isn't my first rodeo."

"Of course not," I bit out, and shoved my recorder into my pocket. "Madam, I'll walk you to your car. Noah, I suggest you stay behind. Sketch is on his way here." I heard a groan, but I paid it no mind as I escorted the Madam out to her brand new Mercedes SUV.

"What's next, Agent?" she asked as we got to her vehicle.

"Honestly, I need you to act like everything is normal. Keep doing what you're doing. If they ask about Jennie, just tell them you had someone take care of it. Don't answer any more than you have to, and stick to the half-truths. Obviously, don't tell anyone anything. We'll tell you what you need to know and that's it, because the less you know, the better it will be. "

She acquiesced, turning her head to gaze back at the hotel.

"What's going to happen to her?" she wondered quietly.

"I don't know," I answered truthfully. "But need to know, Madam Sin. Need to know." She pursed her lips again, and bowed her head slightly, then got into her SUV and pulled away.

I rubbed my forehead to relieve the tension building. The case was becoming more complicated than I thought. Just as I walked over to my Jeep, the engine from Sketch's 1969 Mercury Cougar roared into the parking lot. I waited until he pulled up next to me, my resentment brewing.

"God damn it, Tink. I told you not to question her until I got here. Why the fuck are you out here?" he growled at me, as he stalked over and got in my face. I pushed him back with all my strength, and even though he was a foot taller than I was, and outweighed me by about eighty pounds, he stumbled back.

"Don't worry, Sketch. She's safe. Her *husband* is with her," I snarled. Of all people, Sketch was the one I felt I could have trusted. He knew my issues, and understood them. He knew that my walls were high, and he kept that shit from me.

Recognition flashed in his eyes, and he winced.

"So fuck you very much. She's in her husband's hands now. My team and I will come up with a plan and let you know what's going on. Just keep her quiet, keep her contained, and for God's sake, Sketch, keep her away from the drugs. Her story is already sketchy at best. I don't need her testimony filled with holes because of the fucking drugs."

"Tink, I'm sorry. I wanted to tell you. I told him to tell you too…" his voice trailed off.

"But you didn't. And honestly, it doesn't matter

anyway. It's not like we were a couple or anything," I snapped.

I climbed into my Jeep and turned up the radio. *Breaking Benjamin* filled the interior while I sped out of the parking lot. I needed to think, to process everything that had happened. The office was closed, and I didn't relish driving downtown so late at night, no matter what I was packing. And I was more than pissed off at my sparring partner, so I headed toward Cole's house. A hot shower would do me good.

But, of course, as soon as I got to Cole's, a brand new, 2016 deep purple Corvette was sitting in my spot. I cursed loudly, then pulled behind Cole's massive truck. Not sure who this gym bunny was, but Lord help me if she wasn't quiet. I let myself in, only to see my brother's bare ass on the couch, going at it at with some moaning, groaning chick.

"Oh dear God, I need eye bleach!" I cried out. Covering my eyes with my hands, I maneuvered blindly through the living room, toward the bedrooms.

"Shit! Sorry Kate! You weren't supposed to see that!" Cole said with a laugh.

"That's what your bedroom is for! Now I'm gonna have to disinfect that couch!" I shouted back.

"While you're at it, make sure you take a good whiff of your pillows too!"

"Argh! You cock sucking asswipe! If you did anything to my bed, I'm cutting off that tweezer size pecker of yours and feeding it to the ducks!" *That jerkoff knows better than to screw some random skank in my bed.*

I shucked off my clothes and turned the water on as hot as it would go, then scrubbed the smell of Baltimore, and the feeling of Noah, off my skin. Only then did I let the tears fall. I could have forgiven him for the shit he pulled in Miami to get me off the case. That was some alpha shit I would have done myself to protect someone I loved. But this? To be married to someone else, when he supposedly wanted to be with me? How fair was that?

No matter how I tried to spin the story, no matter how hard I tried to see it his way, I couldn't come up with a good reason why he couldn't have told me. But, it didn't matter, really. Jennie deserved a fresh start, and what better way to do that than to be with her daughter, and the man that made her. Me? I'd just keep doing what I was doing. I didn't need someone to make me whole. And I sure as hell didn't need any weaknesses.

# CHAPTER 18
## Noah

I KNEW I SHOULDN'T HAVE let her go. I watched her walk out the door of that disgusting motel room, with her head held high. But I knew that I had just broke her heart. I wanted to rush after her, but the grip on my hand held me back.

"I'm ready to go see our daughter," she said simply. Her gaze of adoration at me had my stomach uneasy. I wasn't about to let her see Aubrey—not yet. Not until she had been clean for a while. There was no point in getting Aubrey attached to Jennie all over again, only to have her leave again. Yeah, I didn't believe Jennie could stay clean; no one did. The whole point to this exercise was to ensure that Jennie stayed clean enough to testify, to put those cartel bastards behind bars. But to actually make a difference in her life? To become clean for good? Yeah, my money wasn't on that. I'd known Jennie for way too long, and yeah, I felt like an asshole for thinking it, but I knew I wasn't the only one.

"You're not going to see her, Jennie. Not tonight. We'll get you over there to see her soon, but I want you clean first." I dislodged my hand, just as Sketch walked through the door.

"Seth!" She ran over to her brother and threw her arms around his neck.

"God, Jennie. I thought we lost you." The rarest hint of emotion came through in Sketch's voice.

"Seth, I'm going to get clean. I promise this time. I need to, for my baby. And for my family." She looked back at me. "But please, Seth, I need to see her. I need to feel her in my arms."

"Of course, Jennie. Anything you need."  His placating tone told me that I was going to have a fight on my hands. He adored his sister, and wanted nothing more than to make her happy. But he wasn't Aubrey's father, I was.

"Not tonight, Jennie. I already told you that," I stated sternly.

"But Noah, I need her! I need to see my daughter! She's my reason for getting clean!" The whining and the manipulation was already starting. I could see it now. It wouldn't be the first time she'd pitted us against each other.

"Noah, dude. Just let her see the kid. How is that going to harm her? Jennie needs this, just as Aubrey needs to see her mother," Sketch demanded.

*Aubrey won't recognize her mother,* I thought bitterly, then shook my head. I bit my tongue, because everything I wanted to say would just cause a shit storm.

"Tomorrow. That's my final word," I hissed, and walked out of the room.   Jennie, teetering on her ridiculously high heels, trotted after me, pleading with me to change my mind. But Aubrey came first, and dammit, it was about time that I did too.

"Noah! Dammit, where am I going to go? Where are you taking me?" I grabbed her arm and hauled her into the truck then whirled around to face Sketch.

"Listen to me, and listen good. You are *not* Aubrey's father. I am. I will determine *when* and *if* Jennie sees her," I seethed, anger rolling off me.

"Fuck you, you prick. Just because you knocked her up, doesn't mean you get to control her movements. She needs her kid. Maybe this is the time, she'll finally follow through."

I arched my eyebrow. "She's had nine months to get clean, for Aubrey's sake, and she hasn't. So that reasoning can get thrown down the toilet, just like the smack she's probably hiding in her underwear."

Sketch groaned, and looked to the skies while he contemplated what I meant, because he knew his sister. And he'd seen her in this sort of situation too many times to believe that this time would be the final time, that this would be her rock bottom. And even though he wanted to have faith that she wanted to get clean, the odds were stacked against her.

"I got ya, bro. Just tell me what you need me to do," he muttered in defeat.

"Help me keep her safe. I'm going to take her to this place I know of in St. Mary's. It's far enough away from Baltimore, that hopefully the Cartel won't come looking for her." I rubbed the back of my neck, and thought about my next steps. "I can't let Kate go through this shit by herself. I don't need her going on some half-cocked, harebrained scheme, just to prove herself."

"Yeah, you need to fix that. I've never seen Kate so pissed. And not just at you. She's furious with me too. She said I should have told her."

I bowed my head and closed my eyes. The sight of those gorgeous blues, filled with hurt and betrayal, gutted me.

"Yeah, I need to make this shit right." I shook his hand. "I'll text you the address of the facility tonight. Come by tomorrow with provisions, okay? And coffee.

A lot of coffee."

"You got it. Do I need to relieve your mom of Aubrey?"

"Nah, I think she's good with my mom. If anything, the grandparents can switch if they need to."

I looked over at the truck to find her tapping on the glass, telling me to hurry along. If she thought I was taking her back to my place, she was sorely mistaken. I hustled over to the driver's seat and took off, before she could plead her case with Sketch. She casted me the evil eye, and folded her arms across her chest in a huff.

We drove for forty-five minutes, and when we continued on Route 2, instead of getting off at Route 260 for Chesapeake Beach, her mood suddenly shifted.

"We're not going to your place, are we?" she mumbled, her voice turning sad. I prayed that we would get to the shelter before she had a cosmic meltdown. We didn't need to get into an accident.

"Not yet," I said slowly.

"Are you checking me in?" Her voice got very distant, and she turned to face the window.

"I will if I have to, but you need to want to do this yourself. I can't force you to get clean."

"I know," she said quietly.

"I don't want to keep Aubrey from you, you have to know that, right?" I pleaded for her understanding.

Out of the corner of my eye, I saw her wipe away a tear. "I know." Her voice cracked with emotion. God, I wanted to believe that she truly understood, but knowing her and her manipulative ways, I guarded myself.

After an hour of silence, we finally arrived at the rehab facility. We'd tried to get her to come to this place before, right after we were married, but she wanted to be close to me in Miami, and well, we all saw how that worked out.

"Do I get a bag or something?" she asked, brushing her blonde hair back. Her hands trembled, and I wasn't sure if that was from the drugs wearing off or nerves. She looked at the lighted door of the single level facility, and gulped.

"Everything is already here," I said. I got out and walked around to her side of the truck opening the door for her. She froze, as if she wasn't sure how to move her legs. I didn't want to give her any false hope, but I took her hand into mine and led her to the door. A couple of friendly nurses waited for us, and escorted us inside.

After an intense intake and medical exam, they took her back for detox. They didn't allow me back for that, and that was when she snapped. She started screaming my name, and fighting against the oversized orderlies that appeared out of nowhere. I choked up. My instinct, even after all this time, was to run and help her. But I knew, deep down, that she needed to go through this—that she needed to get the crap out of her system. We could have regular contact with her doctors, but not with her. Not for a few days, at least.

I sent a quick text to Sketch, letting him know her status, and made plans to meet up the next day. I spent the next hour and half on the road, in thought. I kept envisioning Kate's beautiful eyes, and the hurt I saw in them. I wanted…no, I needed to have her in my arms. I needed to see her. I needed to make her see how sorry I was. Suddenly, the path was clear for me. I made the sharp left onto Birdsville Road, and made tracks toward Odenton, where I hoped she would be, at her brother's house.

I breathed a sigh of relief when I saw her jeep parked outside. I hurried to the door and knocked. The dog barked, but no one answered. I banged loudly, and called her name. Finally, the light clicked on and I was suddenly staring down the double barrel of a shotgun.

"Whoa, Cole. It's just me." I held my hands up in surrender, and took a step back.

"Why the fuck are you knocking on my door at three in the morning?" he growled, putting the gun down at his side.

"Look, I need to talk to Kate. I need to see her," I

begged, and took a step toward the door. He jacked the gun back up.

"You stupid bastard. What the hell did you do?"

"Look, this is between me and her. Let me in."

"Listen here, asswipe. I told you once already, you hurt her, I'll rip your damn heart from your chest."

"Cole, go back to bed. I got this," her soft voice said from behind him. He glared at me, then turned and kissed her on the forehead.

"I'm down the hall if you need some backup, Kate," he muttered, leaving her the shotgun before heading down the hall.

"Hey." I couldn't get another word out. She was a vision. Dressed in sleep shorts and a white tank, her tan skin made the white of her tank top stand out. I could clearly see the outline of her nipples, and the bars that were in them. The ache in my jeans grew, and I wanted nothing more than to pull her into my arms. But instinct told me to hold back.

"Hey." She crossed her arms over her chest, which only emphasized what she was trying to cover.

"Can I come in? I want to talk about what happened tonight."

"No. There's nothing to talk about," she declared. Her entire body was tense, and guilt ran through me.

"Yes, there is. I want to make sure that you don't get

the wrong idea."

She snorted in disgust, and threw open the screen door, charging out at me.

"What idea should I be getting, Noah? The fact that you were sleeping with me when you were married?"

"Kate, I'm sorry, if you'd just listen—"

"Listen to what? Excuses? More lies? I was fucking a married man. Do you know what that makes me? A fucking homewrecker. That makes me feel like a cheap whore."

"It wasn't like that, and you know it!"

"Fuck you and your God damn bullshit, Noah. You lied to me. Everything you've said is nothing but lies. How can I trust you now?"

"I didn't mean to hurt you, but if you would just let me explain, please!" I shouted back, frustration tearing me apart.

"There's nothing to explain, Noah. Just go. You're wasting your time here." She turned around and quietly shut the door.

I wanted to scream, but Lord knew, I didn't need to have the cops called. I hopped back into the truck and drove. Just. Drove. I needed something to clear my head, and it was too late to do anything constructive. I knew sleep wasn't an option, so I drove. I drove all around Anne Arundel County, from the outskirts of

Baltimore, down to the backroads, close to my parents' house, where my daughter was hopefully sound asleep. The sun was starting to rise as I pulled into the driveway. I went onto the back porch and sat, looking over the South River, and watched the sun.  And as it rose, so did my resolve. Kate would listen. She would have to listen. And I would die trying to make her see that I loved her too much to let her go.

# CHAPTER 19
*Kate*

I WOKE EARLY THE NEXT morning with sandbags the size of my suitcase under my eyes. *Fucking men.* If you can't be happy, you can at least look good. Thankfully, I was a master at disguises. While I was sitting at home, pregnant, at the age of sixteen, and my college exams were over, I dabbled in cosmetology. I constantly changed my looks, going from girl next door, to goth, to vampiress, to glam. I learned from the pros, pouring over websites and magazine articles. And as makeup tutorials became a big thing online, I would soak in everything I could. So I had a plethora of makeup, wigs, and hair colors. My mom called me her chameleon, because my looks adapted to whatever mood I was in.

After an hour in the bathroom, making myself look

like I wasn't a heartbroken homewrecker, I was ready to take on the world. My face was done, with the slightest hint of lash extensions, and my outfit was on point. Nothing said 'I got this' better than some skinny black cropped pants, a loose white chiffon tank, and fitted dark gray blazer. I slid on my three-inch black Jimmy Choo's and grabbed my bag. I was going to take on the day, and make it my bitch.

"You're looking like you're about to handle some business," Cole remarked, as he buttered his toast.

"Something like that," I said, as I poured the magic brew into my travel mug.

"Did you save any for me?" A voice asked from the living room. I glanced over my shoulder to see a beautiful woman with curves I'd kill for walk in, dressed in nothing but one of Cole's T-shirts. She placed a kiss on my brother's bare shoulder, then made herself at home at the kitchen island. I coughed, and gave my brother a quizzical look. He rolled his eyes and mouthed, "Do not make this a big deal."

Which meant, this was totally a big deal.

"Hi. We sort of met last night. I'm Traci," she beamed with a wave, then had the grace to blush.

Oh, I liked this girl.

"Hi, Traci. I'm Kate, this rude ass's sister." I nudged Cole with my elbow, then reached out to shake her hand.

"Pleased to meet you," she said with a big smile.

"Sorry to have barged in on what looked to be a romantic moment," I said with a sly glance over at Cole. His back tensed while pouring two cups of coffee.

She rolled her eyes. "That wasn't anything special." He dropped the cup into the sink and stared at her, with his mouth opened in shock. I burst into laughter, and had to hold onto my sides.

"Really?" he sputtered, which only made me laugh even harder. "Do you think you could, um…you know, not say shit like that to my sister?"

"Stop, you know I didn't mean it like that." She ignored his shock, and continued to drink her coffee, with a sly smile pursed around her lips.

"Woman, I have no clue what the hell I'm going to do with you," he quipped, shaking his head.

"Oh, I could think of a few things. One involves that ball gag, and…"

"La la la! I don't need to hear this crap. Let me get out of here." I put my hands over my ears as I rushed over to grab my stuff. "Traci, I'm so glad I met you. I'll see you around."

I pointed to my brother. "I like this one. She doesn't moan like a porn star wannabe, and she sure as hell can put up with your ass. Keep her around."

"Oh, sweets, I'm not going anywhere. He likes the

pussy too much," she divulged with a wink.  I left the house, laughing the entire way to the office. Oh God, I needed that. I needed to feel free, even if it was for just for a little while.

Then the challenges of the day slammed into me. Not only did I need to ensure that Jennie got the protection she needed, but I needed to plead her case, and the case of Madam Sin's, not only to my boss, but to the special prosecutor. I pulled into the unground parking garage and headed inside. I was early, for once, so the activity was at a minimum. I took advantage of the quiet and got to work. The first thing I did was write up a report from last night. Everything had to be documented, and I couldn't leave anything to chance. The only thing missing was Jennie's whereabouts. I wasn't sure where Noah took her, and truth be told, I didn't want to imagine her in his bed.  A pang of jealousy hit, but I swatted the emotion away. *There was no time to get jealous.* Lives were on the line.

After an hour, and three cups of coffee, my report was done and sent to Rapoles.  And, I may have called the special prosecutor in to discuss a plea. So I was going to beg for forgiveness, rather than ask for permission. But I knew in my gut that it was the right thing to do. The office was buzzing with the sounds of printers, people complaining about the commute in, and general office bullshit. I maneuvered my way around the people gabbing for no reason, and knocked on Rapoles' door.

"What's up, Parker?" he asked, his eyes trained on the monitor in front of him.

"I sent you the update on the events from last night. I wanted to forewarn you, I have a meeting with the special prosecutor in about three hours. "

His eyes bugged out of his head. "Are you kidding me? I haven't read the report, and you're already offering a plea deal? That's not the way things are done around here, Parker. Rescind that meeting."

"With all due respect, sir, you owe me this," I stated firmly.

"The hell you say? I don't owe you shit, Parker. You either rescind that meeting and any sort of mention of a plea deal, or you can walk your ass out of here like you did in Miami."

Fury seethed in my veins, and it was all I could do not to drop kick the fool in his nuts.

"I beg your pardon, Special Agent Rapoles, but you do need to take my word for this. You've ignored everything I've told you thus far. I have used my knowledge from the Bureau, as well as my natural instincts, the ones you said that I had, to get this far. You've been wrong on ignoring what I've had to say. And I'm telling you, if you ignore this, lives will be at risk. Dr. Sinclair will end up dead in some alleyway, and we would have lost our only penetration into the Cartel."

He rolled his eyes and finally looked at me. "What sort of deal are you planning?" he inquired, his voice weary.

"Full immunity on all solicitation charges for the Doctor. And medical care, drug rehabilitation, and the reduction of all charges for Jennie Russo, also known as Jennie Davis."

"In exchange for…?"

"Dr. Sinclair knows the ins and outs of those club members. She can provide descriptions, movements, information that we can only dream of. In time, she could possibly wear a wire," I declared, knowing full well that the Madam hadn't agreed to any of this. *Yet.*

Rapoles thought for a moment. You could practically hear the hamster wheel squeaking inside that pea-sized melon, but finally, he nodded.

"Get it done. Get me what I need, Agent Parker. If shit goes south, it will be your ass in front of the review board."

"Yes, sir." I almost gave him my one finger salute, but I figured that may be pushing it. I hurried back to my cubicle, and pulled the phone out of my purse. I sent a text to the Madam, giving her a head's up, and advised her to bring her lawyer with her. My next call was to Noah. I hesitated. I didn't want to get into any sort of conversation, so I took the pussy way out. I sent a text to Sketch, telling him where and when I needed him, or whomever Jennie's power of attorney was. I also inquired on her location, but Sketch never responded. Finally, the phone vibrated in my hand and I looked down.

Figures, the only man that would vibrate me would be Noah.

*She's at Rachel's Place, an inpatient rehab facility in St. Mary's.*

The rehab place he brought her to was top-notch, and I quickly dispatched local PD units to the facility to stand guard. I gnawed on my lip, as I debated on whether to send the next text. Technically, I didn't need to do anything more. But then again, as her husband, he had a right to know what was going on. I pushed aside any feelings of bitterness and jealousy, and sent Noah a text, advising him that her attorney was meeting with me today to discuss a plea deal, and I left it at that.

I focused my energy and attention on other tasks, primarily getting the plea deal together with the prosecutor, and hammering out any lingering issues. I made contact with Rick, who didn't have much to add to the situation. The only tidbit he had was that Jessica

Knowles had been spotted by a fellow agent on the outskirts of New Orleans, and he was on his way to check it out. My cynical mind immediately thought it was a trap, but Rick was a fantastic agent. Every move he made was calculated, and assessed for risk, entrapment, and failure.

"Agent Parker, your one o'clock is here," a pleasant voice called over the intercom. I gathered up my paperwork and walked into the glass enclosed conference room. The lead prosecutor, Lizette Malfy, sat next to Sketch, with Dr. Sinclair and her attorney across from them. My eyebrow arched as I surveyed the room.

"Mr. Davis, are we waiting on the attorney for Mrs. Russo?" I asked, setting down the stack of files and my traveler's mug, filled with my umpteenth cup of coffee.

Dressed in slacks, and a gray button-down shirt that matched his eyes, Sketch nodded slowly. His gaze pierced mine, and a pang of sadness hit me. No matter what my feelings were toward Noah, no matter how pissed off I was at Sketch for lying, it was incomparable to the fucked up situation they were in. No one deserved that.

"I'll be representing Mrs. Russo in this matter," a voice called from behind me. Megan's uncle, Bob Connors, walked in, with Noah following close behind him. "My apologizes for the delay. There was an accident on Lombard."

I smiled gratefully at the man who was responsible for getting Shane back on track. I was glad I'd put a call into Megan and her uncle. Bob was a great attorney, and had a compassionate heart for those who hit rock bottom. We quickly got down to business and, thankfully, the legalities were ironed out relatively easily.  Jennie's record was expunged, provided she completed her stint in rehab, and Dr. Sinclair received immunity for aggravated promotion of prostitution, solicitation, and engaging in an organized criminal activity.

With the legal issues set aside, it was time to get into the weeds. After dismissing the lawyers, Rapoles came in, along with the rest of my team that wasn't in Florida, looking for Tommy and Jessica.

"So, you got what you wanted, Madam. It's time to tell us what you know," I urged. Her panicked eyes shot toward me, and I tried to reassure her with my smile.

"Right." She heaved a sigh. "There are four major partners in the Cruz Cartel. Christian, Tomas, Elias, and Sebastian, with Christian holding the majority share."

"Wait. Last night, you told me that you weren't sure if Sebastian was part of the family or not," I interjected. Lying during any point of the investigation was wrong, but after I went to bat for her, she pulled this shit? Oh, hell no.

She shrugged. "I wasn't sure if I could trust you, Agent."

"How the hell can I trust you now, after you lied to me within the first three minutes of this interview?" I demanded, slapping the table.

She jumped, then narrowed her eyes. "Don't be ridiculous. You have me over a barrel now. If I don't get you this information, the Feds will be up my ass faster than a john with a pegging fetish."

"Continue," I seethed, my jaw clenched.

"Elias handles the drug trade. He meets with their suppliers, gets the product on the streets."

"What can you tell us about Elias?"

"He's about thirty years old, olive-toned skin, large and in charge. He has both arms covered in tattoos, and his hair is thick and long. I last saw him about three weeks ago, when I was sent to the Miami club."

Miami. "We'll get back to that. Tell us more about Elias."

She rubbed the back of her neck. "He's strong. Crazy. Has a nasty temper. I've had quite a few of my girls request to not be with him. In fact, I've had to ban him from the house in Baltimore. The guy fights MMA on the side, illegally and underground. The Cartel have a ring located in an industrial park near Port Orleans, and that's where they get the girls sometimes."

I arched my eyebrows and leaned forward. "What do you mean, that's where they get the girls?"

"Sebastian is in charge of the women. He's the one that brings them through the house, ensures that they're up to par. Women who come for the cruise ships and the night life are 'invited' to the fights, and some come to the fights. They come on their own accord. From there, Sebastian seduces them, tricks them into coming to his room or his house. He talks up the brand, how women like them are going to make a lot of money. Some stay, some leave. Those that he finds will make the most money, and won't be given the chance to leave." She paused, and looked around the room. "That's when Elias comes in. He makes them submit with enough drugs to get them feeling good, and to keep that edge going."

"You said in your statement, that they don't like the women to be strung out. But now you're saying that they're purposely keeping some women high. Which is it?"

"I don't see them after I get them cleaned up. Elias makes sure that the women who are too high to function are escorted off the property, never to be seen again."

"You don't know what happens to them?"

The Madam shook her head. "No, but I have a feeling...a terrible, gut-wrenching, sickening feeling, that those women…the ones that can't get clean, or can't get off the drugs, are used elsewhere."

"Doing what?" Sketch snapped.  I cut him a quick glare, but he didn't pay me any mind.

"As drug mules, maybe? I'm not entirely sure. I know some go to Vegas and Miami, but I never see them in any of the clubs."

"What do you know about the Port of Orleans?" I asked, shuffling my papers.

"There's always someone headed there, at least twice a month. Nicholas said they're trying to open a Ravenous in New Orleans, but I haven't seen any corresponding paperwork to say that's a fact."

I glanced over at Rapoles, who was intently listening to the Madam's story.  He cleared his throat, then looked over at me.

"What do you know of Sebastian's women, once they get to the clubs? Do you see them? Are they well and healthy? Do you know if they're safe?"

Madam looked down at the table, and for the first time, I saw guilt written across her face. "I only go to the other clubs a few times a month. I don't see all the girls when I'm there, so no. I don't know if they're safe."

"Do you keep records of the women that go through your establishments?"

She looked me straight in my eyes, her lips tightened

with anger. "I may not know where all my girls are, Agent Parker, but I do keep explicit records of those women. Who they are, who they've been with, their medical history, their preference bios. I keep track of my girls, and try to maintain a safe environment for them."

"Safe environment? You call this a safe environment?" Rapoles tossed a packet of photos onto the table in disgust. "When you brought us your records this morning, we traced the names against the list of women we've found over the last six months. Dead, either near Port Everglades, or Port Orleans. They weren't just smuggling drugs, Dr. Sinclair. Those women were being sold on the black market."

Her mouth dropped open, and a strangled gasp was heard. Those sinister green eyes welled up with tears as she flipped through the pictures.

"I...I...I didn't know," she managed to say.

"The fuck you didn't know they were up to something, Madam. In one way or another, you helped these women to die. That makes you a direct accessory," Rapoles bellowed. The veins in his neck bulged, and for a moment, I thought he was going to have a heart attack. It was time to step in.

"Whether or not you knew it then, you know it now. We need to get in there, to help those girls. Women are dying in Miami, Dr. Sinclair. They're dying in Vegas, and they're dying in New Orleans. We need to take the

Cartel down, and you're the one that is going to have to help us do it," I advised. The impact of her inaction rattled through her tense body, and she looked at me and nodded.

"Please. I can do anything. Anything," she begged. Her cold façade shattered, and all that was left was a frightened woman, who wanted to pay penance for her sins.

"When do you go to the other locations?" I asked, gently.

"I leave for Vegas tonight. We just flew a few girls over there, and they refurbished the house with new equipment."

"Good. I'll be accompanying you." The plan was coming together in my mind, and before I could utter another word, I heard a booming, "No."

I turned my head toward the offending voice. "While I appreciate your opinion, Mr. Russo, your input is neither required, necessary, or wanted. In fact, you may vacate this room." The ice in my voice would have frozen anyone else over. Noah, however, was so furious, that fire would have shot from his eyes.

"We'll work out the plan and give you the details. But remember, Dr. Sinclair, we need to keep this quiet, from everyone."

Dr. Sinclair nodded, looking overwhelmed with emotion and dread. She stood and followed her expensive looking attorney, who did nothing more than offer his unsolicited opinion about nothing. Once the door closed behind them, I snapped my head back around to Noah.

"You were out of line."

"There's no reason for you to go," he growled.

"Mr. Russo, you have no jurisdiction. Your team is not in control here, we are. My team. So I'm going to tell you to be quiet and back the hell off, or you're going to be escorted from the building. Do I make myself clear?" I warned, barely holding my fury back.

"Don't push me, Princess," he said with a sneer.

"You need to leave. There's no reason for you to be here. Don't you have a wife to check on or something?" I snarled.

"He can stay, Agent Parker," Rapoles said, his teeth clenched.

"Excuse me, sir?" I cocked my head, as if that could help me understand what a monumental jerk Noah was being. "So what? Our entire investigation, everything we've worked on, gets handed over to them?" I asked, aghast.

"No, this is a joint effort. You'll be running the mission, but they'll be right alongside you. So you have to work together."

# CHAPTER 20
## Kate

"IT'S NO LONGER ONLY A Cartel matter. The Syndicate is just as involved, if not more so, than the Cartel." Noah gave me a smug smile, and it was all I could do not to punch him in his beautiful teeth.

"You want to run that by me again? When were you going to tell me this?" I demanded from Rapoles. He didn't look too happy about it either.

"I just found out about thirty minutes before the meeting. We have reason to believe that Sebastian and Elias Cruz are auctioning off women to members of the Syndicate organization," Rapoles answered. He handed me a file, with a rash of evidence enclosed. Pictures. Text transcripts. Emails. And the smoking gun itself, a signed testimony by a Jane Doe.

"Where did you get this?" My eyes widened as I read through the reports.

"Courtesy of Triton's Edge. We have a penetration inside the organization. She's obviously not able to testify in person, but what she's captured for us is a gold mine." Noah crossed his arms over his chest and leaned back. "And without us, you wouldn't be able to get into their Ravenous location."

"Do we have any evidence of auctions at the Baltimore location?" I questioned, still reading through the reports.

"Not yet. There's nothing to say that they haven't, but we don't have any evidence of that."

I looked over at Rapoles. "Well, our best option is putting in a plant of our own."

He turned to me. "This is your case, Parker. You tell me what your plan is."

"I'll travel with the Madam, and go in as one of her auction girls," I informed. "The answer is simple, really. The only way to decimate the Syndicate and the Cartel is from within. Shane got some traction when he was a narc, but this time, we'd be ready."

Noah jumped out of his chair. "No, we're not putting you in there. Not with them."

I leveled a stare at Noah. "I'll be fine. We'll have a team in place. But this way, we'll have some ground truth in knowing where those girls are, and where they're taking them."

"Over my dead body," he seethed.

"That can be arranged, Mr. Russo. Just tell me how you'd like it done," I countered, with a saccharine sweet grin.

"That may work." Rapoles' response almost surprised me, but any agent worth his salt would understand that this was the best option. Hell, it may have been the only option.

"You can't be serious! I'm not going to leave you out there for those bastards to put their hands on you, Kate," Noah growled.

"Then your men need to figure out something else, because by nine am tomorrow, Kate will be on a plane to Vegas," Rapoles ordered, then he turned to me. "I want a full write up of your plan in one hour, Parker."

"Yes, sir."

"Parker, Russo has point on this. You will work together with Triton's Edge. Is that clear?"

I arched my eyebrow at Rapoles, then narrowed my gaze on Noah. "Crystal." I gathered up the papers from the table as Rapoles stalked out. Noah, much to my dismay, stayed behind.

"Look, if you're trying to get back at me…" he started, but I threw up my hand to cut him off.

"Whatever we had is the furthest thing from my mind right now, Noah. I wouldn't stoop so low as to risk my job, just to piss you off." I snorted in disgust and turned to leave. Immediately, I felt a hand on my elbow.

"Just let me explain. Please."

"What the hell is there to explain? It doesn't matter right now, does it? I have shit to do, and if you're not helping, then you're in my way." I brushed his arm off me and ignored the electric shock of our skin touching, and ignored the way my heart raced when I was around him. And I ignored the ache in my chest at the sight of the emotion on his face.

"It's not what you think," he said loudly.

I whirled around. "You're married. It doesn't matter what the hell I think."

"Don't act like that, Kate." He rolled his eyes.

"Don't act like what?" I replied coolly, walking out of the conference room. Noah followed me, his long stride catching up with me quicker than I had liked. He grabbed my arm and pulled me into an empty office, shutting the door behind us.

He pushed me against the wall, then braced his arms next to my head. "Don't act like you don't care, Princess."

"Fuck you, asshole," I gritted out, pushing against his muscular chest. He smirked, but didn't budge. "Why should I be jealous, Noah? We were fuck buddies, that's it. It's not like we thought it would go anywhere."

His jaw clenched, and his blue eyes darkened with anger. "That's bullshit, and you know it, Kate."

I pushed him back harder. This time, it took him by surprise, and he stepped back enough for me to move around him.

"Is it? Don't make this any more than it is. Am I pissed to find out that you were married? Hell yeah, but you know what? I should have known. We would go out, but it was mostly about the sex. Why? Because I was living a lie down in Miami, and so were you. So hey, no big fucking deal, right? Because you were nothing more than a casual fuck, someone to get my rocks off with," I snapped.

"So that's how you feel?" His lips drew into a thin line, and his glare pierced my body, as if flaming hot knives were shooting out of them.

"Yeah. That's how I feel," I lied. All the fight I had left was drained out of me.

His body hardened, and he jerked his chin at me. And then, without another word, he threw open the door and stalked out.

I exhaled the breath I'd been holding, and willed the tears tingling in my eyes to go away. *I won't let this get to me. I can't let him see how hurt I am. It was just a casual fling, nothing more. Pull up your big girl panties and focus, Kate!* I took a deep breath and readied myself for the potential stares. I composed myself enough to shoot glares at anyone who dared to cast a glance in my direction. I hurried down the corridor and through the maze of cubicles before I reached my own office of solitude.

Thanks to modern technology, I was able to Facetime with Rick while he was in New Orleans, and we started to hatch out a plan. But, we couldn't get very far without the input of Triton's Edge. I debated about sending Noah a text, but before I could pull up his name in my contacts, a large figure loomed in the doorway.

"Can I help you?

The huge, bald-headed, burly man waltzed right into my office and plopped down next to me. He threw his motorcycle boots onto my table, and stretched out his legs in front of him. I quickly noticed the badge around his neck, which only meant that he was not here to kill me. Yet.

"And you are…?"

"I'm Torin. Noah told me to help you out." His gravelly voice sent shivers down my spine, and not the yummy kind Noah gave me. It was obvious by his gruff nature, the size of his body, and the sleeves of tattoos running up and down his arms, that he didn't care what anyone thought, and no one really messed with him, either.

"Kate Parker." I reached over and shook his hand. "Here's what I have so far, and you can tell me where your crew will fit in."

We spent an hour working on the plan, and then the counter plan, then plans B-D. We had backups to the backups.

"You'll mobilize your units and get to Vegas by twenty-one hundred tomorrow?" I asked, pulling my blazer back on.

"Don't worry about us, we have you covered. Noah made sure of it," Torin said with a grin.

I rolled my eyes. "Great. Thanks." I gathered up my messenger bag and headed toward the door.

"Kate." His tone stopped me. "Whatever it is you think you know, you don't. That man's been through a lot of shit, shit you have no idea what to do with."

I turned and faced him. "What I do know, is that whatever is going on between myself and Noah is our business, not yours. While I appreciate the fact that you're trying to be his wingman, don't. We're professionals, let's keep it that way," I retorted back.

I charged forward, not waiting for a reply. I moved through the cubicle maze and out of the office doors. *Come on.* The urge to get away from the office was strong, and I needed...something. My pent-up negative energy needed to be released, and that would normally mean that a session with Sketch was in order. Which was exactly what I'd planned to do. I jabbed the elevator button and just as it opened, I charged ahead, bumping into a wall in the process.

"I'm sorry, I..." I started to say, but my voice was lost the moment our eyes met. He snaked his arms around my waist and pulled me into the elevator. My arms hung limply at my sides, and I just took him in. A flurry of emotions swam through me. He didn't have to speak. He didn't have to say or do anything, but the touch of his hands on me had those damn butterflies going crazy. Those beautiful brown eyes swirled, and were filled with sadness. I wanted more than anything just to tell him that it was okay. To forgive him. His sharp jaw unclenched, and before I knew it, his lips crashed onto mine.

His tongue swept in, plundering and taking whatever I could give him. I threw my arms around him and pulled him close. I wanted to climb him, to arch into him, but the voice of reason, that damn bitch, reminded me that I was still mad. I broke the kiss off, panting. Noah wasn't having any of it, though. He cupped my face in those calloused, large hands, and gently kissed my lips. His lids were heavy with lust, but I saw something different in his eyes—hope.

"I'm not giving up on this. I can't. You have me in too deep," he murmured. He punched the button to open the door, and walked out without looking back. My hand immediately touched my lips, tracing the effects of what he did to them.

I shook off my aroused haze, and pushed the button for the garage. I needed to get my head in the game, and Noah Russo wasn't helping.  I finished my errands in a desire-induced fog, but thankfully, they got done. Thanks to the work of my favorite stylist, I was able to go back to a beautiful platinum blonde hair, and for a hint of flair, I added some high pink highlights. Very few people had seen me blonde, and while I cherished the richness of my previous color, blonde would be the best start of my disguise.

It was time to put Kate Parker on the back burner for the time being. I had several alter-egos that I could use, and Vegas would be the perfect time to introduce one of my favorites to the world. Using disposable contacts, I changed my vibrant blue eyes to a subtle brown. By using some makeup putty I purchased from a cosplay online shop, I was able to transform my chin and nose into something more narrow. I added a nose stud, for an added touch.  A pair of black rimmed glasses, with a micro camera attached, finished off the look. A little much? Possibly. But I couldn't take the chance of anyone from Tommy's crew recognizing me.

I gathered up my items and put them into a regular old black suitcase. I took everything that was Kate Parker and put her away, because it was time for Sabrina Carpenter to come out and play.

# CHAPTER 21
## Noah

I BARELY FOUGHT THE URGE to go back into that elevator, to grab her in the parking lot and hide her away. The idea of her going into the lion's den gutted me on all levels. My instinct, my need was to protect her. I didn't give a shit about her training, or if she was good at her job. Or hell, if she knew what she was doing. She was mine. Mine to love. Mine to protect. But deep down, I knew that this was what she needed to do. And I'd be damned if I just sat back and watched her do it alone.

I met up with Torin as he walked out of their office suite.

"I need all eyes on her, every step of the way." The order didn't need to be said, but I said it anyway. Torin smiled.

"I got you, man," he smirked. "It looks good on you."

"What the hell are you talking about?" I barked out in annoyance.

"You're in love with this chick, and I'm damn happy to see you all pussy-whipped and shit. But she's a smart broad. She knows what the hell she's doing. No need to get your panties in a bunch."

"Fuck you, dickwad." I didn't deny it. Not when it hit me like a fucking freight train. Love. I loved her. And the bitch of the matter was, that she didn't know it.

"Nah, I'll let Kate handle that for me." He slapped his meaty hand against my chest. "Let's go, lover boy. We got shit to do."

We headed down to the garage, where he had parked his Harley. I got into my truckand followed him out to the open road. We made the distance between Baltimore and Odenton fly. Sketch was waiting for us when we pulled up.

"What's the plan?" he asked with grim smile.

"She's going in as one of the Madam's favorite girls. We'll have a wireless mic attached to her at all times, recording everything. Her glasses have the micro camera, so we're set on the tech. We just need to ensure that we have the proper credentials to get in. Each of us have already received honorary membership to the

Ravenous clubs, backdated from a year or so. We're good to go on that. We just need to ensure that one of us is there at all times."

"Artillery?"

"Right this way, gentleman." Sketch led us to the back area of the warehouse, the area in the place that had walls and a locked door—a highly secure locked door. He punched in the code, and opened the door, and we entered the nirvana of guy's toys. Guns and ammo of different types and sizes were stored behind locked cages on two of the walls. Flak jackets, hazmat suits, and body armor hung on the other two. In the middle of the room, was a long table and a tool chest. Knowing Sketch and his inclination for extracting the most information out of people, I shuddered to think of what was in that chest.

"What's the transportation looking like?" Cole asked, coming into the room. We greeted him with grunts as we got back to stocking the cases full of what we needed.

"There's already a military flight headed to Nevada. We're jumping on board with them. Zeke has his place ready for us." Zeke was originally from Vegas. He loved the desert, and had a place outside the Strip.

"What I want to know is, do we get to use the services offered at Ravenous?" Torin joked.

I slapped him on the back of his bald head. "Any services offered by Kate will not be taken. Is that understood?"

"I hear ya, but others are open for business?" He asked lasciviously, wiggling his eyebrows.

"Okay, perv. Let's worry more about the gear, and less about your cock."

We got the gear crated up and loaded into Torin's truck, so we could run it by the base near Washington, DC, then we'd split. We made plans to meet up later on, so I headed back to the house. I hated leaving Aubrey so often, but I knew my parents and Jennie's folks would take great care of her.

Using the Bluetooth, I made a quick call over to the rehab center where Jennie was located. It had only been twenty-four hours, but I wanted to get a quick check in before I left. A nagging feeling had my nerves on edge. Fuck, this whole mission had my nerves frayed.

"Yes, this is Noah Russo. I'd like to check on my wife, Jennifer." I cringed at using the word *wife*, especially for Jennie. But it was the only way I could check her status.

"Mr. Russo, the doctor would like to speak with you."

My stomach dropped, and I pulled over to the side of the road. This was never good.

"Mr. Russo, this is Doctor Angela Montoya. When

we spoke yesterday at the intake exam, you stated that you wanted to do everything you could to get Mrs. Russo well," her brisk voice stated.

"What's going on with Jennie, Dr. Montoya?" I demanded.

"She checked herself out over an hour ago. We tried to place several phone calls to the number listed, but all calls went to a voicemail that wasn't set up."

"You couldn't hold her?" I shouted out in rage.

"No, Mr. Russo, I can't.  You know that I can't hold her against her will. She came in voluntarily, she leaves voluntarily. "

"Fuck!" I punched the steering wheel.  "What happened to the guards stationed there?"

"They were there, and they left when she did. They followed her out." *And no one thought to tell me?* Confusion and fury swirled together until I thought I would scream. *Kate is going to kick my ass.*

"Does anyone have any information on who picked her up, or the car they were driving? Anything?"

"We have camera footage, but they came so quickly. Almost as if it was planned."

"I'll get to the bottom of this." I hung up on the doctor and rubbed my face. There was something more to this, more than Jennie wanting to leave. I dialed Kate. As much as it was going to piss her off, she needed to know.

"What Noah?" She answered without a greeting, just like I figured she would. "I'm about ready to board."

"Jennie left rehab, and the guards that were stationed there left with her."

A string of curses came out of her perfect mouth. "Let me call the agent on duty. I'll touch base with you." And then she hung up the phone.

I put the truck in drive, and headed toward her parents' house. Thankfully, my folks still lived down the street from Jennie and Sketch's old place, so I took a gamble that she would be there. When I pulled up to the old Cape Cod style home that I lived in for six years, I knew my gamble had paid off. I sent a quick text to Kate, then made my way to the front door. I let myself in, and was greeted by the scene of Jennie, all sweaty and pasty from detoxing, holding my screaming daughter in her hands. My mom stood by, trying to coax Jennie into letting her take the baby, but Jennie wouldn't have anything to do with it. Two agents stood there, their hands out, trying to assist, but nothing was working.

"No! No! She's mine. She's my daughter, Diane! I can hold her if I want to."

"Jennie, sweetie, I know. Truly. But she doesn't know you," my mom coaxed her, which made Jennie scream in rage.

"She's *my daughter*. Your fucking son took her away from me. I'm going to take her back!"

"Jennie! Stop what you're doing right now!" I roared. The shrieks from Aubrey intensified dramatically, and Jennie jumped in surprise.

"Fuck you, you bastard. She's mine. I don't need you in her life anymore. She's mine," she screamed back.

"Jennie, just give me Aubrey. I won't take you back to rehab. I just want to make sure Aubrey is safe." My voice was calm, but my body was tense and coiled. One wrong move, and she could snap. She could do anything. She could hurt Aubrey, or herself.

"Fuck you. You're just going to leave her here. You don't love her. Hell, I'm pretty sure you're not her father. Just because I conned you into marrying me, doesn't mean you're her father any more than it means you're my husband. I was hoping you'd die overseas so I'd get those benefits, but no! You had to play hero and live to tell the fucking tale. So fuck you, Noah. We don't need you. I'm going to sue your rich ass for as much child support as I can, and live the fucking high life with my daughter," she snarled.

The venom that spewed from her mouth bothered me, but not as much as the grip she had on Aubrey. Her nails were drawing blood on Aubrey's back and chubby thighs.

"You're making our daughter bleed, Jennie. Please, just give her to me," I begged.

"If you don't let me leave with her, she's going to bleed more!" she cried out. Mom started to plead to her even more, and I caught the eye of the agent next to me. He was ready for whatever I was about to do. I knew I had to time it right, and catch her off guard. With her attention on Mom, I managed to slip around her and put her in a choke hold. She released Aubrey, and in a split second, the agent dove to grab her.

"That will be the last time you ever put your hands on our child again. Fuck that, you will never see her again. *NEVER!*" I roared in her ear. Her arms went limp and she fell unconscious.

"Local just pulled up," the other agent said, as Mom frantically looked over Aubrey.

"Good. I want her locked up." I let her fall into a slump, and moved to hold my baby girl.

"Daddy's got you, baby doll. Daddy's got you." I pulled her into my arms, and kissed her sweaty head. She hiccupped, and put her head on my shoulder, as I took stock of her injuries. Just bruises from where Jennie's hands had been, and scratches from her nails. I sighed as the EMTs hauled Jennie out on the stretcher.

"I want her ass in cuffs. I don't want her to take a piss without a guard right next to her," I ordered in a low, threatening voice. He nodded, and followed them out to the car.

"Noah, thank God you came when you did." Mom sighed and put her arms around my waist.

"I was actually coming to say that I have to roll out. Our timeline got pushed up, and we're going wheels up in two hours," I informed her, and kissed her forehead. My mom sighed again. She hated when I left. My brother Evan was also Special Forces, and paid the ultimate sacrifice. He never made it home alive. "Mom, if you knew what these animals did to Jennie. I mean, hell, she's not my favorite person right now, but they tortured her, Mom. They're torturing these other girls, selling them to the highest fucking bidder. I need to go stop them."

"I know, Bub. I just worry." She raised herself up on her tiptoes to kiss my cheek, then pulled the sleeping angel from my arms.

"I'll take care of Bree. You just come home safe."

"Always, Mom." I headed for the door and looked back at my mom swaying with Aubrey in her arms. I knew that I would be back, and Kate would be with me.

# CHAPTER 22
## *Kate*

I RECEIVED THE MESSAGE from Noah that Jennie had been found, but that still didn't put my heart at ease. Something was amiss. Something just didn't seem right, and I wasn't sitting pretty. It wasn't the normal pre-mission angst, either. I checked my nerves at the door, and pushed through the airport terminal in Vegas, and grabbed a cab to the place I would be staying. I knew that meeting up with the Madam right off the bat would be a bad idea, and I needed to make sure I had my head in the game, and a place to lay low if I needed to. Luckily for me, she had two friends that I could stay with.

The cab pulled up to a lovely, one level stucco home on the outskirts of Vegas. Knowing nothing about the two women that lived there, I was going in unprepared, and slightly nervous. This wasn't what I did. I was normally more prepped for something like this.

And boy, was I unprepared.

"Darling! Welcome to our home!" A beautifully made up woman, about six feet tall, with porcelain skin, fire engine red hair, and startling blue eyes popped out the door. My eyes widened at the sight of her. I paid the cabbie his fare, and lugged my suitcase out of the trunk. I walked up the sidewalk and reached out my hand in greeting, and she lightly slapped it away.

"We don't shake hands here, Love. We're huggers!" And that was the only warning I got before I was swept up in an overzealous squeeze. My face was smooshed against her enormous, yet surprisingly soft breasts. About ten seconds into the hug, I gently eased myself away.

"Hi! I'm Sabrina," I said awkwardly.

"Yes, Love. Do you think we introduce ourselves like this to just anyone? The Madam told us about you! We're dying to have you stay with us for a while. I'm Penny Johnson, but you can call me Pancakes."

"Nice to meet you, Pancakes," I said with a big smile.

"Now, come on in. We have a room all set up for you." She led me through the door, into an exquisitely appointed living room, decorated in rich jewel tones. Through the archway, I could see the gorgeous kitchen, and off to the side, a long hallway.

"This is Bubblezzz, my sister in crime," Pancakes gestured proudly. A sister from another mister, maybe? While Pancakes was statuesque and flamboyant, Bubblezzz was small and prim.

Until she opened her mouth.

"Oh my fucking God! You're fucking *gorgeous!* Girl, are you a stripper? Are you a hooker? If you're working with the Madam, you're probably a hooker. You need to tell us everything! The Madam is so secretive when it comes to Ravenous. We perform there every week, but we don't get to hear all the dirt."

*Light Bulb.* That was how the Madam knew these ladies. They were performers.

"Unfortunately, I've signed several contracts and a non-disclosure agreement, so I can't spill the beans," I said in a sly tone, giving them a wink.

"Shoot, honey, a bottle of tequila for a woman like yourself and you'll be singing like a canary," Pancakes retorted, flipping her red hair behind her.

*Mental note, no drinking around Pancakes and Bubblezzz.*

"Why don't I take you back to your room, and you get settled. We're having martinis in the lounge, so you can know us better. And we can hear all the gossip from you."

"Sure!" I plastered a big smile on my face and

followed Bubblezzz down to the room I'd be staying in. Deliciously decked out in whites and creams, the bedroom and accompanying bath were almost like staying in a five-star hotel. I quickly unpacked my clothes, and ensured that the gear I would need was safely secured. My plans to meet up with the Madam at seven were on track, so I had two hours to kill. Two hours to get information out of my hostesses. I meandered my way back to the lounge area, which was really the lanai on the back of the house.  Several bottles of wine, both red and white, were displayed on the table, surrounded by an antipasto platter, trays of crackers and veggies, and holy cow, were those truffles? If these women ate like this every day, I was sure to gain a couple—or twenty—pounds.

"Ladies, what a spread!" I plastered on that fake smile again as I walked in.

"Oh, Love, we do this every day before we go to Ravenous. It's our cocktail hour, before all cock," Pancakes said suggestively.

"So what do you ladies do at Ravenous?" I asked, pouring myself some wine.

"We're performers, dear. You mean to tell me that you haven't been witness to the Pancakes and Bubblezzz show before? I mean, I know we're only located in Vegas, but we're world renowned! We were trending on social media before social media even took off!"

I shook my head, amused at their disbelief. "Sadly, no. I just started with the Madam at the Baltimore establishment, so I haven't been privy to your show. Tell me, what do you do? Are you dancers?"

"We are the hostesses of the Ravenous Burlesque. We put on sexual skits of the most innocent of fairy tales and stories. The skits are short, about ten minutes long, and they only take place three times a week. As the hostesses, we get to make sure that everyone is having a good time," Bubblezzz informed me, taking a sip of her martini. Her long, ruby red nails drummed on her thigh. "You know, you could make for a fantastic Alice in Sexyland."

"Yeah, my acting skills aren't that great, but thanks."

"So tell me, Sabrina. What brings you to Ravenous?" Pancakes asked coyly.

"I just graduated from High Point University, and I'm looking for a good time, and also to pay down some of my student loans." The lies, although practiced, flowed easily.

"Oh, those dreaded student loans. Yes, Love, with your looks, you should have no problem paying those down."

I took a sip of the dark, luscious wine, and pursed my lips. "I hope so. I'm not going to make much with my teaching degree, so as much as I can get paid down, the better." I caught the knowing glance between the two women.

"What does that look mean?"

"Exactly what do you think you'll be doing at Ravenous?" Pancakes asked softly.

"Oh! The Madam told me all about the place. It's where the super wealthy come for conversation and companionship. "

"You're sweet, Love, and you seem like a great person, but you may not be able to last long at Ravenous," Bubblezzz said conspiratorially.

"What do you mean?" I asked, innocence all over my face. I needed to project the girl-next-door attitude.

"The men at Ravenous, they're...how do we say this for your poor ears...used to a different sort of woman? They're used to women who like to provide activities in the most sexual of nature."

"Well, yes, I understand that. But the Madam assured me that if I wasn't comfortable doing something, I didn't have to."

"Hmm..." hummed Pancakes. She glanced at Bubblezzz, who already had her eyebrows raised.

"If that's what she promised you, then you should be fine. Have you received your schedule yet?"

"No, ma'am. That's what I'm going in early for

today. I'm supposed to meet her at seven."

"Oh God! That's in less than two hours. Quick! Shake a leg, Love! We got to get you prepared!" Pancakes shot up from the loveseat and hurried me into the bathroom. "Wax, shave, and buff everything. The Madam likes her girls clean and smooth. Then we'll get to work on your hair and makeup."

*Oh dear God, these women are going to be the death of me.* I did what they commanded, though, and scrubbed, buffed, and shaved until I was silky smooth. Thankfully, I already had my wax taken care of, because I had a feeling that Pancakes would have done something about that herself. I dressed myself in the lingerie that the Madam recommended, along with the strapless, tight dress that I had brought with me. I was just slipping on the shoes, when Pancakes poked her head in.

"Ready, doll?" And before I could answer, she threw open the door. She dropped her bag of hair products, rollers, flat irons, and curlers. For the next hour, she blow-dried, ironed, and curled my hair. Then she attacked my face with makeup from the stars. Thankfully, I already had my putty in place, and smoothed over it with some pancake makeup.

By the time she turned me around, I was stunned. I looked like myself, but way better than I could have ever done. My makeup was dramatic, but flawless. I thought I had seen all the tutorials, but nothing could have prepared me for what Pancakes could do.

"Wow, you really have an eye."

"I wasn't born this beautiful, Love. Hell, I wasn't born a woman, but I was born to have a great sense of style and looks. You have good bone structure. You can pull off any look." She bent down to whisper in my ear. "You can also be anyone you want to be. Even the naïve girl next door." I looked up at her, and she gave me a knowing smile.

Before I could open my mouth, she said, "I may not know why, or what's going on, but I'm no fool, Ms. Sabrina. And I know when people are hiding something. But I ain't mad at you. Your soul is good. I can see that. I just hope to hell that you know what you're doing."

I nodded. "I appreciate your discretion, Pancakes."

"Child, I also know when to keep my lips sealed." She smiled, then hesitated. "I'm sure you know that Ravenous caters to a dangerous sort."

"I do. And please, trust me when I say, I can take care of myself." She squeezed my shoulder.

"There's something about you, Love. Truly, there is. But your true strength is what you show others once those walls are down." She kissed the top of my head. "Should we attend this evening's festivities?" She inquired, worry filling her face.

I thought for a minute, then shrugged. "You have a better idea of what's going on than I do, Pancakes. Let's play it by ear, okay? But I promise, I won't let anything happen to you or Bubblezzz."

She smiled wearily. "That, we can do. Come on, we're just waiting on Bubblezzz to find that perfect pair of shoes, then we can get going."

I squeezed her hand and reached for my cell phone. I received a text from the Madam from her burner phone.

*Auction is tomorrow night.*

I was glad that the ladies weren't going to be performing tomorrow, so I sent off a quick text to the guys. They'd be on-site tomorrow, and we'd have a quick powwow in the morning to go over everything. If everything came together, then Ravenous and the Syndicate would be taken down by tomorrow evening.

# CHAPTER 23

*Noah*

We touched down at midnight, and made tracks to Zeke's house in the desert. The huge house was set apart from any other residences by miles, and we made prime use of the land by setting up a shooting range. My body was coiled like a fucking snake, ready to strike. After all the bullshit with Jennie yesterday, I needed to get some of my frustrations out. My preferred method was now playing prostitute in some brothel, so the next best thing would be shooting some gear. We received the text from Kate that the auction was to be held tonight, and that we had to look the part, whatever the fuck that meant. I guess we had to look wealthy and shit.

We stored our gear at Zeke's, after lighting up the

morning with the beautiful smell of gunpowder, and before long, it was time to get ready. The auction began at eleven, but we were supposed to meet up with Kate around six to ensure the gear was working, and make sure our plans were ready. We had contingencies after contingencies. Local PD was not yet informed, and only a select few on Kate's team even knew about what was going down. Rapoles was in town, and coordinated their front, along with Commander Wells. Bravo Team, the slick fuckers, hadn't been invited, and that was a good thing. I found out it was Jose Martinez running his mouth. I should have known that the motherfucker was talking shit. He'd had a hard-on for me since we both graduated from BUD/S. He was pissed that I was leading this team, and he was back to playing second fiddle.

A Benz pulled up in the long driveway, and we all grew tense. Our trigger fingers were itching to get some relief, but the only thing that got any relief when that car door opened was my cock. The long, tan legs went on forever, and it took a minute to realize that the blonde bombshell getting out was Kate. *My* Kate. Torin went to whistle, and before he could get the note out, I socked him in his gut.

"That's my girl, fucker. Don't even think about it," I growled, as she walked down the driveway. The teal dress she was wearing was like a second skin on her. Those breasts were practically pushed up to her chin, and God almighty, she looked hotter than sin.

All business, she walked up to our crew and looked at everyone. I quickly made the introductions, and we went over the plan. Myself, Trey, and Torin would be stationed throughout the facility, and to Torin's elation, they were supposed to be enjoying themselves. At eleven, those with sufficient cash would be escorted into a lower-level for the auction. Zeke would be our eyes and ears, while Benji, Sketch, and Cole would be waiting in the wings. Because Tommy had seen them before, we were limiting our chances of them being recognized.

"Security will be at the door, checking for weapons. It's expected that those coming for a visit would be armed, so they're not going to cause a ruckus if it's minimal. Just limit whatever you have on you to one handgun in the holster, and that's it."

"Anything else?" Benji asked, checking the magazine on his 9mm.

"Yeah, the rooms have cameras. They're live feeds, and watched on a closed circuit TV. Supposed to be for security purposes, to ensure that the women aren't getting roughed up. But really, it's to make sure that the women are doing their jobs."

"And what job would that be, Princess?" I huffed.

So help me God, if she had to service anyone, I couldn't guarantee that we'd get out of there alive.

"Whatever the customer wishes. Most of the johns are nice, but there are some I'd like to stay away from," she replied with a grimace.

"Have you seen any sign of Tommy, or his brothers?" Cole asked her.

"I met Sebastian Cruz earlier, just in passing. He didn't get a good look at me, and I'd like to keep it like that."

"What happens if you get put up for auction?" The question slipped out of my mouth before I could think. We weren't supposed to let it go that far. Benji, Cole, and Sketch were going to track the vehicles as they left, and remove the girls from harm.

"Then I go," she said simply. The beast inside roared with anger, and it was all I could do to control my temper. "I go, Noah. That's the only way we'll learn where they're taking them, and who is doing the buying." She held up her hand when I went to interrupt. "That's final. I have the permission of Rapoles and your commander."

"That's fucking bullshit," I spat out. "How the hell are we supposed to protect you if you're out of our sight."

"You're going to have to trust in the fact that I can do my job, and I will do whatever it takes to get those girls out," she retorted. Her brown eyes flashed angrily. I hated that color on her. It didn't look natural.

"Kate, I need to get you mic'd up," Zeke called from the minivan that we commandeered.

*The hell he's going to mic up that skin.* "I'll do it," I declared harshly. Kate rolled her eyes and headed over to Zeke. With his short dark hair and glasses, you would think that the nerd wouldn't be able to fight back. Only a few of us knew what sort of warrior he really was.

I took the mic from his hand and glared over at Zeke. "Get out," I snarled. With his hands up in surrender, he quickly backed out of the van with a chuckle.

"Really? Do you have to be an ass?" she complained, letting the dress fall to her waist. I ignored her while taping the mic to the under curve of her breast. She'd already mentioned that she wouldn't have to get fully naked at the auction, so I felt somewhat comfortable with the mic being there. However, we did take precautions, and used nude body tape that was similar to her skin tone. Unless someone was really looking, it wouldn't be noticed.

I traced the curve lightly with my finger, going all the way up to her jawline, then tucked a blonde strand behind her ear.

"You look good as a blonde." Her breath hitched as my fingers cupped the back of her head. I leaned my forehead against hers and closed my eyes, taking in the delicious scent of coconut, citrus, and...her.

"God, I miss you, Kate. Please, come back to me. I'll tell you everything. Fuck, I was going to tell you everything."

"I don't know if I can, Noah," she whispered sadly. My heart ached at the sound of her voice. I knew I'd screwed up, but damn if I didn't wish I could take it all back.

"Please, Princess. Please. I need you." My grip tightened around the back of her head, and I lowered my lips to hers.

Tentatively.

Patiently.

Waiting.

Asking.

She pulled away and gave me a sad look. "I just can't. Not right now, okay?" She walked over to Zeke to ensure that coms were working, then got back into her rented Benz.

"Dude, she'll come around," Cole muttered. I shot him a quick look.

"I didn't think you wanted her to be with me, after everything that happened."

Cole shrugged. "You broke her heart. But, your reasons are valid. She needs to hear them from you, though. And I know you love her. That's what every brother wants for his sister."

I nodded, then looked over at Torin as he gave the signal. It was time to roll out. We got in our separate vehicles to get to Ravenous, so we didn't look like we came together. We arrived close to nine, and the line to get in was two blocks deep. Being the members of good standing that we were, we were able to cut the line.

"Sir, glad you could join us," the host at the door said, checking the customized wrist band that was given to all members. "Please see the Madam once you arrive, as she has the auction sheet available."

I filed in behind everyone else, and took a sheet. And damned if Kate wasn't listed in the first round. I just had to make sure that I would be the one to win her.

Everyone milled and mingled around, drinking out of fancy glasses and swilling champagne. The atmosphere was festive, but the guys and me weren't in the mood. Torin and Trey were making their rounds, flirting with the women, and doing their best to show that they belonged. But my eyes never left the blonde bombshell in the teal dress. She flirted and spoke with the people in the room, engaging them with her seductive smile and beautiful laugh. But I could see it. I could see her sizing up each person she met.

There was a rustle at the front of the room, and a

crowd formed. Several men, of varying ethnicities walked in, and went straight for the tucked away elevator in the back hallway. I caught Kate's eye, and nodded to the left, ever so slightly. She looked down, and then up at me, confirming my question. I ambled my way over toward the hallway, ready to be shot down.

"Sir, may I help you?" a tuxedo wearing man asked.

"I'm sorry, sir, I was bringing this customer down to the rooms," Kate said from behind me. I gently grasped her hand. The guard acquiesced and keyed us entry into the elevator. The flight down was quick, and we stayed quiet. But I let the rubbing of my thumb on the underside of her wrist do the talking.

We walked down the candlelit hallway, testing the knobs of each room. Most rooms were open, except for one. With a quick look at me, she stopped at the last door on the right. After walking in, she quickly locked the door behind us. The room was filled with a trunk, a king size bed with white satin sheets, and a cabinet full of any toy someone could want. Kate flicked on the stereo next to the bed, and the sounds of D'Angelo's "How does it feel?" came over the speakers.

Immediately, I took her in my arms and held her close, relishing the feel of her body against mine. I ducked my head next to her lips.

"Auction is in the next room over."

"How long do we have?" I whispered, inhaling her scent.

"Thirty minutes before we have to go back upstairs. Sixty minutes until the auction." Her voice came in soft pants, and I groaned.

"Then let's get it done." I swayed her over to the wall, and pushed her up against it, next to a massive chest. My head dipped down, letting my tongue trace down her neck, and nibbled my way down the V of her dress. She draped one arm around my neck, letting her other hand caress the package in my pants. "God, please," I begged quietly.

She cupped the small disk that was in the front of my boxer briefs, and pulled it out, as her thumb traced the big vein on the underside of my cock. I groaned, and my cock strained against the fabric even more. She put the circular disc in my hand and I palmed it. Hitching her legs up around my waist, I slammed my hand against the wall, holding it there so the audio mic concealed in the disc would engage. This disc could penetrate all sorts of walls and materials, and would be able to hear whatever we couldn't. It was a custom job, created by Zeke for situations similar to this one. The shadows would conceal the disk until we were finished, and we pushed the self-destruct button.

I ground my pelvis against her, feeling the heat

between her legs. "God, I want you. I've always wanted you. It's always been you, Princess. Please know that." I managed to get out, in between our frantic kisses. Our lips crashed together, our tongues pulsated with the same rhythmic motion as our hips. I broke off the kiss, needing to know where this was going before I lost all control.

"I need you, Princess." I cupped my hand around her throat, using my thumb to tilt her chin up. "I fucking love you. I need you."

She gazed into my eyes, and I swear there was love hidden underneath the hunger.

"Please, Noah," she begged me in a soft voice.

"As much as I love to hear you beg, I need you to say the words. Tell me you love me, because I know you do. I can see it in your eyes," I pleaded, slipping my finger up her thigh and sliding her panties to the side. She let out a soft whine, and I caressed her silky wetness.

"Oh God, Noah." She arched herself into my hand, and gasped when I added another finger. "Oh God, please!" She started riding my hand, searching, cresting.

"Princess, I need to hear those words. Please," I begged urgently.

Her breath came in quick pants, and I knew she was almost there. Hell, I was almost there myself, and I was about to nut in my pants.

"Yes! I love you…God, I've loved you for so long!" Her whispered wail was music to my ears, and I couldn't last a minute longer.

"Fuck me." I pulled my fingers out of her soaked pussy and shoved them into my mouth, sucking off her arousal.

Pure honey. I pulled her body close and twirled around to the bed, where I laid her down. I shimmied her dress off her body, noticing at the last minute, the mic was taped to her breast. Fuck! I covered her body with mine, and as I paid attention to her gloriously pierced nipples, I placed my lips next to the mic.

"Fellas, radio silence, please. Fifteen minutes max," I ordered through gritted teeth. A chuckle came through my earpiece, then there was blissful silence.

"Cameras," I reminded her. She ignored me, and dug her hands in my scalp as I made my way down her body, suckling and nibbling at her everywhere.

"I'm too far gone to care right now, so please, don't stop!" she cried out.

My balls were about to burst, so I climbed up her body, and rubbed my bare cock against her folds. With no time to lose, I slipped in as far as I could, bottoming out against her ass. She arched into me, her back coming off the mattress. I pulled out, then thrust back in quickly. The walls of her pussy clamped onto my cock so tightly,

I almost lost my load right there. I rocked back on my heels, and pulled her body up to mine, wrapping her legs around my waist. It would be quick, but the angle alone was worth it. I slid in, and the new angle had me hitting that sweet G spot of hers with each thrust.

"Oh God, yes! I'm so close," she cried out again. My thrusts became quicker, and the sweat from our bodies made us slick and wet against the satin sheets. Then she exploded with a scream, as her pussy clenched around me and milked my cock of everything I had. I couldn't hold back anymore, and I let go with a roar. With our quick breaths, I pulled her up, with my cock still inside her, so she was in my arms again.

"I love you, Princess. And I'll spend the rest of my life trying to prove it to you," I said, kissing her.

# CHAPTER 24
*Noah*

"HATE TO INTERRUPT THE lovebirds, but movement has a large contingent of people coming down the stairs. Need to get a move on," someone snarled in my ear.

"Roger that. We gotta roll." We detangled our legs from each other and moved to clean up and get dressed. A loud knock came through the door.

"Miss Sabrina, the Madam requests your company once your client is satisfied."

Kate rolled her eyes. "Sure thing. I'll be right up."

"Be careful," I said, kissing her lips. I zipped up the back of her dress and opened the door for her, only to smack that ass when she walked by.

I took the opportunity to do some checking around.

The ten other doors in the hallway were now locked, and from the muted noises, they were also occupied. I opened the last door at the end of the hall, right next to the room where we planted the device, , and not surprisingly, it was the the size of a small auditorium. Several seats were arranged in a semicircle, surrounding a small stage. This was where they did the auctions.

"I'm sorry, sir, but the auction hasn't started yet. If you'd like to wait, I can escort you to the library where all the other participants are waiting," the butler with the beady black eyes said from behind me.

I gave him an arrogant smile and raised my chin, then followed him out. Suddenly, the faint buzzing in my ear crackled with activity.

"Updated info, Noah. There are two auctions taking place tonight. One is the willing, and Kate's among those. That one is taking place upstairs in the Observatory."

"And the next one?" I muttered quietly under my breath.

"Downstairs. There's a sublevel that wasn't on the original plans." Zeke paused. "And Noah? Jennie is among the women that are being auctioned off."

*Shit! How the hell did she get here?* "Where?"

"Back where you were. There's a door on the wall somewhere. But you won't be able to find it yourself. You need to get in on the next auction."

*Motherfucker.* Having to choose between Kate and Jennie was a no-brainer. I'd pick Kate every time. But I couldn't leave Jennie to the Syndicate.

"Who has eyes on Kate?" I asked, barely moving my lips.

"I got her, brother. Go get Jennie," Torin insisted. I grunted my acceptance of the change in plans, and headed out to find the Madam. Her eyes widened at the sight of me, and a look of confusion came over her face.

"Madam! Thank you so much for having me tonight. Unfortunately, I'm not exactly happy with the service. My tastes run a bit more...aggressive," I said loudly. The tall, dark-haired gentleman behind her, turned his head slightly to eavesdrop.

"Oh, Mr. DePandi, I'm so sorry tonight was not to your satisfaction. We truly appreciate your business. Perhaps if I can find another woman...?"

"I'm looking for a long-term commitment, Madam. While I appreciate being invited to the auction, a week of companionship is not something I'm looking for. It's barely enough time to...mold her to my needs."

"Oh, of course," she demurred.

"Ah, a man after my own tastes." The dark-haired bastard behind her finally turned his attention to us. "Sebastian Cruz. And you are?" He held out his hand.

"Gavin DePandi. It is nice to meet you, Mr. Cruz,

but I'm in the mood for something more than your establishment can provide." I made a motion to move along, but just as I figured, he stopped me.

"I believe I have something you may be interested in," he offered, cryptically. "Why don't you join us, as my private guest? We can see if your money matches your desires."

Seeing as how a bank account with a minimum of ten million dollars was required to join in on the auction, I had no doubt that my money, however fake it was, was welcome. He gestured for me to follow him, which I did. We went down the halls I was just in, and into the room with the semicircle of chairs, and the small stage.

"This location is for those of a particular nature," he advised, dialing a code into a hidden panel on the wall. The door swung open, revealing another set of stairs. "Right this way."

We made our way down to what could only be described as a dungeon. Cement and cinderblock walls, and florescent lights lined the place. The smell of sweat and fear filled the room. Several men, and a couple of women of various ethnicities and cultures, sat in rows of cushioned chairs, their focus to the back of the room. Several women lined the back wall, with a sole spotlight on them. They shivered, trembling and naked, in horror. A couple of them were also drugged, based on their lethargic stances. Or maybe they had just given up.

"Welcome, friends! For tonight's delight, we offer you fourteen women, ready to be modeled and taught your most delicious desires. And for tonight only, we will have a special sale. If you buy one, you may have a companion from the upstairs' auction at only half the price!" Sebastian boasted. His voice boomed against the cinderblock.

"Starting bid is at one million dollars."

One million dollars for drugged out, sick women? What the hell good would they be? Apparently, the more drugged up, the better, because as each woman stood, quivering in fear, the price rose higher and higher. Each party, once the woman was won, was escorted with their prize to an exit door near the stage; another exit that we didn't know about. I tried to mumble to the crew, but my earpiece was shot.

"And lastly, this firecracker right here. Yes, she has some miles on her, but she is completely submissive, requiring nothing but your cheapest heroin, and has the most pleasurable scream." Sebastian brought Jennie to the forefront, and I winced. Her body was beaten. There was no place where she wasn't bruised. But, of course, she didn't realize what was going on. She was so high, she could barely stand.

"Bidding starts at three million." I looked around as

the bidders' paddles rose in the air. The bids rose to an astronomical level, that before I knew it, I was about to be outbid.

"Ten Million dollars!" I shouted, my paddle raised high in the air.

"Ten million! Going once. Going twice. Sold, to Mr. DePandi for ten million dollars!" Sebastian announced with a sneer. Then he pulled out a gun and held it to her head. "Ten million is a good price for your wife, isn't it, Mr. Russo?"

"You don't need to do this. Hand her over, Cruz," I warned.

"Sure thing. I mean, hell, the customer's always right." And before I could blink, he pulled the trigger and fired. Jennie didn't have a chance. She went down. My eyes widened in horror as I watched her blood spill from the wound, coating the wooden stage.

"You fucking bastard!" I seethed. I raced toward him, but the sound of guns cocking back had me stopping in my tracks. Everywhere I turned, a gun was pointed in my direction.

"Now you see, Mr. Russo, I've seen your parlor tricks. I've seen what you and your team can do. Did you think we didn't have an informant within the Special Forces, just as we have with the FBI?" A low chuckle came from behind me, and the ugly, scarred face of Jose Martinez came into view. A Triton's Edge member, Bravo Company. That son of a bitch.

"Mr. Martinez has been extremely instrumental in assisting us. We know that you're here, and your teammates are upstairs, as well as your girlfriend. What a strange predicament you're in, soldier. You had to choose between your wife or your girlfriend. Don't you know you should never mix pussy?" He waved his gun at me, nonchalantly. "Get rid of him. I'm done."

And just as I was waiting for the bullets to fly, the building exploded into gunfire. I threw myself down on the ground, seeking cover behind a fallen chair. I aimed my Glock and fired, taking out three of the Syndicate members. Chaos ensued, and no one knew where the bullets were coming from. I used that to my advantage, taking weapons from those that had fallen, and using them against others. A hot white pain gripped my shoulder, and I looked down to see the blood spread. Fucking hell. I continued to fire, at anyone and anything. I needed to get to Sebastian, and put the final bullet in his head.

"Noah!" My name was screamed out, and my blood boiled. I looked up to see Kate rushing down the stairs, with Torin and Trey behind her, guns in hand.

"Alpha Team, in place." Fucking Benji's ass grabbed my shoulder and pulled me up.

"About fucking time you pussies got here," I said through gritted teeth. I looked around at all the carnage. "Where's Sebastian?"

"We lost him in the fray, but we've managed to round up several high-ranking members of the Syndicate. The local PD has the girls, and they're assisting us in processing. Commander Wells is here too."

"Where the fuck is that jackass Martinez? He's the informant on the squad."

"We took care of him with a bullet to the brain," Cole seethed, gesturing to the side of the room.

"Fuck! Jennie!" I bounded up to the stage, where Sketch held his sister in his arms, staring into nothing, while tears rolled down his face.

"Buddy, I'm so sorry. I tried..." I tried to apologize, explain. I didn't know. I didn't know what to say to ease his pain.

"I know. God, I know. I just wish..." and he broke down. I put my arm around him while he shed silent tears.

"Come on, guys. We have to get out of here," Kate said quietly. I moved to pick up Jennie, but Sketch carried her in his arms and up the stairs. I looked helplessly to Kate.

"You did everything you could, Noah." She pulled me upstairs and into the night.

"Not enough."

Guilt crashed over me. I could have done more, done something more, to save Jennie, to help her get clean. I may not have loved her, but she was the mother of the greatest gift I'd ever received. Then, I looked over at Kate, and knew she could have ended up just like Jennie. Anger coursed through my veins. There wouldn't be enough protection in the world to save them from the destruction I would lay down, had Kate been killed.

We walked into parking lot that was crowded with police, SWAT, and FBI. The locals had the buyers separated from the group, with Kate's partner overseeing them. EMTs were everywhere, catering to the wounded, and the women high on God knew what. Carnage was everywhere, but I was detached. I couldn't feel anymore. The numbness had taken over.

After I got checked out and bandaged up, we gave our reports to Commander Lewes and the Special Agent in Charge, and assisted with processing of evidence and suspects. We managed to save the women, but Sebastian and Elias got away. Again.

As the sun started to rise in the eastern sky, we were finally released, and it was about time. The team was dog-tired, and running on fumes. And the beast inside of me demanded to be released.

"I need you tonight," I muttered, taking Kate by the

hand. I despised feeling this way, and the only person who could make me feel sane again was her. We jumped into her rented Benz and shot off toward Zeke's house.

I was on her the second she got out of the car. I yanked up that dress to her waist and dropped to my knees, feasting on her delicious pussy. The taste I had been craving was finally on my tongue. Thrusting my two fingers inside her, while flicking her clit with my tongue, her release flooded my mouth. My name was on her lips as she screamed, riding my face like I knew she could. Before she could come down from her high, I picked her up. Her legs wrapped around me, with her drenched core right against my painfully throbbing cock as I marched into the house.

Once the door was shut, I made my way down the hall to the guest room I had been staying in. I dropped her onto the bed with a bounce, and we both made quick work of my clothes. We were covered in sweat, grime, and blood, but that didn't stop me from pushing her onto the bed and putting her legs on my shoulders. I slid inside of her, groaning her name as her pussy tightened like a vice around me. I rocked against her, my balls slapping against her skin as the pace became frantic. Her quickened pants and unintelligible moans were what I needed to keep going.

"God, Noah. Yes! Oh God, yes!" she screamed. Her

pussy tightened, and with that, I exploded. The stars shone brightly behind the back of my eyelids as I pulsed inside of her. In my crazed state, I again failed to put on a condom, but by that point, I didn't care. I would give anything to see her belly blossom with my baby. To know what she was mine, always.

"I love you, Kate. God, I love you so much," I muttered, tracing my tongue down her jawline.

"I love you, too, Noah."

Reluctantly, I pulled out and walked into the adjoining bathroom for a rag to clean her up.

"I guess we need to talk," I said, after we cleaned up and got dressed. Luckily, she had a bag in her Benz that contained a spare set of clothes and sneakers. The dress I tore off her was now hanging in shreds.

"Noah, your wife just died. Our mission just combusted in heavy gunfire. Lives were saved tonight. Let's process this before working out any drama between us. I love you. God, I love you. There is a whole lot to talk about, but right now, let's not. Go be with your team. Go be with Sketch and your family," she said gently.

"I'm going to make you a part of my family," I murmured, cupping her face. Her freshly cleaned skin glistened with her tears.

"I'm going make sure you stick to that," she said with a soft laugh.

I grabbed her by her neck and pulled her close, burying my head in her neck.

"Don't forget about me, Princess."

"Never."

I crushed my lips to hers, tasting her one last time.

And then I let her go.

# EPILOGUE

*Kate*

THREE WEEKS HAD PASSED by, since that crazy night in Vegas. Three weeks since I'd seen Noah. Three weeks since our last kiss. I missed him. God, I missed him so much.

I saw him at Jennie's funeral, dressed in black, and carrying little Aubrey. She was too young to know what was going on, but the sadness overwhelmed her. We figured out how Jennie got to Vegas. A member of the Cruz Cartel had posed as an orderly at the hospital where Jennie was taken. He snuck her out the back door, and into a waiting ambulance that flew her out to Vegas. Was it in hopes that we would crash his party? No. Sebastian Cruz knew what we were up to the entire time, which meant that we could no longer trust anyone. It was time to go black. Everything we'd done up until that point, had had FBI approval. No more. My confidence and trust in the system was shattered. So shattered, that I turned in my badge and gun. I was no longer Agent Parker.

I'm Kate Parker, member of Tactical Redemption. My brother's company went underground. It was what we needed to do in order to take down the Syndicate, and the Cartel. Would we succeed? I hoped so. But I knew, if not, we would die trying.

But right now? We needed to take a step back, revisit our ways and means, and look at things from a better picture. And refocus on the things that mattered.

Love.

Which was why, at one thirty in the morning, I was on route 214. I pulled into his tiny community next to the water. Tiny shells and rocks crunched under my feet, as I made my way to his backyard. And as I'd predicted, he was sitting on the back porch, the soulful sounds of Chris Stapleton playing softly in the background.

"I thought you might be up."

"I haven't been able to sleep without you," he confessed.

"Me neither," I whispered.

"Look," he ran his hands through his hair, "you need to know, that I never thought my marriage would be an issue."

"Wait, what the …?"

"No! Hear me out. We got married because she was pregnant and needed insurance. She was also a user, and in need of rehab. She told me I wasn't the father, but she would be without insurance or help if I didn't marry her, so I did. We got married in a quick ceremony, and I immediately put her in a residential home in Miami. Her family had no idea we got married until after the fact. She needed to get better, for Aubrey's sake, and her own. When she left the center, before I got back, I had no clue where to find her. So I filed for an annulment. But, because I kept getting called away on missions and trips, I wasn't able to follow through with it. And honestly, I met you, and everything with her fell by the wayside."

"Until Aubrey."

He nodded. "Until Aubrey. When they called me and told me she had the baby, I had this gut feeling. And damn if my feeling wasn't right. She was mine. Always mine. "

I stepped closer, running my hands up his arms.

"Why didn't you tell me?"

"What would I have said, Kate? Oh, by the way, I'm married to a junkie who may or may not be carrying my kid, and it's really a matter of guilt because I didn't really love her?" He said dryly, taking a pull from his beer bottle.

"It sure as hell would have been better hearing it from you, than finding out the way I did."

"Yeah, I know. And let me tell you, I wanted to tell you. Hell, Sketch was on my ass about telling you. But I couldn't let you go again. Going without you next to me in Miami was hell for me. I needed you like I needed air to breathe." He stood, and pulled me with him. "I need you with me. I need you all in."

"But you have Aubrey. I haven't even met her yet. Well, officially, anyway. What if I'm horrible at this?" I said nervously.

"I've seen the way you interact with baby Katie, and everyone else. You're going to be fine. You're a natural with kids. Tell me you're in this with me, that you're going to fight for us."

"I think about Vegas, and how close I was to possibly losing you." I wrapped my arms around his waist. "I can't let you go again either. So yes, I'm in this. All the way. You've broke down my walls, Noah. Just don't break my heart, too."

His lips brushed against the sensitive part of my neck. "I know you weren't looking for a relationship, but I promise, I'll spend the rest of my life, making sure you know that you're mine. And that starts tonight."

He put his lips to mine, and as the soulful strands

of Tennessee Whiskey faded into the night, I finally realized that when it came to matters of the heart, rules were always made to be broken.

*The End.*

# ABOUT THE AUTHOR

*Melissa grew up in Maryland by the Chesapeake Bay, where her favorite memories took place near the water. Now she lives near Washington, D.C. with her family, dog, and a lot of fish. In between the chaos of laundry, chasing after her three children and trying not to burn dinner, Melissa continues to find her escape by feeding her addiction of reading and writing about love, suspense, and humor.*

*Melissa loves to hear from readers! She can be contacted at:*

*Email — melissa@melissahuie.com*
*Website — www.melissahuie.com*
*Twitter — www.twitter.com/melissahuie*
*Facebook — www.facebook.com/melissadhuie*
*Goodreads — www.goodreads.com/melissa_huie*

# ACKNOWLEDGEMENTS

I'm keeping this short and sweet this time. I promise!!!

Brian – Thank you for everything. Taking the kids out of the house so I could get this done, to keeping the wine glass full, and making sure I ate. I love you.

My Family – Thank you for supporting me, for buying my books, and for keeping me on my toes.

My Publishing Crew — Emma, Dana, Cassy and Robin—Thank you for putting up with my bs and my antics. We kick ass together. Thanks for being on my side. I love you ladies so, so much.

To My Street Team – Jenny, Lizette, Candace, and the mistress of hookas herself, Traci – I love you ladies. I'm so honored that you guys decided to be my pimps. And you pimp with class!!! Thank you for everything. First round of drinks are on me.

Paulette & Jen – My boozy brunch bitches. I love you girls. Thank you for being my sounding board, my voice of reason, and the monthly excuse to go hang out at Grafton Street. Mimosas anyone?

The Amazing Photog – Shauna Kruse, Aurora O'Brien, and Zack Salaun – Thank you for the amazing cover. I'm so glad we finally got to show the world your killer photo!

To the crew I have in my corner – Harper K, Natacha, Emma, Dana, Cassy, William, Katheryn, Judi, Tyf, Brooke, Heather – and so many more — I love you all more than you know. Thank you.

To all the amazing blogs who have shared my teasers and my releases – Thank you for your hard work and taking a chance on me. <3

And to the ones who make all this worthwhile – My Readers. Thank you. Thank you for your support, your patience, your encouragement and love. I truly hope you love this book. Without you, there wouldn't *be* a series.